Crimson Crisp

CAYTLYN BROOKE

Crimson Crisp
Copyright @ Caytlyn Brooke
All rights reserved.

First published by Kindle Direct Publishing 2023.

First Edition

ISBN paperback: 979-8-9877402-2-4
ISBN ebook: 979-8-9877402-3-1
Visit Caytlyn Brooke's website:
http://caytlynbrooke.wixsite.com/booksbycaytlyn

Editor: Samantha Moran
Cover Designer: Neil J Hart

Other Works

Dark Flowers
Wired
Among the Hunted
The Baker's Wife

Crimson
Crisp

To my dad, I wish we had been enough

8

Chapter 1: Avery

Mid-morning sunlight licked Avery's exposed arm where it dangled off the edge of the mattress and elicited a wonderful tingling sensation along her skin. It was even more delightful than the wet tongue licking the outside of her pussy. That's when she realized she was bored of fucking Todd.

Tucking her chin, she glanced down to where a handsome head of dark hair rested between her thighs. His big blue irises looked at her, no doubt eager for a groan or a pleasurable sigh to fall from her pursed lips to relay the satisfying assurance that he was the most skilled lover she'd ever had. Avery held her lips in a firm line. She refused to inflate *fucking Todd's* ego with a pity moan. He was below average, in every way, and she didn't have the energy to pretend otherwise.

Avery laid back on the mussed sheets and closed her eyes. Maybe she could catch a short nap before the sun shifted its touch away from her. *Fucking Todd's* tongue moved faster, desperate to regain her attention. The sound of a keycard sliding out of the slot, followed by the signature click of the lock, stalled his movements.

Avery turned her head. Lying at the bottom of the bed, she had a great vantage point of the foyer, not that she needed to visually confirm what she already knew. The dim lighting from the carpeted hallway illuminated two silhouettes, one in front of the other. The shorter of the two waved its hands, but the taller one forged ahead into the suite.

"Sir, you can't go in there. We have strict instructions not to let anyone—"

"It's perfectly fine. I won't be long," a deep voice answered dismissively before the intrusive figure shut the door in her face.

Avery pulled the sheet up to cover her chest and kicked Todd in the shoulder with her foot. "You're going to want to put some pants on."

Todd withdrew his tongue and wiped his chin with his thumb as Avery's father strode into the room. With a sly smile, she watched *fucking Todd's* dimples disappear and eyes bulge with familiarity as he took in the crisp designer suit, sleek silver hair, and permanent scowl etched on his new boss's face. Glancing from their guest to Avery, he scurried off the bed and grabbed whatever clothing was within reach and slammed it over his erection.

Avery's father's polished shoes halted their progression on the granite floor, and he held his hands in his customary manner, precisely aligning his steepled fingers in front of his stomach. He remained silent at first, his cold eyes assessing *fucking Todd's* naked form and flushed cheeks.

"Mr. Sterling, I . . . this isn't . . . I didn't know she—"

"I understand, Mr. Collins." Avery's father adjusted his left cuff link. "Mistakes happen."

Todd exhaled, relief palpable in the sag of his shoulders. "Thank you, sir. It won't happen again, I swear—"

"Save your vows, Mr. Collins. You're fired. Feel free to pick up your first and last paycheck on Monday with my secretary, along with a personal letter of recommendation for your next employer regarding your skills in the art of cunnilingus."

Todd's face blushed an even darker shade of red. Unsure whether to break eye contact with her father, he stumbled to locate the rest of his clothes. Avery smirked when he gathered her lacy pink bra along with his pants and shuffled into the bathroom. He closed the door harder than necessary, only to open it a moment later and toss her bra back out. The lingerie slid across the tile and came to rest inches from her father's shoe.

Neither Avery nor her father spoke or moved from their positions. This was a game they had played many times, and it was necessary for any extra parties to vacate the premises before the tongue-lashing on both sides could commence.

Muffled shouts and curses rained like violent drops on the other side of the bathroom door as *fucking Todd* dressed and attempted to collect what little pride he had left. Avery kept her cool gaze on the sunlight tickling the few freckles adorning her arm while her father stared at the closed door, indifference giving way to ennui.

Two minutes later, the bathroom door swung open, emitting Todd—who was buttoned back up in his knock-off suit. His collar was undone and highlighted a sliver of his chiseled chest, one of the features that drew Avery to him in the first place. His messy hair she'd pulled while she sat astride him was gelled back with water and whatever wholesale product the hotel provided. He looked sophisticated, but nothing could hide the humiliation and rage burning in his eyes.

"Bye Todd," Avery called lazily from her sunny perch.

Todd gritted his teeth and took a step toward her. Avery's father turned ever-so-slightly, angling the toes of his shoes level with his ex-employee.

"Goodbye, Todd. I think it's high time you were on your

way," her father said.

"Cunt," Todd muttered under his breath and marched to the exit. He didn't slam it as Avery expected. Instead, he left it wide open, as if he hoped to display her humiliation to the world.

Avery smiled. She had quite enjoyed *fucking Todd* until he tried too hard. Last night and that morning hadn't been about pleasure or embarrassing *him*. Before yesterday, she had no idea who her father's new recruit was. No, last night and that morning were about something far bigger.

Mr. Sterling strolled toward the gaping door and closed it with a gentle click. He didn't bother to turn the lock. He wasn't going to linger long. Crossing back to the edge of the main room, he scooped up her bra and flung it at her. One of the golden embellishments caught Avery in the eye, but she refused to flinch.

"What a shame," Avery said. She cocked her head and tightened the sheet across her chest. "Todd showed real promise."

"Shut up, Avery." Her father's fierce voice lashed out like a cracking whip. He raised his hand. She could see the way his fingers shook with barely controlled rage. "Why do you do this? You knew that man was recently hired, knew how long it took me to select him after you screwed the last chief marketing executive. At least with Kenneth, you waited a month."

Avery shrugged and pursed her lips. "I didn't want Todd to get too comfortable."

"Christ, you are a nasty little thing, aren't you?" Mr. Sterling spat. "You're deliberately trying to run my company into the ground. Do you want me to fail? Do you want your lavish lifestyle to evaporate? What is it you want, Avery?"

Avery bit the inside of her cheek and brushed her bleached

blond bob out of her eyes. "I can run circles around those clowns you continue to hire. I just want a chance to prove that I can do it."

Her father scoffed and plunged his hands into his pockets. "Enough, Avery. We've been over this. You don't have the necessary experience."

"I went to Cornell. I double-majored in International Business and Marketing and graduated Suma Cum Laude. I excelled at my internship at Wells Fargo, and all my professors have written excellent letters of recommendation."

"Yes, and during your time at Cornell, you were also rushed to the emergency room to have your stomach pumped for acute alcohol poisoning, were caught streaking in a National Park, and totaled your Lexus."

"The trip to the ER was freshman year and a plow smashed my car when it was parked on campus."

Mr. Sterling held up his palm and shook his head. "The point is you are not mature enough for the requisite amount of responsibility and visibility in my company. I need someone I can trust."

Avery sneered. "No, you need a son. If I were a man, you would have hired me the moment my degree was in my hand."

Mr. Sterling arched his eyebrows and closed the distance between them, his eyes cold and calculating. "You're right. Having a son would make this much easier, especially because I wouldn't have to worry about finding him beneath my employees."

"Actually, I was on top."

"Enough, Avery. This is exactly what I mean. You think you're hurting me by throwing these little temper tantrums. There are plenty of men I can replace Mr. Collins with. Several hundred apply every day who will bend over backwards and sacrifice twenty hours a day to make sure the job is done."

Avery pressed her hand to her collarbone. "So will I. Give me a chance to prove it to you."

Her father paused and narrowed his gaze. "You really want to show me you can do this?"

"Yes, sir." Avery sat a little straighter, tucking the sheet tighter beneath her arms, though the wrinkled fabric wasn't exactly professional.

"Fine. I'll give you one chance to demonstrate a strong worth ethic, maintain a strict schedule, and become a dependable member of a team."

Avery's stoic expression cracked into a hopeful smile. "I promise you won't regret this, sir."

"Good. Get dressed and meet me downstairs in the lobby. I'll have a car drive you."

"Right now?"

Mr. Sterling raised his chin. "Is there a problem?"

"No, but it's Friday afternoon. I don't have proper business attire and my briefcase is at my apartment."

Mr. Sterling waved his hand. "I'll have my assistant Melanie pack you a bag and bring you some things. You won't be dressed like a floozy for long and you'll need a tour to become acquainted with the way everything will work."

Avery's stare hardened at the insult, but she held her tongue. Her father was finally giving her a chance to make a positive impact in his company. She didn't want to blow her opportunity with a snide retort.

"Okay. I'll meet you downstairs." Avery agreed.

"Wonderful." Her father gave a curt nod and pivoted on the heels of his shiny shoes. "Do be quick. We have a long drive." With a purposeful stride, he exited the suite and closed the door behind him.

The moment she was alone, Avery exhaled all her anxiety and trepidation. At last, her father was giving her a shot. Growing up in his shadow as the pampered princess, no one expected anything from her, but she was never content to play the dimwitted heiress. She had plans and the vision to take her father's company to new heights, and finally he was taking her seriously.

Yes, she had endured a few moments of "disgrace" as her father mentioned, but every one of her past transgressions had been meticulously planned. She had known he would be in town, and if her achievements and accolades weren't worth his attention, then she found something that was.

Pushing off the twisted sheet, Avery ran to the bathroom, her bare feet hitting the cold tiles. She pulled the stainless handle and a stream of water burst from the showerhead. Giving it a few seconds to warm up, she slipped under the pressurized rainfall as shivers raked her skin.

Avery tipped her head back, and a contented sigh fell from her lips as the massaging droplets danced on her hairline. She knew she had to be fast. Her father wasn't a patient man, but she wanted to enjoy the moment. She felt dizzy but in a good way—that lighter-than-air feeling as you stand over a great precipice and imagine what it would feel like to fly. She couldn't wait to soar.

Chapter 2: Avery

Twenty minutes later, Avery sat in the back of her father's Mercedes-Benz EQS with her legs crossed at the ankles and her hands resting on her knee. Her short hair was slicked back with the same gel *fucking Todd* took advantage of, in hopes of turning her form-fitting red sequined cocktail dress into a sophisticated ensemble. She had also found Todd's black blazer hidden under the coverlet. Thankfully oversized blazers were trending. Overall, she thought she looked quite put together for the minimum amount of time she'd allotted herself to wash Todd's saliva off her inner thighs and present herself as a worthy adversary in her father's game.

Her father sat in front, neck bowed as his fingers flew across his new Samsung, no doubt wheeling and dealing with another high-profile client. Avery yearned to open her beaded clutch and lose herself in social media, but she resisted. From the moment her father issued the challenge, she was on stage, always performing. She had to show she was above the mundane urge to mindlessly scroll, no matter how soothing it would be on her nerves.

The car accelerated onto the on-ramp, heading toward Newark. Avery frowned and knocked her knuckles on the window. "Where are we going? I thought we were headed to your office."

The driver didn't respond and kept his eyes fixed on the merging lanes. Her father raised his head but didn't look at her.

"No. As you said, it's nearly the end of the day. Everyone will be rushing to wrap up. It's not a good time to introduce you."

Avery was silent for a moment. "Then where are we going? Have you opened another office outside the city?"

"Not quite, but before you begin at Sterling Management, it's important to understand our foundation."

"The foundation of what?"

"The company's ideals and humble beginnings. Once you understand the power of our strong work ethic, it will give you the proper inspiration and expectations." Her father glanced out the window as the city began to shrink behind them.

Avery pushed her sunglasses back into place on the bridge of her nose. "Humble beginnings? Are you talking about Schuyler County? I went to Cornell. I'm familiar with the back-woods town you grew up in."

Mr. Sterling chuckled. "Oh, Ithaca is a little different than Millport, especially in my day. Sure, you've got Watkins Glen next door that brings in tourists during the summer for the NASCAR race, but it's a whole different way of life than what you're accustomed to. I believe there's a valuable lesson in spending a few days up there."

Avery's stomach sank. "A few days? Like a weekend trip?"

"Maybe a bit more." Her father kept his eyes straight ahead.

"But I thought . . . on Monday. I thought I was going to be—"

"I told you I would give you an opportunity to prove yourself. Do you remember Uncle Stanley? He's got a large orchard up here, one of the largest in New York state."

"Does he need a new marketing campaign for the fall?"

Avery asked, but she already knew the answer. She cursed her fragile hopes. She had fallen for another one of her father's tricks. He had no interest in giving her a job or a chance to show her merit. He just needed a place to stick her that was so far removed from the rest of society, she wouldn't be able to corrupt anymore of his bright young stars.

"As a matter of fact, the apples tend to sell themselves. Thousands of folks flock to Stan's orchard from September to October, so many that he can hardly keep up."

Avery furrowed her slender brows behind her large shades. "And it's the beginning of June. What, pray tell, will I be doing for three months before the tourist season?"

Her father lowered his visor and made eye contact with her in the small rectangular mirror. Humor, or possibly revenge, made his blue eyes sparkle. "Well, Stan doesn't only cater to the wonderful people of New York City and their desire for wholesome Instagram content. His crops are shipped out to grocery chains all over the country, and he doesn't just grow apples, but corn, berries, pumpkins, and zinnias."

"What the hell is a zinnia?"

"I'm sure he'll show you when we get there," her father said.

"So, I'm meant to be what? A pack mule for manual labor? How, may I ask, will spreading manure and picking strawberries prove I can handle a cutthroat Manhattan marketing firm?" Avery didn't care if she sounded like a spoiled child in that moment. The two jobs were polar opposites, and the pain of his betrayal made her feel eight years old again.

Her father had promised to attend her school ceremony to watch her accept an award for Outstanding Leadership. Avery recalled the obsessive way she had stalked his calendar and called his then assistant, Caroline, to double-check that her ceremony, complete with the school's address, was secured on his schedule.

The morning of the ceremony arrived, and her father kissed her on the forehead and looked her in the eye, promising he would be in the crowd to wave. Yet, when the principal called her name and held out her certificate, complete with gold foil stars and beautiful cursive lettering, her father's face was not smiling back at her among the sea of proud parents. No one was there to cheer or clap obnoxiously as she walked out. The other parents regarded her with kind smiles and glazed eyes as they counted the moments until their child was called and they could leave the musty gymnasium. To them, she was just another name.

That night, Caroline tucked her into bed and explained her father was in San Francisco, meeting with a Japanese silk company, an arrangement that had been in place for weeks. Her father never planned on watching her accept her award, but being the sly salesman he was, he had ballooned her hopes. Better to ask forgiveness than permission, right?

The buildings raced by as her memories faded. Her father heaved a dramatic sigh and dipped his neck. The little screen in his hand commanded his attention once more. "One summer of fresh air and hard work won't kill you, Avery. Show me you aren't afraid to get your hands dirty, then we'll talk about New York."

The finality in his tone relayed her father had nothing more to say about abandoning her in the middle of nowhere, or in conversation in general. Avery tilted her neck and rested her forehead on the window. She watched the gray and black aesthetic of the concrete jungle she yearned to dominate shrink on the narrow shore as they crossed the George Washington Bridge.

Most city dwellers looked forward to traveling upstate to see the beautiful greenery and lush fields, but to Avery, the stifling vastness of upstate held no appeal. In college, she had already experienced the beauty of the gorges and yawning farmland. She was done with that part of her life. She belonged in the city but had the unfortunate happenstance to straddle the odd limbo where although she lived in Manhattan, she hadn't achieved enough of anything to make it feel like she truly belonged.

Avery glanced down at the sparkling water that separated the city from the rest of the world and identified with the lolling waves. She wished to make a powerful impact, but she held no control, forced to carry on where the current saw fit.

Chapter 3: Jonah

A heavy groan sounded as Jonah hefted three wooden crates onto the pile. As the first farmhand to arrive for the new season, he didn't waste any time collecting the supplies out of winter storage. His boss—and longtime friend—Stanley Sterling, entered the dusty barn with his signature Buffalo Bills cap pulled down low on his forehead.

"Jonah," Stan called. "You do know you're two days early?"

Jonah straightened the tower of crates and removed his thick gloves. He turned away from the project and tucked them into his back pocket before he reached out to take Stan's hand in a firm shake. He clapped his old friend on the shoulder.

"This spring has been so dry. Thought you'd need all the help you could get. Have you already gotten the extra hoses out?"

Stan released Jonah's hand and frowned. "We talked about this, Jonah, remember? We agreed you'd take this year off."

Jonah shook his head and adjusted his own faded blue baseball cap. His freshly shaved head itched as the baby hairs pushed through the skin. He had forgotten the feeling after months of inattention when he'd let it grow out. "I'm fine, Stan. I can't stay there anymore. I need this. I need to do *something*."

Stan's frown deepened. "It's only been seven months. No

one is going to judge you for taking more time—"

"I told you. I don't need more time. This right here is what I need, okay?"

Stan put up his hands and walked closer to the well-stacked crates. "I won't say nothing more on the matter then."

Jonah slid his hands back into his gloves. In the few short months since he'd been away from the orchard, his callouses had grown soft. He didn't regret the weak skin, but he'd always regret the reason why.

"I appreciate that, Stan. I already threw my things into cabin four. Are Jesse, Marissa, and Mac coming back this year too?"

"Mac and Marissa are, but Jesse was invited to join a research group overseas, and I don't anticipate him being back before August."

"Oh." Jonah's eyebrows arched under the brim of his hat. "It's going to be tight with one less hand, but I'm sure we can make it work."

An odd look crossed Stan's face, and he hooked his thumbs into the denim loops of his worn jeans. "That's why I came to find you. I hired another hand."

Jonah crossed the hay-strewn floor to the supply closet and dug out another two crates. "Nice. When he gets here, I don't mind showing him the ropes."

Stan cracked a smile. "I'm glad to hear you say that, except he is she. My niece is up from the city."

Jonah pivoted and braced the large crates on his raised knee. "Your niece? How old is she?"

"Twenty-seven. Smart as a whip but as green as they come." Stan chuckled.

Jonah gritted his teeth and expelled his breath as he carried the crates to the table and set them down. "I'm going to stop you right there, Stan. No. I don't have time to follow some snooty city slicker around and clean up all her mistakes. Stick her with Marissa."

"Marissa won't be here 'til late next week."

"So?"

"My niece will be here around five."

"What? Today?"

Stan shrugged. "I just got off the phone with my brother. He said he was driving her up to help me out for the summer. I didn't ask why, but I'm sure he's got his reasons."

Jonah straightened and rubbed the gathering sweat off his brow with the red flannel that covered his bicep. "No offense, Stan, but I don't want to be responsible for babysitting some brat with daddy issues for the next five months. I've got my own problems to deal with."

"How do you know she's got daddy issues?"

"Please, a rich heiress being shipped upstate for the summer? Fifty bucks says her Pops scooped her out of some party and presented her with an ultimatum. Why else would he drive all the way up here with no notice?"

Stan smirked. "You may have a point, though last I heard she had a big internship with Wells Fargo back in college."

Jonah rolled his eyes. "Great, that's all I need. Some princess who thinks she's smarter than me trying to tell me how to do my job."

"She won't be like that. Besides, I think she'll be good for you." Jonah shot Stan a dark look, but he was quick to throw up his palms. "Not like that, tiger. I just meant, helping her will take your mind off—"

"I can manage my own mind, thanks."

Stan crossed his arms. "Wasn't saying you couldn't. Just thought managing her might help get you out of your own head for a bit."

"Thanks for the concern, but I can talk to Mac and Marissa if things get heavy again."

"Okay," Stan said. He cocked his head and gestured to the main house. "When you're finished getting all those crates out, come grab some late lunch. Carrie's making sandwiches."

Jonah adjusted his cap again and fixed Stan with a look. "Thanks, man. I'm sorry for being harsh. I want to be a team player, but I'm not in the best head space right now, you know?"

Stan shook his head. "Nothing to apologize for. I'll see you in a bit."

Jonah watched his friend leave the utility barn and cross the dry grass that led up to his house. Jonah hung his head. Disappointment clouded his mood. He hated letting anyone down, but he refused to be some rich bitch's errand boy for the summer.

Chapter 4: Jonah

The massive grandfather clock in Stan's living room chimed five at the same moment a black Mercedes rolled up the gravel drive. Jonah snickered and wiped the yellow mustard off his bottom lip with his napkin. He nodded toward the window. Stan sat across from him and propped his left elbow on the back of his chair, glancing out the panes.

"Curtis was always punctual," Stan said as he pushed back in his chair. "Come on, let's go greet her."

Jonah followed suit and dropped his napkin onto his plate. "Let's get this over with is more like it."

"Be nice," Carrie, Stan's wife, said with a frown. "Show the young lady some manners."

"Of course," Jonah agreed. "I'll clean these plates up and meet you out there." He reached for the other dirty plates, but Carrie smacked his hand away playfully.

"Nice try. You go on out with Stan and help her with her things. I'll tidy up. I'll only be a minute. Knowing you, you'd find some way to drag out washing three plates to sundown." Carrie winked and took Jonah's out of his hand, then stacked it atop hers.

"Thank you, Carrie."

She answered with a kind smile. "Git."

Jonah nodded his thanks and watched her retreating figure. Carrie and Stan were in their late sixties. Stan had gone gray in recent years, but Carrie still had rich mahogany hair that she wore in a long braid down her back. Compared to last year, she had a few more wrinkles around her eyes, but the previous months had been hard on everybody. Jonah couldn't remember the last time he'd looked at himself in a mirror. It hurt too much to see the pain in his reflection. No doubt he appeared far older than his thirty-one years, but it didn't matter. Nothing mattered anymore.

Stan called over his shoulder as he waltzed onto the back porch. "Come on, Jonah. Want to make sure I don't lose ya."

"As if you could, you old bloodhound."

Stan laughed and led Jonah outside to where the black car waited. Jonah sighed and retrieved his ball cap from his back pocket. Bending the weathered brim, he put it on his head once his feet hit the stones, standing to the side slightly behind Stan. He pasted a robotic smile on his face and kicked a nearby pebble with the toe of his dirty boot.

The passenger side door opened first and an older man with sleek silver hair emerged. His navy-blue suit and paisley tie reeked of money, as did the manner in which Stan's brother carried himself, like a visiting noble sent to mingle with the common folk. He took off his designer shades and slipped them into his breast pocket. Curtis was older than Stan, but it was easy to see the resemblance.

"Stanley," Mr. Sterling greeted. He embraced his brother in a stiff hug. "It's good to see you. The trees look lovely." He pointed vaguely behind himself.

"Good to see you too, Curt," Stan replied. "And thanks. We have a lot of work ahead of us seeing as how the rain is holding out, but the fruit is budding, so I'm hopeful."

"Good." Mr. Sterling nodded, and a glazed look filtered over his eyes. Jonah guessed he had little interest in exchanging pleasantries, especially with the long drive back to the city. "Then I'm glad I've brought you an extra set of hands." He smiled with all his teeth, forcing exuberance into his voice, no doubt to compensate for the little thunder cloud he was about to release from the back. "Come on out, my dear."

Mr. Sterling angled his body back toward the car and held his hands before him in an almost arrow-like manner, touching every fingertip to its mate. The car door opened, but the tinted windows kept the occupant a mystery.

The first thing Jonah saw was a nude stiletto, followed by a long, tanned leg. A second foot joined the first on the uneven gravel and the young woman slid out and stood tall, clutching the top of the door frame for support.

Big brown frames covered half her face and her bleached blond hair must have been slicked back at one point, but now it resembled the fluffy down of a duckling. Jonah couldn't see her eyes beyond the large sunglasses, but her lips were tightly pinched. From under his hat, he watched her leave the safety of the car and stroll to her father's side. Her first few steps were smooth, that is until one of her heels rolled atop the dusty stones and she wobbled like a baby giraffe.

He cleared his throat, masking a chuckle as the heiress's arms shot out to steady herself. This girl was a deer on ice.

She pulled herself together and completed the short walk so that she stood before them. Jonah noted the careful distance she put between herself and her father.

Ten points for daddy issues.

Confident his brim hid most of his face, Jonah let his eyes roam from top to bottom over the orchard's new addition. Along with the ridiculous heels, she was clad in a scrap of a dress that barely reached mid-thigh. The red material hugged her curves and forced her breasts to swell above the tight fabric. An oversized men's blazer hung off her shoulders. He wondered if the frat boy she took it from knew it was missing.

"Avery, you remember Uncle Stanley," Mr. Sterling introduced.

Jonah scoffed under his breath. Even her name sounded entitled.

Stan opened his arms and invited his niece into a warm hug. Jonah was surprised to see a genuine smile crack her stoic façade as she stepped into his embrace.

"It's good to see you, honey. Geez, you're almost taller than me in those death traps."

Avery grinned and gave his arm a light punch. "Yup. I'm not the same scrawny kid who fell out of your apple tree when I was eleven."

Stan laughed and fixed his cap. "No, you sure ain't. I do hope you brought a different pair of shoes for running up and down these rows though."

Avery shrugged and twisted her lips. "This is all I have. I wasn't exactly briefed before coming up here."

Ten points for indentured servitude.

Mr. Sterling snapped his fingers. "That's right. I almost forgot your bag, my dear. Wouldn't that have been tragic. Perkins, can you fetch Avery's bag from the trunk please?" The driver hopped out, popped the trunk, and delivered the solitary bag a minute later.

Jonah's eyebrows arched. Was everyone on Mr. Sterling's staff so well trained? His eyes wandered back to where his daughter stood, her arms crossed under the big jacket. Maybe not everyone danced to the beat Mr. Sterling demanded.

Mr. Sterling accepted the offered bag. "Ah, thank you,

Perkins. Here, my dear. Melanie packed your essentials and a few clothes." Her father handed the droopy bag to Avery.

Jonah wasn't certain, but for a moment he thought he caught a flash of malice in the old man's eye.

Avery weighed the bag in her hand, and her eyes flashed to her father. "A few clothes and essentials?" She rooted around in the light bag and withdrew a toothbrush, a wrinkled shirt, and a pink lace panty that looked no bigger than his boot strings.

Jonah averted his gaze before the image of her clad in nothing, but the tiny lace garment could form.

"Is this a joke? What am I supposed to wear all summer?"

Her father put up his hands. "Perhaps Melanie misunderstood."

Avery stuffed the insulting items back into the bag and drew her bottom lip into her mouth, sawing it with her teeth.

Stan cleared his throat and gestured to Jonah. "I'm sorry for the mishap, but my man, Jonah here, can drive Avery into town to pick up some things."

"Stan—" Jonah started to argue, but Mr. Sterling cut him off.

"Excellent." Mr. Sterling's voice boomed with false enthusiasm. "See? It all worked out. Thanks again, Stanley, for letting Avery help you this summer. I'll have Perkins pick her up at the beginning of October." He turned to his daughter and slid his hands in his pockets. "I expect a good report. Then we'll talk about a position in the fall. Work hard."

Without another word, Mr. Sterling spun on his heel and strode back to the passenger seat. Perkins started the car once again, and the engine purred. Stan waved, and Jonah gave a quick salute, but Avery didn't move, keeping her back to her father. The sleek sedan's tires spun atop the gravel for a second before gaining traction and pulling away. A fine cloud of dust trailed in their wake.

Stan reached out and gave Avery's upper arm a light squeeze. "It's good to have you here, honey. And don't you worry. Like I said, we'll take you to town and get you some things so you can settle in and feel comfortable. This is Jonah. He's been my right-hand man around here for five years now."

Avery rubbed her nose and sniffled once. "Thanks, Uncle Stan. I appreciate it." Now that the sound of the black car had faded, she exhaled a deep breath and removed her sunglasses. Light amber eyes, the color of new boots, flashed to Jonah's face. "It's nice to meet you. I'm Avery."

Jonah closed the distance between them and accepted her offered hand. "Jonah," he mumbled. "Nice to meet you."

Her hand was warm in his, the skin soft from a lifetime of manicures. She gave him a small smile when they touched, and her gaze lingered on his for a moment longer than necessary. He was shocked to find that beneath her shades, her face was void of makeup. Wild freckles dotted her cheeks and nose. He dropped her hand and adjusted his cap, pulling it higher on his forehead.

"Come on. Let's say hi to Carrie before ya'll head to town and see if we can find you something a little more comfortable to wear." Stan hooked his arm around Avery's shoulder and steered her toward the house.

Jonah brought up the rear. He glanced once more at the dust still swirling along the lane. His first impression of the heiress was that of a pampered diva, but the moment her father left, it was as if her cold demeanor thawed. He had serious reservations about the quality of work she'd contribute, but he'd be lying if he said he wasn't intrigued to see who she was beneath the hard shell.

Chapter 5: Avery

The scent of warm biscuits welcomed Avery as she stepped inside the cozy farmhouse, transporting her sixteen years into the past. The last time she'd run through these halls, she was a scrawny string bean who snuggled the barn cats and enjoyed chasing after her cousin Jesse. She'd changed so much, but the farmhouse was like an old hoodie that cocooned her in comfort. She noticed little modernizations here and there, but the floorboards still squeaked, and the same happy photos of Uncle Stan and his family lined the walls.

Avery paused before a new photo, barely recognizing her cousin. He was far from the little gapped-tooth boy she used to race to the top of the hay bales. "Is that Jesse? Wow, he's so handsome!"

Uncle Stan nodded and pointed to the sandy shore in the foreground. "Yup, he went to San Diego with a group of friends last year for spring break. Learned how to surf on the last day. This was the only wave he caught, but to hear him tell it, you'd think he'd won first prize in some competition."

"That's so cool. I bet he's thankful you made him haul all those apple crates and pumpkins now, huh? Look at his abs!" Avery said with a laugh.

Uncle Stan chuckled and removed his hat. "He's popular

with the ladies, that's for sure."

"Does he have a gaggle chasing him?"

"Naw." Uncle Stan shook his head. "He started dating this girl from Tennessee, Wendy, his freshman year. They've been inseparable since. Sweet girl, Wendy is."

Avery craned her neck and scanned the open living and dining room as if Jesse was waiting to jump out and scare her. "Is he outside?" Her gaze brushed over the burly farmhand behind her. She hadn't realized he had followed them in. Averting her eyes, she glanced down the hallway toward the bathroom, but that was empty as well.

Uncle Stan snuck past her and directed her toward the kitchen. "No, Jesse ain't here, honey. He took a group of students to Melbourne this semester and decided to stay a little longer after the program is completed. He and Wendy will be there until early August."

Avery's eyes widened with surprise. She hadn't been anywhere abroad, yet here was her country cousin living it up and traveling around the world. "That's amazing. It's so cool of you guys to let him go."

Uncle Stan shrugged. "His department awarded him a scholarship for half, but he paid for the rest himself. He earned it, waking up at 4 a.m. every morning to help me dig the irrigation canals and keep the tractors up to snuff. Plus, don't tell him this, but we've saved a fortune on groceries since he's been out of the house."

Avery laughed. "I bet. I remember him eating everything in sight when we were younger. I can't imagine his appetite has decreased."

They rounded the corner and stepped into the kitchen. Gone were the outdated brown shaker cabinets and Formica countertops. In their place proudly hung glistening white cabinetry complete with a gorgeous granite slab that lined the counters and the large island. In the center hung a wire rack of shiny, bronzed pots and pans.

Situated near the six-burner stove was Aunt Carrie. Her signature brown braid hung to the middle of her back and an old apron hugged her waist. At the sound of their entrance, she stopped stirring something in a medium-sized pot and rested the spoon on the blue and white checkered trivet. She spun around and a bright smile lit up her face.

"Avery! It's so good to see you! Look at how beautiful you are and so tall!" Aunt Carrie wrapped Avery in a big hug and rubbed her hands along her back as she held her. Taking her by the fingertips, Aunt Carrie looked her up and down. "Those shoes are lovely, but how do you walk in them? Are you hungry? I put on some potato soup. I thought something heavy and warm would be nice after your long drive. Where's your father?" She looked over Avery's shoulder, but only Jonah brought up the rear.

Avery sighed. "Sorry. Daddy couldn't stay."

Aunt Carrie scrunched her lips and furrowed her brow as she patted Avery's elbow. "It always seemed to me your Daddy was too busy running toward the next big thing to appreciate the gift he had right in front of him." She waved her hand. "Oh well, more for you. Feel free to freshen up in Jesse's room and come sit down."

Avery bit her lip. "Uh, this is all I have. Dad didn't exactly tell me I'd be helping you guys out." She felt warm color spread to her cheeks and worried a loose thread on the sleeve of Todd's blazer between her fingers.

Stan retrieved a can of Bud Light from the fridge and popped the tab. "Jonah here is going to run Avery into town to grab a few things after she has a bite to eat."

Aunt Carrie's gaze slid from Avery to Jonah where he leaned against the edge of the island. A ghost of a smile tugged at the corner of her lips. "Well, isn't that nice. Then, here. Let me pour you a bowl before you leave."

Avery slid onto one of the stools and balanced her elbows on the countertop. Out of the corner of her eye, she watched as Jonah settled against the pantry. She didn't know what to think of him, but his dark and broody manner was starting to grate on her nerves. Aunt Carrie set a big bowl in front of Avery and handed her a napkin and spoon.

"Thanks, Aunt Carrie. Do you have an extra pair of shoes I could borrow?" Avery asked. She dipped the spoon into the creamy broth and brought it to her lips. It tasted of nostalgia and love, easily one of the best meals she'd had in a long time.

Aunt Carrie came around the counter and placed a sweet kiss on Avery's cheek. "Of course, honey. Let me go check my closet. I'll be right back."

Avery swallowed and smiled as the warm contents settled in her stomach.

Her aunt left the kitchen and Avery ate in easy silence. Uncle Stan and Jonah started up a casual conversation, but she didn't pay attention to their words. Her mind drifted and their voices morphed into a buzzing hum. It wasn't until a harsh tone echoed somewhere behind her that she shifted out of her dissociative trance.

"What?" Avery looked up from her near-empty bowl and dropped her spoon. Uncle Stan studied the floor, his face hidden under the brim of his hat. She turned over her shoulder, shocked to see Jonah's face was a dark shade of red. Quickly, she tried to sort through the garbled sounds that made up the exchange she'd missed, but nothing stood out. "Is everything okay?"

Jonah sucked his teeth and grimaced. "Nothing for you to worry about. Meet me outside when you're ready. I'll be in my truck."

Before Avery could say anything, Jonah stalked out of the kitchen, back the way they'd come and through the door. She hadn't been out of it for that long, had she? Uncle Stan took a long swig of his beer and sighed.

"What happened? What'd I miss?" Avery asked as she slid off the stool.

Uncle Stan shook his head and drummed his fingers along the aluminum can. "Nothing, Avs. Jonah's dealing with some things is all."

Avery bit the inside of her cheek. "It's me, isn't it? He's mad about driving me into town."

"No, honey. It ain't you," Uncle Stan said. He put his empty can in the sink and rubbed his eyes. "Jonah's never been much of a people person and let's just say life hasn't exactly been kind to him."

"What do you mean?"

Uncle Stan opened his mouth to reply, but before he could utter a word, Aunt Carrie returned with an old pair of high tops.

"I think these should fit. Mind you, they're a bit worn but will suit just fine until you find something else. How was the soup?" Aunt Carrie asked. Her voice was bright, but the lines around her mouth were tight.

"It was delicious. Thanks for making it for me," Avery said.

"Good. A warm belly does wonders for the soul. Did I hear Jonah head outside? You should put those on and get going. That way we can get you settled in before dark."

Avery nodded. She wanted to ask Uncle Stan for more details about Jonah's outburst, but she sensed Aunt Carrie was pushing her out the door for a reason.

"Okay." She kicked off her heels and stuck her bare feet into the old sneakers. They scrunched her toes but were otherwise comfortable.

Aunt Carrie bent down and retrieved Avery's shoes. "I'll put these with the rest of your things, honey."

Avery nodded in thanks and started to leave the kitchen, but Uncle Stan stopped her. "Do you need some money, darling?" He reached into his back pocket and pulled out his wallet.

Warmth flooded Avery's chest at the kind gesture. "No thanks." She gestured to the clutch hanging across her body that contained the black card her father gifted her on her eighteenth birthday. "Seeing as how this was Dad's idea, I figure he won't mind footing the bill. Can I pick anything up for you guys?"

Uncle Stan chuckled and withdrew fifty dollars from the folds. "Nah. We're fine, honey, but thank you for the offer. Take this just in case." He handed her the crisp bill. Avery cocked her head in question. Uncle Stan's neck burned red. "I just want to make sure you'll still be able to get some things if he canceled your card."

He sounded embarrassed to even suggest such a thing, but Avery's jaw dropped. She hadn't considered the fact that her father might cut her off. Wasn't dumping her there for the duration of the summer cruel enough? She tried to remember how much cash she presently carried, but she had relied on her credit card for years. The idea of needing cash never crossed her mind.

Avery accepted the bill and popped it into her purse. She gave her uncle a weak smile, her humiliation palpable. "Thanks, Uncle Stan. Hopefully, I won't need it."

"Don't worry. We're just happy to have you."

Aunt Carrie seconded her uncle's sentiment and squeezed her niece's arm before Avery left them in the kitchen. With her aunt's shoes on her feet and her uncle's love in her clutch, her throat swelled with emotion. Shame flushed her cheeks, and she was thankful she was alone as she navigated to the front door. The whole drive, she had mentally cursed her father for leaving her with relatives she hadn't seen in over a decade, pitying herself. Yet already they had shown her more care and compassion in half an hour than her father had in years.

Swallowing the rising lump in her throat, Avery banished any threatening tears from her eyes. She gripped the doorknob and exited the farmhouse into the muggy afternoon air. Jonah's old red Ford sat in the driveway. The paint was faded, and a large patch of rust deformed the hub over the right rear wheel. He sat in the driver's seat and stared out the window. Immediately, her vulnerability evaporated as she remembered the way he had stormed out.

She understood he might be put off about chauffeuring her around, but it wasn't like she was a little kid who needed babysitting. He was older than her, but that didn't give him any right to be rude. Her earlier anger simmered to a boil once more as her feet crunched atop the gravel drive.

She only prayed it wouldn't be a long drive to town.

Chapter 6: Jonah

The front door closed with a solid thud, drawing Jonah's attention away from the gently blowing leaves of the Honey Crisp trees. Avery stalked out of the house with her purse pressed against her stomach as she glared at the ground. Gone were those ridiculous heels. Instead, a ratty old pair of Converse hugged her feet. At least he didn't have to worry about her falling spread eagle on the driveway.

Their gazes locked when she glanced up. The second she realized he was watching her, she straightened her posture and held her head high. A cold expression transformed her features. Jonah's lips twitched. Maybe she'd heard the argument after all.

Avery wrenched open the passenger side door and hopped into the cab with an audible huff. Jonah started the truck but didn't look away from her. After several long seconds, she turned and wrinkled her nose.

"What are you waiting for? Don't you want to get this over with?"

Jonah nodded once and clucked his tongue. She had heard, or Stan filled in the blanks. "I do, but I can't go anywhere until you put your seatbelt on."

Avery rolled her eyes. Jonah was pleased to see she left her obnoxious sunglasses inside. "Are you kidding me? I'm fine unless you plan on rolling the car."

"Truck." Jonah corrected. "And even though I don't plan on driving into a ditch, you never know what someone else might be up for. Seatbelt."

"I haven't worn a seatbelt in years. Will you just drive?" Her tawny eyes flashed with anger and annoyance, but Jonah held firm.

"Sure thing, just waiting on you."

"This is ridiculous. Stop treating me like a child."

Jonah shrugged. "Rules are the same for anyone who gets in my truck. Now I have other things to do other than play your chauffeur, so let's go."

Avery crossed her arms and fixed him with a hard stare. "No."

Jonah wasn't in the mood to play her game. Unbuckling his own seatbelt, he reached across the console and her body to where her buckle hung. The movement brought his face inches from her own, and the scent of her shampoo wafted over him. Her startled little gasp sounded in his ear and sent a pulse of warmth to his groin.

He held his breath, grabbed the metal buckle and dragged it diagonally across her chest. Careful not to touch her, he secured it in the lock at her side. Jonah let out a long breath, trying to get his body under control. He hadn't expected to react to being so close to her. The involuntary response sent a wave of guilt crashing over him that immediately relaxed his thickening cock.

Shifting in his seat, he refastened his belt and gripped the steering wheel. "There. That wasn't so hard, was it?"

"Are you done proving you're a big, strong man, now?" Avery frowned and squeezed her arms tighter against her chest. Was she aware she was forcing her breasts even further out of the top of her dress?

Jonah put the truck in drive and stepped on the gas, eyes on the road. "If you're done actin' like a toddler."

A few tense minutes passed in utter silence as the truck eased onto the pavement that led away from the orchard and onto the main thoroughfare. They passed a dairy farm and a large field with a herd of black and brown cows all congregating at the fence line, eating the sweet grass.

Avery chortled under her breath. "You don't see that every day." She looked at Jonah out of the corner of her eye and pursed her lips. "Well, I guess you do."

"Yup." Jonah nodded. He dropped his left hand out the window and held the steering wheel with his thumb.

"What kind of stores do you have around here?" Avery asked. "Is there a Macy's?"

"Nope. The only one we had was up in Big Flats, but that closed a few years ago. You could go to Sears, but that one closed, too."

"Sears?" Avery repeated. "You've got to be kidding me? What about Aerie or American Eagle?"

Jonah shrugged. "If we had those, they'd be at the Arnot Mall in the same town, but I don't want to drive that far."

Avery pouted, a small divot forming between her eyebrows. "What then? Last time I checked, gas stations don't sell intimates."

"Nah, I got a better idea."

Avery studied him and narrowed her eyes. "You're not taking me to Walmart, are you?" The disgust in her voice was tangible. "No. Please, can we just drive a little farther? I don't shop at Walmart."

"I thought you needed supplies like toothpaste, deodorant,

and shit," Jonah said. "Walmart is the best place to get all that. Besides, I'm hungry. I'll grab something while I wait for you."

"You could've had some of Aunt Carrie's soup."

"I didn't want soup."

"What do you want?"

Jonah glanced at the fiery young woman beside him and found he didn't have an answer. He knew she expected him to say something like "cheeseburger" or "fried chicken," but for reasons he couldn't understand, he wanted to confess to the tumultuous sea raging inside him.

He wanted his life back, the life he'd chosen three years ago that was pulled out from beneath his feet. He wanted his friends to stop looking at him with pity. And most of all, he wanted to quell the rising guilt that swirled in his mind every time he looked at this woman.

Jonah cleared his throat and pushed up his flannel sleeves. He set his eyes straight ahead and shrugged. "I don't know."

Avery's pink tongue licked her bottom lip before she worried it between her teeth. "Are you sure I can get everything there?"

"I don't know."

"What?"

Jonah held up his hand. "Look, I don't know what you deem essential. Let's poke around, and if you're missing something, ask Carrie to take you someplace else when we get back."

Avery exhaled loudly through her nose and tucked one of her feet onto the cloth seat. "Fine."

"Fine." Jonah adjusted his hat and tried to ignore the now visible soft flesh on the underside of her thigh. He turned up the volume and sang along to the country song on the radio.

"Ugh, I forgot how popular country is out here," Avery said.

"Let me guess, you're into rap."

"It's better than this crap."

"This is poetry."

"All they do is whine." Avery stretched out and raised both her legs up to balance on the dashboard. Her Converse strings blew in the breeze. Jonah's heart ached as he imagined a different set of feet dancing on the windshield.

He shook his head. "And all your artists do is cuss."

"They do not."

"Okay, name two rap songs off the top of your head that don't have to be edited for the radio."

Avery opened her mouth to reply, but then shut it and furrowed her brow. "Country swears too, you know. Always going on about their damn truck or what a hell of a dog they have."

Jonah chuckled. "But you'd rather listen to men rattle off their body count and objectify women?"

"No! That's not . . ." Avery's argument fizzled. "They're not all like that."

"And all country songs aren't about a man's dog or his truck."

Avery pursed her lips. "Touché, sir."

Jonah drummed his thumb on the steering wheel. He liked the title she'd addressed him with more than he cared to admit. "Country as a genre is just nice to listen to and family-friendly. You don't need to worry about turning down the volume every other word."

Avery stared out the windshield, and the razored ends of her short blond hair fluttered against her jaw. "Do you have a family? Pretty wife with two-point-five kids waiting for you to bring home supper once you're through with me?"

Jonah stopped tapping the wheel and gripped it. His knuckles turned white. "Nah, it's just me."

"Really?" Genuine surprise colored Avery's tone. "Can I ask why?"

Jonah gritted his teeth and looked at the trees racing by. "Just hasn't happened yet."

"Oh. You strike me as the type of guy who marries his high school sweetheart." Avery's tone was casual, but she couldn't possibly understand how painful her comment was.

Jonah eased on the brakes and came to a stop at a red light. He swallowed the blooming emotion in his throat and nodded in her direction. "What about you? Did that blazer come with an engagement ring?"

Avery snorted and removed her feet from the dashboard. "No way."

"Can I ask why?" Jonah smirked and peeked at her out of the corner of his eye. The light changed to green, and the engine rumbled when he stepped on the gas.

"Har-har." Avery rolled her eyes. "I'm twenty-seven, not old like you."

Jonah coughed in surprise. "Old? How old do you think I am?"

Avery wiggled her head. "I don't know. Not as old as Uncle Stan, but . . ."

"Wow. Thanks." Jonah knew this last year had put him through the wringer, but he didn't realize he could pass for Stan's slightly younger brother. "I turn thirty-two in October."

Avery slammed her hand over her mouth. "For real? I'm sorry. It's not that I think you look old, but you act more mature than most of the other thirty-something's I know."

"There's a difference between country life and city life I suppose." Jonah felt Avery's eyes roam down his frame. Did she like what she saw, or did she view him as a grungy old man?

"Yeah," Avery said. A few minutes passed in silence as they merged into downtown traffic. "I went to school out here."

"Where?"

"Cornell. I thought it would impress my dad."

"Mhm," Jonah grunted. "Did it?"

Avery shook her head. "No. Nothing I've done ever has."

Jonah didn't know what to say, so he hummed a few more bars of the song coming through the speakers. He turned into the parking lot and found a spot close to one of the cart bays.

"And here we are." Jonah put the truck in park and leaned his head against the head rest. "I'll wait here."

Avery's eyes widened as she turned to face him. "You're not coming in?"

"Ah, no."

"But I thought you were hungry."

Jonah lifted the brim of his hat and arched his eyebrows. If he didn't know any better, he would say she was nervous. "I'm always hungry."

"Great, let's go then." Avery unbuckled her seat belt and was out of the truck in a handful of seconds.

A low hiss slithered through Jonah's teeth as he turned the key and took it out of the ignition. Climbing out, he locked the doors and saw Avery was already headed in. He shook his head and followed. This girl was making him dizzy.

Chapter 7: Avery

Automatic doors breezed open with a hushed whoosh. Avery strode inside and snagged a cart haphazardly parked to the left of the inner doors. She guided it with the tips of her fingers and grabbed a sanitizing wipe from the wobbling stand, cleaning the entire surface of the handle.

"People actually use those things?" Jonah's deep voice vibrated in her ear. His proximity sent a small shiver down her back. He smelled of lumber and warm grass. Avery swayed on her feet, thankful she'd exchanged her heels for the sturdy Chucks.

"Are you kidding? Do you know how many people touch these?"

Jonah fell into step beside her and nodded to the elderly greeter perched on a wooden stool. Avery drove the cart forward and was met with a large crate of oranges. Jonah pointed to the right.

"Essentials are that way, and women's clothes are diagonal and to the right."

"Great, let's start with clothes. I need to get out of this dress."

"I bet."

"What?" Avery shot him an annoyed look.

"You seem like you're being squeezed, is all."

Avery hooked her fingers into the top of her dress and hiked up the shiny fabric. "I only planned on wearing it for a few hours." She tried to cover her cleavage, but the material slipped back to its original position. Defeated, she settled for buttoning the blazer instead.

Jonah didn't say anything. They walked in silence, passing racks of men's shorts and a disheveled bin of sneakers and flip-flops. Avery followed a path to the left and spied a wall of women's intimates ahead. She smirked. She couldn't wait to see the grumpy lumberjack squirm as she picked out panties.

Parking the cart over to the side, she started combing through the display. Most of the panties available were large bikini-cut in obnoxious patterns like leopard and polka dot. She grabbed a few. No woman liked to wear thongs during that time of the month.

"Interesting choice," Jonah said behind her as she threw the underwear into the cart.

"Underwear shouldn't always be sexy."

Jonah pursed his lips. "You could have fooled me with that little pink shoestring you pulled out of your bag earlier."

Avery flushed. She hadn't realized he'd been paying attention, but the thought of him picturing her wearing the tiny panty was empowering. "That pink shoestring, as you called it, is for special occasions and honorary eyes only." As she traveled down the wall, her fingers skipped from style to style. Jonah stayed by the cart, but his gaze trailed her movements.

She reached up and removed a pair of simple gray boyshorts from the hook. "These, for example, are my favorite. They provide adequate coverage, don't ride up, and pair perfectly with a t-shirt for bed."

Jonah cocked his head. "I'll take your word for it."

Avery sifted through the colors and piled her selections atop the rest, before turning to the thongs. They weren't nearly as sexy as the designer brands she usually purchased in the city, but the lace was soft. Plus, she didn't exactly have a booked calendar of events, and she doubted there would be many opportunities that called for sexy attire at the orchard. She tossed a few pairs in though, just in case.

It was easy to see Jonah liked to keep his distance, but she was shocked at his maturity. Most guys she hung around with would never have stood by while she shopped for underwear, at least not without making sexual comments or lewd jokes, but Jonah simply waited, content to let her browse.

Avery meandered down the aisle and found two push-up bras in her size. Just in case she found an ideal path for jogging, she snagged a white sports bra. As for the rest of her wardrobe, she managed to find several pairs of cut-off shorts, a few tanks, and one oversized sweatshirt for the occasional chilly mornings.

"I think I'm set. Where's the shampoo and stuff?"

Jonah hooked his thumb back the way they came. "You should grab some socks, too. Otherwise, those shoes will cut up your ankles."

"Thanks, I didn't even think about that."

Jonah nodded in his sturdy, silent manner and pushed the cart. Avery chewed the inside of her cheek while she tossed a pack of a dozen low-rise socks into the cart's swelling belly. They changed direction and passed a multi-tiered greeting card stand and Jenga-like display of brightly colored microwaves. Catching sight of the haircare and feminine hygiene product aisles, Avery took the lead.

"What size shoe are you?" Jonah asked as they neared an end cap decorated with loofas.

"An 8 ½."

Jonah nodded and pointed to the bathroom supplies. "If you're all right to finish up here, I'll grab you some shoes. I don't know how long Carrie's pair will last."

Avery glanced down at the ratty Converse, touched by his concern. "Thanks. That'd be awesome."

"Be right back." Jonah left before Avery could say anything else. She watched him go, noting his subtle swagger as he maneuvered around old ladies in motorized scooters and mothers wrangling children as they dangled off the noses of their carts.

Her first impression of the farmhand was that he was a cocky asshole, but the more time she spent with him, the more she wanted to chip away his tough exterior and reveal the center he was trying so hard to cover up.

She pushed the cart toward the deodorant and body wash, thinking maybe this summer wouldn't be so bad after all.

Chapter 8: Avery

Satisfied the contents of her cart would be sufficient to get her through the next couple of months, Avery wandered through the towering shelves and miscellaneous bins back toward the registers. Farther down, a few self-checkout lanes were free, but the thought of having to scan and then balance everything on that notebook-sized platform wasn't appealing. She stretched onto her tiptoes and searched the sea of faces for Jonah, but the cowboy's scowl was nowhere to be seen.

Avery grumbled to herself and got in line behind a dad and two kids. He stared at his phone while his boys stealthily snuck candy bar after candy bar through the slits in the cart. An elderly woman in front of them was torn between two different packs of cigarettes at the register, giving the kids plenty of time to smuggle their contraband.

"There you are."

Again, Jonah's rough timbre sounded close to her ear and made her knees go weak. She frowned. What was wrong with her? She was the one always in control. She didn't swoon over guys. They were tools to be used, nothing more. She cleared her throat and steadied herself.

"Yeah, hey. I just finished over there," Avery said, pointing to the cardboard unit of sunblock.

"Nice. I found these. What do you think?" Jonah held up a pair of white New Balance with purple slashes along the side.

"Wow." Avery took the offered sneakers and stuck her finger inside. A squishy pad of memory foam bounced under her touch. "These are great. Thank you."

Jonah raised his other hand. Suspended from his thumb was a pair of black sandals, punctuated by a delicate floral pattern. There was no heel, but they were perfect for an evening orchard stroll.

Touched by his thoughtfulness, Avery accepted the sandals and ran her nail along the dainty silver buckle. "That was sweet of you. Thanks, Jonah."

Jonah nodded curtly. "Glad you like them."

The line started to move. Avery was pleased to see the father in front of her unknowingly loaded the candy with the rest of his purchases while his kids stood to the side with large smiles plastered on their faces.

Once it was her turn, Avery placed her items onto the conveyor belt and stepped back. She dug in her purse for her credit card, but the moment her fingers brushed the solid edge, her heart raced. Uncle Stan's words flooded her mind. She regarded the small mountain of clothes and toiletries with a sinking feeling. The fifty from her uncle would help but would never be enough to cover it all.

Blind to her panic, the cashier scanned item after item. The loud beep of the machine matched Avery's pounding heart. Biting her lip, she stepped forward and pushed the cart closer to the growing pile of large paper bags stacked on the carousel. The flashing display totaled $118.64.

"Cash or card?" the cashier asked.

"Um, card please." Avery withdrew the credit card from its little pocket on the side of her clutch.

"Go ahead and insert."

Avery offered a silent prayer to whichever saint looked after children forsaken by their parents and slid her card into the reader. She held her breath and waited for the soft pinging command to remove her card. Instead, an abrupt buzzing sounded.

"Your card was declined. Do you have another form of payment?" The cashier regarded her with an apathetic stare.

"Ah, yes, I have some cash." Avery fumbled with her purse and threw the useless credit card to the bottom as she tried to stem the gathering tears. She grabbed the fifty, a crumpled five, and a few ones. "I have um . . . fifty-nine dollars. Is there any way I can take a few things off?"

Avery didn't miss the way the girl eyed her expensive dress. Humiliation burned her cheeks.

"What don't you want?"

Avery glanced to her left. Jonah was reading a magazine with a large fish on the cover. Thankfully he seemed oblivious. "The hair dye, the hair dryer, the mascara, the eye makeup remover, and the sandals please."

The cashier nodded, popped her gum, and removed the large hairdryer and box of blond hair color from the belt, then placed them into a bin behind her. The sound roused Jonah from his article, and he glanced up. Avery kept her eyes on the shrinking pile.

"Everything okay?" Jonah asked as he returned the magazine.

"Yup," Avery said in a tight voice.

The cashier tossed the mascara and makeup remover in as well but paused before the sneakers and sandals. "Which ones didn't you want again?"

Avery brushed her hand through her hair to block Jonah's

view. "Um, the sandals please." She felt his broad body sidle up closer.

"Sorry, I thought you'd like them."

Hearing the disappointment in his voice made Avery want to crawl into a hole.

"She doesn't have enough money," the cashier explained in a bored tone.

Jonah turned to Avery. "What do you mean? Why didn't you say something?"

Avery shrugged and held up her inadequate cash. "Dad cut me off. My credit card was declined. Uncle Stan gave me fifty bucks, but I . . ."

She had never shopped on a budget before and had always dismissed the numbers beneath each product as mere decoration. There was also a part of her that refused to believe her father would not only abandon her, but leave her with no means to support herself as well. Her bottom lip wobbled with the realization that after all these years of excusing her father's behavior and absences, the truth was, he didn't care about her.

Jonah's face softened. "How much do you need?"

"For all of it, it's $118.64."

"I have fifty-nine and I really don't need the hairdryer and color."

Jonah turned to the cashier. "What's the total without those two things?"

The cashier scanned the mascara and makeup remover back into the total. "$72.36."

"Great." Jonah dug his wallet out of his back pocket and handed the cashier a twenty.

Avery passed her wrinkled bills to the girl as well and exhaled as a single tear fell. "Thank you, Jonah. I'll pay you back. I promise."

Jonah waved his hand as the cashier handed him his change. "It was like ten bucks. No big deal." He reached past her and piled the bags into the cart. "Thank you very much." He waved to the cashier and slid his hand on Avery's lower back, gently guiding her forward.

Avery's steps faltered as the heat from his palm radiated through both the blazer and her dress.

"Whoa, I got you. Was there anything else you needed?"

Avery shook her head and allowed Jonah to walk her out of the store and back into the parking lot. He didn't remove his hand, but she didn't ask him to either. "No, I'm all set. Thanks again." She wished her voice didn't sound so small.

His truck came into view as they jogged out of the path of an oncoming minivan. "Like I said, it was no big deal. Everyone needs help." They walked the rest of the way in silence, then Jonah removed his hand and tossed her the keys. "Hop on in and get her started. I'll load these up."

Avery caught the flying keys and unlocked the driver's side door. She climbed into the cab and slid across the bench seat. An image of herself straddling Jonah—his large hands squeezing her hips—flashed through her mind as he sat behind the wheel. She shook her head and focused on the cooling skin above her backside where he'd held her.

She needed to get a grip.

Avery slid the key into the ignition and the engine roared to life. Outside, Jonah shut the tailgate and joined her a minute later.

"Ready?" he asked. He put the truck in drive and eased out of the parking lot.

Avery regarded him with narrowed eyes.

Jonah seemed to sense her concentrated stare and arched his brow. "What's up?"

"You're too good at this," Avery said.

"What?"

Avery waved her hands. "All this—the shopping, the shoes, the swooping in to save the day. Most guys don't know how to do that. The thought doesn't even cross their mind."

"So?"

"Who taught you? And don't say your Mama because as hard as moms work to teach their sons, the second they get out on their own, those lessons evaporate from their tiny brains."

"Why does it matter?"

Avery shrugged and angled her body toward him like a needle on a compass finding true north. "We're going to be working together all summer. I want to know who you are."

Jonah fixed his eyes on the road. "Seems presumptuous. I don't see you volunteering your life story."

Avery rolled her eyes. "Fine, what do you want to know?"

"Nothing." Jonah's answer was flat.

"What do you mean?" Avery frowned.

"I don't care. I don't need to know what kind of person you are to work beside you at the orchard."

"I'm just trying to be friendly."

"By demanding I spill my past trauma? I don't think so."

Avery threw up her hands. Ire prickled the back of her mind. "It was a simple question. And I didn't demand to know your trauma. I asked who taught you to be so intuitive when it comes to women. Christ, I assumed you were going to say your wife, that's all." She crossed her arms and slammed her back against the seat, determinedly staring out the window.

"I'm not married," Jonah grumbled. Once more his knuckles tightened to sharp peaks over the steering wheel.

"Great." Avery spat, not taking her eyes off the road. Jonah turned to her but didn't say anything. They spent the rest of the drive in tense silence. Part of Avery weighed heavy with guilt. They'd had a nice time at the store, and Jonah was a gentleman, but his nice guy side warred with another personality, a true asshole.

Avery sunk lower in her seat. Warmth spread to her cheeks as her thoughts drifted to the memory of her earlier fantasy. Gone was her desire. Jonah could join the list right next to *fucking Todd* for all she cared.

Chapter 9: Jonah

Jonah flinched as Avery slammed the passenger side door and stalked to the back. He climbed down and closed his door as well before meandering to the truck bed. He knew Avery wouldn't know how to put the tailgate down, and part of him was looking forward to watching her struggle.

His boots crunched on the gravel as seconds later, a flurry of cuss words broke their stalemate. Sure enough, Avery was trying to yank it down.

"Slow down. You're going to hurt yourself," Jonah said.

"I don't need your help." Avery shot back. She jumped up onto the bumper and leaned over to hook the bags with her finger.

Forgetting her limited wardrobe, Jonah watched as Avery's arm flailed around, not even close to the bags. The movement caused her cocktail dress to ride up over her thighs and exposed the round swell of her ass. She leaned further, and he caught sight of white panties cupping the sweet mound between her legs.

Jonah knew he should look away, knew that staring at her most vulnerable part without her knowledge meant he was being a creep, but he was only enjoying the view. He would stop as soon as she stopped being so damn proud and asked for help.

As Avery stretched, her dress scooched higher, revealing more of her perky ass. Her thong rose as well, pulling the fabric taut. Jonah swallowed. He could see the definition of her pussy through the thin white cotton. His cock pulsed, growing thick under his jeans. It'd been so long since he was with a woman. Even the urge to pleasure himself had fled after everything that happened.

He shifted and took a step back. The desire to reach out and stroke her sweet pussy was overwhelming. He wondered what she would do if he brushed her panties aside and slid a finger into her warm center. Would she smack his hand away, or moan and arch into his touch, inviting him deeper?

Jonah licked his bottom lip. His cock strained against the stiff denim, growing uncomfortable in the confined space. He imagined undoing his pants and letting his shaft spring free. Then he'd climb up behind her on the bumper and slide his dick into her wet slit. He'd grab her hips and thrust while she held onto the tailgate, and they'd rock the truck like in the old movies.

He took an involuntary step forward and rubbed the front of his jeans with his palm. She was at the perfect height. He could press his face against her panties and feel the heat from her pussy, pull the fabric away with his teeth . . .

"Yes!"

Avery cheered and dispelled Jonah's daydream. Had he spoken out loud? Quickly, he stuck his hand down the front of his pants and pulled his hard length up to hide its bulge in the waistband of his boxers.

"Told you I didn't need your help." Avery wrinkled her nose and glanced at him over her shoulder. A loud whooshing sound echoed as she slid the bags to the edge. Using both her arms, she scooped the first one up and turned. "Can you take this?"

Jonah fixed his hat and reached up. He gritted his teeth as she passed him the crinkly paper bag. Could she read all his dirty thoughts? He shifted the bag to his hip and took the second one she offered. Then he stepped back to give her room to dismount.

With the last bag in hand, Avery jumped off the bumper and landed on the balls of her feet. "Oops!"

Her dress hiked up even farther when she landed. A toned thigh winked at him, as did the triangular front of her panties. A rose emblem decorated the intimate fabric, and Jonah wondered if she smelled as sweet as the flower.

"Were you staring at me?" Avery asked. She balanced the bag in one hand while the other righted her dress.

"A little bit." He didn't see a reason to lie.

"Hmm." Avery raised her chin and started walking to the main house. "See anything you like?"

Her brashness caught Jonah off guard. He fell into step behind her. "Maybe."

Avery's brown eyes burned as she held his gaze. He wished he could tell what she was thinking. Was she offended? Flattered?

"I wouldn't get my hopes up if I were you, sir."

Jonah's cock stirred again. The way she called him sir stirred some primal instinct. Avery spun back around and continued walking. He couldn't be sure because her blazer was so large, but she seemed to be wiggling her ass as if daring him to come after her. The curtains swished. Carrie's silhouette was visible through the sheer fabric. No doubt she was spying on them.

Jonah swallowed his desire and followed Avery into the house. At least her interrogative nature seemed to have subsided.

"How was it?" Carrie asked when they stepped through the doorway.

"Great," Avery answered. "I think I got everything I need." A sigh crept into her voice. "But you were right, Uncle Stan. Dad cut me off. I'm sorry I had to use your money. Jonah even pitched in a few bucks, too."

Carrie gave him a kind smile. "That was nice of you, Jonah. I'm sorry to hear about your father, Avery. I don't understand treating one's children so . . . but it's not my place to say anything."

Stan waved a hand in front of his face and set aside his large book of sudoku puzzles. "No problem at all, short stack. If you need any money from here on out, just let me know, okay?"

Avery blushed and nodded. "If it's all right with you, I'd like to earn what I can. I don't know how much my take home will be after room and board, but I don't want to be a freeloader."

"I appreciate that, honey, but don't worry. I won't lose any sleep putting you to work."

Stan snorted, and Avery laughed. Jonah couldn't wait to see how the Barbie did on her first day.

Carrie motioned to a row of small cottages standing a few hundred yards away from the main house, lodging for the summer help. "I'll help you carry your things and get you set up."

Jonah cleared his throat and hoisted the bags he held. "Don't worry, Carrie. I can help her get settled. I'm heading that way anyway."

Carrie paused and gave him a long look. She knew he wasn't interested in starting a new relationship so soon, but Jonah could tell she still wasn't comfortable with her niece living so close to him.

Stan answered before Carrie found the words to refuse his

offer. "That sounds great, Jonah. Y'all get settled in. I'm about to throw some burgers on the grill, so come on up after and we'll have supper."

Jonah gave him a curt nod and gestured toward the door. "After you."

At first, it looked like Avery might ignore him, but then she pivoted on her heels and walked outside.

"You're in cabin four, Jonah, and put Avery in one," Carrie said. The veiled warning simmered in her eyes.

"Yes, ma'am."

Jonah bit his tongue, grateful she hadn't witnessed the scene in the driveway. She would've smacked him into next week if she had.

They walked together down the slightly sloped lawn to a row of four mini-cabins. Each was identical with a small, covered porch large enough to stand beneath or decorate with a flowerpot. Two windows framed the front door. In truth, they looked more like the children's play set over by the signature, giant Adirondack chair for photo-ops than real residences.

Avery marched toward the third cabin, a woman on a mission. Jonah called out to her. "Carrie said to put you in cabin one."

Avery paused her stride and angled her body toward the designated building. A wrinkle formed between her eyebrows. "I don't want to be on the end. It's too exposed."

Jonah huffed and pointed to the second one. "Take the one next to it then."

"The path to the front door is all muddy. I want that one." Avery pointed to the third cabin, the one right beside his.

"Marissa usually stays there."

Avery tossed her short, cropped hair over her shoulder and winked. "Too bad. I got here first this year." She continued and wrenched open the door to cabin three. Jonah groaned and looked to the sky. A few lazy clouds painted the golden canvas. He couldn't wait for Carrie to give him an earful.

Jonah crossed the porch and entered the cozy cabin. They all had the same interior layout: a twin bed along the right wall, a narrow table-desk to the left with a fold-out seat, a microwave and a hot plate beside that, and a closet wide enough to hang several shirts and to kick your boots into at the end of the day. It wasn't a huge space, but with working in the orchard 'til dusk, there wasn't any reason why it should be.

"Whoa . . . this is . . . quaint," Avery said as she set the paper bag on the table.

"It'll keep you warm and dry. Can't ask for much more." Jonah placed the rest of the bags on the bed. A square window looked directly into his cabin. He frowned at the sheer panel curtains. This was going to be interesting.

"Where's the bathroom? Behind the closet?" Avery opened the closet door and pushed on the back wall as if a bathroom would appear like Narnia.

"Bathrooms are out back. They're co-ed with two stalls and one shower head. I recommend getting there early. Otherwise, it can be quite a wait."

"Seriously? What if I have to pee in the middle of the night?" Avery stared out the window, fear in her wide eyes.

"We're on an orchard . . . not in the middle of the woods. Take a flashlight."

Avery frowned. "Everything is so much spookier at night."

Jonah snickered. "Big city girl is scared? Don't you have muggings and gun-shots going off all night long?"

Avery fixed him with an icy stare. "Not all the time. And the lights never go out in the city. Don't you find it smothering? I remember hating that part when I was younger."

The small space forced them to stand close together, and the tips of their shoes kissed. Avery tilted her head and sighed. Her breasts almost brushed Jonah's chest. Suddenly, the room was too warm. He caught the faint scent of her shampoo and floral perfume once more. She was so close.

If he leaned down and kissed her, would she push him away? Jonah gazed at her, drowning in her amber eyes. What was wrong with him? He'd only met this woman a few hours ago, and already he was fantasizing about what she tasted like.

Jonah leaned back and pushed up his sleeves. "Well, I'll let you settle in. I need to unpack my stuff, then I'll meet you up at the house."

"Okay." Avery breathed. She shrugged out of the blazer and threw it in a heap on the bed. "It'll be nice to get out of this." She brushed a hand down the front of the tight material. For the first time, Jonah was able to see her full figure. Her hips were wider than he'd originally guessed. His cock pulsed again.

"Okay, I'll see you later." Jonah turned his hat around so the brim faced the back and exited the cabin. He shut the door firmly behind him. Was he the only one who could feel the tension between them? He didn't even like the little brat, but there was something about her that drew him like a moth to a flame.

Turning to the left, Jonah stepped onto his front porch and pulled open the cottage door. The sight of the bag he'd thrown onto the bed earlier greeted him. The straps flopped over the side of the mattress like the arms of a satisfied woman. He pictured Avery sprawled there, a big smile on her face as he played between her thighs.

"Shit," Jonah cursed under his breath. She was already in his head, and that was a dangerous place to be. He walked inside and kicked off his boots. There was no way he would be able to make it through dinner in his current state.

Confusion and guilt warred within him, threatening to pop. He dug through his bag and fished out an old pair of sneakers and a pair of gym shorts. A hard run through the orchard would clear his mind and hopefully the dirty thoughts that had his body in a chokehold.

Jonah changed and headed back outside a minute later. He'd grabbed his ankle and relaxed into a stretch when Avery's curtain flickered. He switched to the other side as her small desk lamp illuminated her house. Her curvy shadow was easy to identify beyond the thin sheers, and he pictured the slow, sensual way she was about to slip off her dress. A guttural groan thundered in the back of his throat.

To hell with stretching. He'd rather get a cramp than be subjected to Avery's strip tease. He started with a slow jog, and his breathing came easier once the cabins began to shrink behind him. The orchard opened before him several minutes later, a serene oasis that stretched toward the horizon. He dug in his heels and exploded into a hard sprint, desperate to outrun the new girl and his guilty conscience.

Chapter 10: Avery

Avery let the thin curtain fall once Jonah disappeared. She couldn't figure him out. He hadn't given the impression that he wanted to fit in a workout before dinner. She was shocked he even owned a pair of sneakers. He seemed far too rustic, but he shot into the trees like Death himself had leveled him with his scythe and demanded his soul.

The cowboy's apathetic demeanor was wearing thin as well. She'd only been subjected to his hooded stares and indecipherable mumbles for a few hours, but she was already sick of the way he regarded her. She wasn't some "woo girl" who spent her nights dancing in clubs. She had an MBA from Cornell and every intention of becoming a proper executive at her father's marketing firm.

Avery reached behind herself and unzipped the teeth that held her body captive in the tight, metallic fabric. Her breasts spilled forward, no longer compressed, and she let out a relieved sigh. Had Jonah fled because she started to undress? Anger swelled within her. She was in her cabin. Did he expect her to change in the bathroom stall like this was middle school gym class?

Avery dumped the paper bag's contents onto her bed and grumbled under her breath. Earlier when she unloaded the truck, she had felt Jonah's heavy gaze linger on her. She wasn't an idiot. She knew he was staring at her ass. Maybe he'd even seen her cunt when she bent forward.

She wasn't opposed to his attention. Being able to control and manipulate a man with a simple pop of her hip was empowering, and Avery craved control. Enough things in her life had been forced upon her: a new nanny every three months to prevent attachments, tortuous piano lessons every other day to ensure she'd become a cultured young woman, strict exercise regimen and dietary counseling since she turned twelve. Image was everything, and according to her father, he'd carefully curated the perfect body shape to guarantee her success. Ironically, it was the selfish bastard's own hand that prevented her from climbing atop that almost unachievable pedestal he'd force-fed her for her entire life.

Jonah had even admitted to staring when she called him out on it. Clearly, he was attracted to some part of her, but she got the impression the majority of him wanted nothing to do with her. Avery expelled an exaggerated breath that sent a strand of hair hanging in front of her mouth into the air. She grabbed a simple white cotton t-shirt and pulled it over her head. Her light pink bra was somewhat visible, but she didn't care. It had been a long day, and she wasn't going to change to make the grumpy cowboy comfortable.

With a quick jerk, Avery ripped the plastic tab from the new denim shorts and stepped into the twin openings. They were a little snug around her hips and hugged the top of her legs, but that wasn't surprising. It was hard to find bottoms that could handle her ass and thighs.

She glanced at her phone screen. It had only been fifteen minutes. She could probably find a home for her new things before it was time to head back up for dinner. Avery thumbed through her Spotify until she found a cool indie rock playlist and lost herself to the music streaming through the tiny speakers as she arranged her belongings.

Forty minutes later, dusk had fallen and transformed the peaceful orchard. Gone were the slanting gilded rays, but in their place was a hazy lavender glow that descended on the trees from the tangerine and violet sky.

Avery turned off her music and stepped onto her small porch. She glanced to the left at Jonah's cabin. She hadn't paid attention to when or if he'd returned from his run, but since he was expected at dinner as well, she didn't want to be rude and walk off without him.

Rolling her eyes, Avery hopped down the few stairs to the well-worn path. Against her better judgement, she marched to cabin four and rapped her knuckles on Jonah's door. Her toes beat a steady rhythm atop the planks as she waited, but no movement sounded from within.

"Nice. The bastard left without me."

Avery spun around and stomped off the porch. Why was she letting him bother her so? He didn't give two shits about her. She increased her pace and studied the unfamiliar terrain. In the darkening twilight, the last thing she needed was to twist her ankle on a hidden gopher hole. She worried her lower lip between her teeth, a habit she'd cultivated when she was little to stem her anxiety. How long ago did Jonah leave? Would Aunt Carrie be upset she'd taken so long to arrive? It wasn't her fault. If the arrogant farmhand had told her.

Avery smacked into a solid wall and bounced backward with enough force to rattle her teeth. Her forehead stung from the impact, but when she looked up to inspect the surprise barrier, Jonah's hooded hazel eyes stared back at her, clearly as shocked as she was.

Slippery skin met her touch as she tried to steady herself, and she realized with abhorrent alarm that she was not only touching Jonah, but that he was also very naked. Naked and wet. Tiny droplets ran from his short dark hair.

Unable to stop herself, Avery let her eyes rove over every inch of him, from the spiky tendrils of hair that hovered over his thick eyebrows to his defined chest, complete with the spectacular 'v' just visible above the terry cloth towel wrapped around his waist. Jonah balled the extra length in his fist, but the material had fallen a fraction when they collided.

"Uh, sorry. I didn't see you there." Avery stammered. Her fingertips traced the curve of his bicep as she withdrew her arm and pressed it tight to her side. Her eyes roamed his body, searching for an innocent place to rest, but every part of this near-naked man set her heart racing. His surprise quickly soured, returning to the casual indifference he'd regarded her with all day. As his posture stiffened, he hiked the towel higher.

She scoffed. He acted as if she were some virtue-stealing villain come to trick him into surrendering his virginity. Slyly, she assessed his firm abs once more. With a body like that, she wouldn't mind playing the bad guy.

"Obviously," Jonah replied.

Avery drove her hands into her hips. "You bumped into me, too. You're just as much to blame. What are you doing over here? I thought you were running?"

Jonah was quiet for a moment. His lips turned up with slight amusement, but his eyes remained dark. "Were you watching me?"

Avery crossed her arms and matched his stare. "A little bit." Déjà vu assailed her. She waited to see if he would recite her own line from earlier, but instead, he hung his head and hitched the towel higher up his torso.

"Excuse me. I need to get dressed for dinner."

Right. Dinner.

Avery snapped out her fantasy of trailing his abs with her nails and shook her head. "Yeah, you do. I mean, you should."

Jonah cocked his head and furrowed his brow before stepping around her and continuing on his way. Desire thrummed in the back of Avery's throat as she caught the way the fading light highlighted the contours of his back. He may not be interested in her, but that wouldn't stop her from enjoying the view. Now they were even.

Chapter 11: Avery

Avery meandered across the crunchy grass toward the main house. The clean air and fragrant flowers pushed the distracting thoughts of Jonah away and brought back nostalgic memories. As much as she hated her father for duping her and forcing her to leave the city, Uncle Stan's orchard was one of her favorite places in the world.

Without all the pressure, noises, and wealth the city demanded every day, Avery was gloriously untethered, a solitary balloon twirling in the endless blue sky. She would take the summer to reset and refocus her life, then show her father she was better than all his ass-kissing lackeys.

Avery followed the wrap-around porch to the west side of the house. The smell of charred ground beef and muted laughter greeted her as her family came into view. Uncle Stan manned the grill, the neck of a beer bottle clutched between his fingers.

"Avs, is that you?" Aunt Carrie materialized on the other side of the grill, weighed down with plates. She set them on the picnic table and brushed her long braid over her shoulder.

Avery crossed the porch and gave Uncle Stan a quick peck on the cheek. "Yup. Just finished putting most of my stuff away."

"Good. If you don't mind, I could use your help in the kitchen," Aunt Carrie called over her shoulder. She didn't wait for Avery's reply before she toddled back inside.

"Thanks, honey." Uncle Stan—used to being the one subjected to his wife's instructions— winked.

She smirked and followed her aunt through the sliding glass door that led to the kitchen. Aunt Carrie stood in front of the stove, stirring a big brass pot of baked beans. Avery balanced her palms on the edge of the granite island. "What can I do?"

Aunt Carrie continued to stir the beans with one hand and pointed to the island with the other. Laid out before them was a large cutting board with two plump tomatoes. One had already been sliced and its slimy innards spilled over the sharp blade beside it.

"Finish slicing the rest of those. Then grab the lettuce and American cheese from the fridge." Aunt Carrie directed.

"On it." Avery picked up the knife and started where her aunt had left off. Her first few slices were too thin, and mushy pulp slid over her fingers, but thankfully the rest of her cuts were useable. She moved the tomato to the cornflower blue and white serving dish near the cutting board and retrieved the rest of the ingredients.

Avery unraveled a few sheets of lettuce and ran them under the cold water. The ripping sound they made as she tore them into smaller pieces made her smile. The cheese was last, and she peeled a dozen slices off the plastic sheets and arranged them in the remaining space on the plate.

"Nice job," Aunt Carrie said when she saw Avery's progress.

"Thanks. Want me to bring this out now?"

"Grab those buns and put them on there too, then it should be good."

Avery located the generic burger buns in the blue cellophane.

"Should I use them all?"

Aunt Carrie scoffed. "With the way those boys eat, we'll probably have to crack open another bag."

Avery laughed and picked up the artfully designed plate. She pivoted on her heel, but her aunt's voice stopped her.

"Speaking of Jonah, what do you think of him?"

Avery's brow wrinkled. "I don't really know anything about him. He kept to himself for most of the ride." A tiny shiver tickled the back of her neck as she recalled the heat of his palm, and the intimidating definition of his biceps as she stumbled against him. Truth was, she was curious to get to know him, but at the same time, his condescending attitude was enough to douse her attraction.

Her aunt turned the burner off and hefted the pan, a blue potholder secured around the handle. "Jonah is a very nice boy. I only bring it up because I want you to keep your distance." Aunt Carrie poured the beans into a matching bowl and fixed Avery with a hard stare.

"Aunt Carrie, I don't—"

Her aunt held up her empty hand and bowed her head. "Now I'm not trying to pry, and I have no reason to suspect, but he's a good man who has been through a lot. He's already had his heart broken into more pieces than you can imagine."

Avery was a bit taken aback. "I just met him."

Her aunt shook her head and returned the pan to the burner. "I know, and I'm sorry to put you on the spot, it's just . . . you're young and very beautiful. Try not to lead him on, okay?"

Avery nodded. There wasn't much else she could do. Embarrassment flooded her cheeks. What had her father told them about her? It was true she had slept with several men, but she had very good reasons to bed every one of them. Jonah was attractive, but did her aunt honestly think she planned to make him her boy toy all summer and leave? She wasn't there to fuck around (*literally*).

Aunt Carrie gave her a tight smile and shooed her to the door. "Good. Now, take that outside and we can eat. I'll be right behind you with these beans."

Avery grabbed the heavy plate and darted back out the sliding glass door, more than eager to get away.

"Perfect timing, honey," Uncle Stan said. "These burgers are coming off the grill right now."

Avery set the large plate down in the center of the table and grabbed a beer from the cooler. She twisted off the top and took a long swig. With a sigh, she lowered the bottle and leaned over the railing, looking out over the orchard. A warm breeze brushed her arms.

"Everything all right?"

Jonah leaned against the rail beside her, careful to keep a conservative distance between them. He had forgone his customary ball cap, and his short hair curled in gentle waves. A fresh black t-shirt clung to his lean torso above clean, well-fitting jeans.

Avery shot a quick glance over her shoulder. Aunt Carrie was still inside fussing over the beans. "Nothing, just my aunt."

Jonah scrunched his eyebrows. "Did something happen?"

Avery exhaled a long breath and took another healthy swig. "She warned me to stay away from you. Apparently, I'm a bad girl who plans to corrupt your morals and shatter your heart."

Jonah snorted. "What?"

"Yup." Avery deepened her slouch and took another deep swig. She rarely drank. She would have to remember to pace herself.

Jonah's nail picked at the label on his beer bottle. "She's right about one thing. You should stay away from me."

The alcohol burned in her stomach. "And why is that? Are you some devilish rogue that toys with women? Or maybe a sexy vampire waiting to consume me during the next full moon?"

"Nah. Vampires don't need to wait for a full moon."

"What then? Did some other woman ruin you for good?"

Jonah took a large drink and pushed off the railing. "Something like that."

Avery frowned. Earlier, she'd said he seemed like the type of guy to marry his high school sweetheart. Maybe he'd tried, but before they could reach happily ever after, she left him for a different knight in shining armor. She wanted to ask what he meant, but the sound of the glass door sliding open pulled her from her thoughts.

"Come on over, you two," Aunt Carrie called. "Food's ready."

Avery gave her hair a quick shake and fell into step behind Jonah. She grabbed another beer and sat down opposite him. He didn't look at her. Instead, he kept his eyes downcast as if purposefully avoiding her stare.

She finished the contents of her first beer and happily piled her plate with a burger, beans, and chips. Her father and her nutrition coach could go to hell. Tonight, she would enjoy herself without worrying about the constant demons that haunted the back of her mind.

She brought the delicious contraband to her mouth and sank her teeth in. Over the curve of the bun, she caught Jonah's eye and was shocked to recognize the pain reflected in his stare. It seemed she wasn't the only one struggling to silence the voices inside.

Chapter 12: Avery

An hour, and numerous funny anecdotes about her aunt and uncle's first year starting the orchard later, Avery's stomach bulged. Thankfully, high waisted shorts were trending. She thought she could brush off Jonah's remark, but it wriggled inside and latched on. Who had hurt him? And how was he coping?

She had only planned to eat half of her burger, but her nerves were fried. It helped to have something to occupy herself with. One and a half burgers later, Avery was about to explode. She finished her third beer and wiped her mouth with the back of her hand. Her head swam with the alcohol. She needed to lie down.

"Thank you for dinner, guys. This was great." She pushed her chair out and stood, tipping back slightly.

"Whoa, you okay there?" Uncle Stan asked.

Avery caught herself with the top of the wooden frame. "Yeah, I don't drink much. I'm going to take a shower and get some sleep."

"All right, honey." Uncle Stan laughed. "Goodnight."

Aunt Carrie scooched her chair back. "Let me walk you to your cottage."

A third chair scraped the deck. Jonah stood, holding his

plate and an empty bottle. "I'd be happy to walk her. No need for you to stumble through the dark, Carrie."

Aunt Carrie seemed to consider Jonah's offer, but she didn't look pleased. Her lips pinched and her eyes narrowed, as if she was mentally chastising him for his chivalry.

"Perfect. Now I can have you all to myself." Uncle Stan waggled his eyebrows and stood up, giving her aunt's ass a little pat.

"Oof, you dirty old man," Aunt Carrie exclaimed, but Avery was pleased to see the tension leave her eyes. "All right, goodnight you two. But head straight to bed. You've got your first day of work in the morning, bright and early."

"Yes, Aunt Carrie," Avery said as Jonah recited a similar acknowledgment. She started to collect the plates, but her aunt waved her off.

"Leave them, honey. We'll take care of this."

"Okay. Night guys, and again, thanks for letting me stay." Her aunt and uncle gave her a kind smile, and she was grateful neither of them mentioned they'd had little choice in the matter.

Jonah waved with one hand, his fingers extended and spread. What would it feel like to be caressed by those hands? Before naughtier thoughts could form, Avery stopped herself. The cowboy was off-limits.

Avery rounded the corner, crossed the long stretch of deck, and hopped down the stairs. Once her feet hit the sloped grass though, her equilibrium sloshed to the right and she stumbled. Rough hands caught her by the waist and kept her from falling into the banister.

"Whoa, easy there," Jonah said. "We haven't even made it to the hill yet."

Avery knocked his hands away. They were too warm, too

big. She didn't want to become familiar with the feel of him. If she did, she'd never want to leave. "I don't need you to hold onto me. I'm fine." She took several more steps, but away from the warm light of the deck, a thick blanket of blackness stretched in every direction. "Um, which way to the cabins again?"

Jonah placed his hand on her lower back to guide her to the left. "This way, but go slow."

"I got it, thanks."

Jonah removed his hand and walked slightly behind her, no doubt ready to catch her when she inevitably fell, but he would be sorely disappointed. Avery kept her footing and reached the door to cabin three a few minutes later. Jonah paused at the foot of her tiny staircase.

"Do you need any help with the showers?" he asked.

Heat flooded Avery's cheeks as the image of their wet bodies pressed together sprung to her mind. She was grateful for the darkness she had cursed moments ago.

"I'm not interested in you washing my back, but thanks."

Avery saw Jonah stiffen and shift his stance. "I didn't mean it like that. I meant finding your way in the dark."

"Oh," Avery paused. "No. Like I said, I'm fine."

Jonah gave her a curt nod and continued to his cabin. "All right, see you in the morning then."

"See you." Avery wandered inside and shut the door. "Shit," she cursed. It was darker than a tomb in there. Reaching into her back pocket, she withdrew her cell phone. The service was spotty, but she only needed the flashlight.

She tapped the screen and pulled down the menu button, activating the strong beam of light at the top. Stumbling to the left, she clicked on the small lamp and sighed in victory. The room flooded with light. Avery looked out the window. Jonah's cabin was dark. Must be nice to slide right into bed.

Avery tossed her hair and rummaged through the remaining paper bags on the bed, but the cavernous black holes were impossible to navigate. She groaned and dumped everything onto the coverlet. Sorting through, she found her shampoo, body wash, and razor, then tossed them into one of the empty bags. She draped her new towel over her other arm and grabbed her makeshift flashlight before heading outside.

The light from her phone revealed the bathroom building, looming like a sleeping giant several yards away. Still tipsy, Avery made her way up the slightly sloping lawn and reached the quiet outpost a minute later. She aimed the beam up and down the wall until she found the switch. A buzzing sounded overhead. There was a single bulb for the whole building which cast an eerie curtain of shadows on the shower stall.

Avery pushed the thought of a serial killer stalking the showers far from her mind and set her phone and bag on the bench across from the cubicles. She scrolled through her playlist and put on something fun and poppy to drown out the fear tickling her spine.

Grateful the shower had a frosted glass door rather than a moldy curtain, she set to work arranging her things. There was even a double hook for her towel. Points to Aunt Carrie for designing this because if it was up to Uncle Stan, it would be a dirt floor and cold water from a hose.

She reached in, cranking the handle to the left, and the water sputtered to life. Avery unbuttoned her shorts and slid the denim and her panties to the floor. Her t-shirt and bra joined the pile shortly after and she stepped inside the warm stream. The water pressure wasn't the best, but at least it was hot and felt wonderful pitter-pattering against her skin after the long day.

Tilting her head back Avery let out a satisfied sigh as the

water ran down her neck. Part of her wished to stand there forever, but it would be her luck to indulge, finally lather up, and run out of hot water. She squirted shampoo into her palm and massaged it along her scalp. Moving on, she reached for her loofa and realized she left it sitting on the bed amongst the mess of the rest of her newly purchased possessions. With little choice, she squeezed a healthy dollop of raspberry blossom body wash into her hand and rubbed it along her body.

Arms, back, breasts, stomach—Avery tried to lather the soap hard enough to create bubbles, but most of it slid down her skin ineffectively. She cursed her forgetfulness and surrendered, deciding to enjoy the warm water instead as it poured down her chest. Her hands cupped her breasts, squeezing gently. Her head lolled to the side, and she closed her eyes.

While one hand teased her left nipple, Avery's other hand trailed down her stomach, her middle finger reaching toward her clit. In slow, rhythmic circles, she moved and pressed the tiny pearl. Pleasure rippled through her. It was amazing to think *fucking Todd* had been between her legs only this morning. Her own touch was so much better than his floppy tongue darting to and fro like he was trying to stab the orgasm out of her.

She dipped her finger into the pooling wetness between her thighs and pushed deeper, eliciting a moan. Enjoying the sensation, Avery forgot about *fucking Todd* and imagined a different tongue licking her pussy, of Jonah's rough hands holding her hips steady while he delighted in her tight center. Another moan cascaded through her as her orgasm built. She remembered the weight of the cowboy's stare as she stood on the truck and imagined him bending her over the bumper and slamming into her. Faster and faster her finger moved, her thumb tapping and pressing her clit in glorious synchrony. She was so close.

A clattering sounded outside the stall, followed by a muted curse. Avery withdrew her hand and shut off the water. She wasn't alone.

79

Chapter 13: Jonah

Shit, shit, shit.

Jonah's toothbrush and toothpaste skittered across the tile floor. He yanked his hand out of his gym shorts and ducked around the stalls toward the pair of sinks on the left. His cock throbbed, aching for release, but the pipes shuttered off a moment later. Avery had heard him. He bent down to retrieve his stuff and the slap of wet feet echoed in the small building.

"What the hell are you doing?" Avery demanded.

Jonah straightened and held his hands up in surrender. "Sorry, I came to brush my teeth and dropped my things. I didn't mean to startle you."

A white towel was hooked beneath Avery's arms. It wasn't long, barely falling an inch below her pussy—the same wet pussy she'd been finger-fucking a second ago. Jonah willed his boner to soften, but the longer he stared at Avery, the harder he grew.

Water droplets ran from her hair, trickled down her neck, and pooled between her breasts. With her hair slicked back, her eyes appeared even larger, and her wet lips shined. The unbidden image of them wrapped around his cock made him thicken. He spoke the truth. He hadn't meant to spy. The plan had been to sneak in, brush his teeth, and get out without her knowing. Because of the frosted glass and condensation, he hadn't even known she was touching herself. Then she moaned, and he couldn't help himself.

Avery's eyes narrowed. "Did you hear me?"

Jonah licked his bottom lip and remained silent for a moment before answering. "Um, I heard the water running."

Avery took two steps closer. "Anything else?" Her voice was quiet and alluring.

Jonah bit his lip. Was this a trap? "Uh, the glass was all fogged up. I promise I couldn't see anything."

She angled her head. "But you heard me. You knew what I was doing in there, right?"

Jonah swallowed as his dick twitched. "Yeah."

Avery looked down at his shorts. The mesh material clearly outlined his erection, as if it were on display. He had discarded his boxers when he changed, so he knew every detail was visible. She glanced down, and her gaze traced his cock over his shorts. The ghost of her imagined touch made him throb painfully.

"Then you know I didn't finish . . ."

Avery's words hung between them. Jonah had no idea what they meant. Maybe it was wishful thinking, but it sounded like an invitation. Heat bloomed in his groin as he took in the beautiful girl before him, from the perfect swell of her breasts over the towel to the cute purse of her soft lips. The most powerful urge he'd felt in a long time—the desire to kiss her and tear the cloth away—compelled him.

Jonah took a step closer and ran the pad of his thumb over her plump lower lip while his other hand settled on her hip. Avery sighed at his touch and her damp lashes fluttered. He arched his neck to capture her mouth with his, but a different face formed in the back of his mind. Guilt constricted his breathing as he heard *her* voice.

"I'm sorry. I can't do this." Jonah dropped his hand and turned away. His sudden withdrawal made Avery stumble and pull her towel tighter.

"I didn't mean to make you uncomfortable." She tucked her hair behind her ear, anxiety shining in her eyes.

Jonah hung his head, gathered his toiletries, and held them against his stomach. "It's not . . . I shouldn't have barged in on you. I . . . I'll brush my teeth outside and let you . . . finish up." He spun on his heels, not daring to look up from the scuffed tile floor. The door flew open and banged shut behind him as he stormed into the moonless night. His cock softened but continued to throb, begging for release, release he could only find with Avery.

He felt terrible for leaving her like he did, confused and discarded. But on the other hand, he would have felt equally awful if he had engaged in the arduous pleasure he'd fantasized about a few hours ago. It was too fast, too soon since Laura. He wished he had listened to his gut and remained outside once he heard the water running, but he hadn't been thinking clearly since she pulled up this afternoon.

Jonah stalked through the grass. He tried not to think of the look of rejection in Avery's stare, or of the pleading look on Laura's face as she begged him to find a way to save her. He forced his mind to go blank and drifted back behind the thick wall he'd constructed where nothing could touch him.

Chapter 14: Avery

The bathroom door slammed shut with an unmistakable finality. Avery stood on the cold tile, barefoot and bereft. A painful exhale slithered through her lips as she found herself alone. Between the hot water and Jonah's rejection, her alcohol-induced rosy outlook paled to a stark reality.

She hadn't meant to make Jonah uncomfortable. She hadn't even known he was out there listening. Yet once she heard his hoarse affirmation and caught sight of his glorious erection, she had been overcome with the need to finish what her fantasies of him had started.

Avery unwrapped her towel and dried her dripping body before she secured the terrycloth around her cropped hair. In agitated swipes, she slapped streaks of lotion along her limbs, then threw on fresh panties and an oversized shirt. She thrust her toothbrush in her mouth and aggressively brushed, taking small comfort in knowing Jonah would go to sleep with stale beer lingering on his breath. Either that, or hopefully he washed his mouth out with pond water.

She spat a foamy stream into the sink basin and wiped her mouth. A pleasurable wave of warmth rippled down her frame as she remembered the intensity with which he'd looked at her and studied her lips. She could feel his erection straining through his shorts. Physically, it wasn't hard to see he wanted her, yet why then had he regarded her with such disgust right before he fled?

Avery groaned and gathered the rest of her things. The summer continued to throw curve balls her way. From the moment she realized she would be relegated to the orchard, all romantic inclinations had fled. The last time she'd been up there, she hadn't even gone through puberty yet. Contrary to Aunt Carrie's belief, she didn't plan on spreading her legs to every farmhand, especially the grumpy, moody ones who didn't know how to engage in equal conversations. It was a good thing the prick wanted nothing to do with her. She couldn't afford to be distracted by anything, including muscular men with commitment issues.

She shot herself one last look in the mirror, satisfied that her shirt came down just enough to cover her ass, and left the steamy building. Her flashlight scanned the encroaching darkness for the reflective eyes of foxes, bears, or other nocturnal wildlife that might stalk her, finding only shrubbery. The night was void of cowboys as well. She could practically hear her father's cruel laughter. Another man who didn't think she was good enough.

Avery's chest fell. She hadn't expected him to wait for her, but it was a hard blow regardless. He knew how much the dark scared her, but any concern he might have had wasn't enough to overpower his need for self-preservation. Scanning the uneven ground, she trekked back to the cabins. The small light she'd left on shined through her windows, guiding her home—a sharp contrast to Jonah's pitch-black cabin. Had he doused his lamp on purpose, hoping she'd crash into metaphorical rocks and sink into the inky oblivion?

She hissed through her teeth and climbed the mini

staircase to her front porch. Tomorrow began the first day of her mandatory work release under the abrasive tutelage of the seasoned lumberjack. He no doubt thought she was a manicured princess who couldn't be bothered to lift a hammer. She couldn't wait to shove his misogynistic predictions in his face.

Chapter 15: Jonah

The slam of Avery's door startled Jonah out of his sordid thoughts. He lay on his bed, cloaked in nothing but midnight's blanket. He dropped his dick and let it bounce against his stomach. He hadn't touched himself in nearly a year, but after today, he craved release.

Images of Avery bent over his truck bed, moaning his name as he thrust into her tight pussy, had plagued him all day. Still, he'd been able to push his need away, bottled it up and locked it behind the impenetrable wall to be forgotten. He nearly succeeded in making it through the day, but then he'd heard her in the shower.

Jonah had told the truth. All he'd wanted to do was brush his teeth. Obviously, he knew she was naked, but it wasn't until she started mewling with pleasure that he realized she was touching herself. Just the thought of her playing with her clit made his cock pulse with excitement, and it was in his hand before he could fully process the scene.

At that point, the plan had been to jerk off while Avery provided the soundtrack to his climax and slip out before she turned off the water. But he'd been so focused on her that he hadn't noticed when his dopp kit came loose and clattered to the cement floor. The next thing he knew, Avery's beautiful face was glaring at him from the narrow breadth of the shower door. He'd barely had time to shove his dick back into his pants. He groaned aloud now, picturing her soapy breasts and the slick taunting him from between her thighs.

You know I didn't finish.

Her sultry invitation caused him to stiffen even more, and he grabbed hold of his shaft. Faster and faster, he pumped as he imagined her pussy clenching around his girth while she straddled him. This time, Laura's face was the farthest thing from his mind. Instead, Avery's tawny eyes regarded him with pure lust, her teeth piercing her baby-pink lip as she fought to control her orgasm.

Avery was all he pictured, and her breathy sighs played on repeat in his mind. Jonah stared up at the ceiling. The dark fan rotated almost as fast as his fist pumped his cock. He remembered the way her white panties had peeked from under her dress and encased her cunt in an irresistible, tight little bundle. He hadn't been able to look away.

Jonah's breaths became ragged and shallow as his climax crested. His pleasure shot straight up and he pumped his cock until all his pent-up desire drizzled out of the thin slit. Groaning with satisfaction, he let his dick fall between his legs. Fumbling to the right of the bed, he scooped up his discarded boxers and wiped his spilled arousal off his stomach.

For the first time in months, he'd been able to maintain an erection long enough to reach climax and fantasize about another woman without being harpooned by guilt or shame. Jonah exhaled a relieved breath and flung his soiled boxers toward the closet. He felt rejuvenated and light, almost as if a curse had begun to lift from his shoulders.

His therapist would say he'd taken a very important step, but that didn't mean he was ready to share his success yet.

Jonah rolled over and pulled the sheet over his lower body. Avery's light was still on, but he couldn't see her. Maybe she was reading in bed, or maybe she was finishing what she'd started in the shower.

Jonah sighed and closed his eyes. Avery didn't know it, but she'd given him a great gift and if they had any chance of working together amicably this summer, he would have to apologize. He only hoped she would hear him out.

Chapter 16: Avery

A cheerful blue jay twittered outside Avery's window the next morning, followed by the haunting melody of a mourning dove. She squinted against the rosy golden light. Gone was the thick layer of smog she'd grown accustomed to that dampened the rising sun's rays. Out here it shone with pure radiance and illuminated every blade of grass adorned with shimmering dew.

The breathtaking view was straight out of a fairytale but Avery groaned. Five o'clock in the morning was too early to appreciate anything other than the inside of her eyelids. She turned her head, eager to escape the cheerful light, but she hadn't thought to purchase a new eye mask, and her plain white sheets offered little aid.

She slammed her palms down on the comforter and stared at the ceiling. Her alarm was set to go off in half an hour anyway. If she got up now, she'd be able to work in a run before she was due to meet Jonah at the utility barn.

An agitated growl reverberated in the back of her throat at the thought of being alone with him so soon after their awkward moment last night. She had no idea if he planned to bring it up. He'd probably tell her off for wasting water, but whatever he would or wouldn't say, she'd refuse to give him the satisfaction of showing that his rejection had affected her.

She threw back the covers and shivered as her feet kissed the cold floor. Standing, she sloppily pulled them up to the headboard and left the wrinkles, a silent fuck you to her father's meticulous expectations. She exchanged her panties for boyshorts and stripped out of her sleep shirt. Avery pulled on a mesh pair of shorts and found the sports bra at the end of the bed. Once dressed, she put on a pair of socks and stuck her feet into the white sneakers Jonah had chosen for her.

Avery wrinkled her nose. She hated to wear anything associated with him, but she had no other option if she didn't want to roll an ankle as she jogged through the orchard. She bent forward to touch her toes and stretch her hamstrings. After she completed a few lunges on both sides, she reached her arms over her head and pulled on each elbow for ten seconds.

Her phone read 5:11 a.m. She could hear her fitness instructor scolding her now for not taking the time to properly warm up her muscles, but he wasn't there, and she had a shrinking window. Avery opened the door and stepped out into the sunrise. The sun had barely cleared the horizon, yet the air was already humid and buzzed with waking insects.

Avery took off, starting with a light jog, and followed the same path she'd seen Jonah disappear down yesterday. The grass was slick beneath her sneakers, and she was thankful for the traction they provided as she cleared the mowed fields in favor of one of the first apple rows toward the side orchard. The sign read "Red Delicious," and the early dawn was tart like the first bite of the scarlet fruit.

Birds chirped happily while they shook sleep from their feathers, and large bumble bees were already hard at work collecting pollen. Confident she had a feel for the bumpy terrain, Avery increased her speed. The row yawned wide, encased by tiny apple blooms running parallel to the path which seemingly stretched for endless miles.

One row ended and gave birth to another, and another, and another beyond that. Avery wasn't counting steps, nor did she have a desired destination in mind. She might even reach the edge of Uncle Stan's property. Sweat beaded on her forehead and beneath her arms, but the strain felt so good, a natural endorphin that chased away all her insecurities and regrets. Nothing could touch her when she ran. It was the one exercise she looked forward to, that clicked with her body.

Avery ran to the end of the row and glanced up. Small, hard, yellow buds bloomed in these trees. She had left behind the Red Delicious in exchange for Golden Delicious. Time to turn back. She tended to lose track of time when she ran, and without a doubt, would be cutting it close to her six o'clock start time.

Touching the ground with the tips of her fingers, Avery leaned into the lunge and shifted direction, racing back the way she'd come. She didn't full out sprint yet. She conserved her energy for that final push, her favorite part when the runner's high kicked in and she could no longer feel her legs pulsing beneath her.

Row after row shrank as she pushed her body, willed her legs to stretch longer. Her arms pumped at her sides, and her breathing adopted a steady three-breath rhythm: one breath in, two breaths out. Up ahead, the utility barn loomed. The rising sun highlighted the front door like a portal.

Avery gritted her teeth, unleashed the final reserve of her energy, and urged her body to its maximum acceleration. Her soles flew over the well-worn path, faster and faster toward the finish line. Her breathing jackhammered, and her heart pounded in her chest. That glorious out-of-body experience overtook her conscious mind and for a moment, she floated above her body, watching as she sprinted the final few yards.

The ground beneath her rounded into a slight incline. Avery began to slow, expecting a clear runway, but instead, a brown boot slid across the middle of the path, followed by a jean-clad leg and Jonah's full, thick as a brick wall torso.

Avery's eyebrows arched in surprise. She tried to call out a warning, but she was moving too fast, and Jonah wasn't paying attention. Her sneakers thundered atop the earth, unable to slow in time. She tried to throw her body out of the way at the last minute, but her ankle twisted on a shallow root. Crashing into Jonah's side with enough force to knock him off his feet, a jolt of agony zinged up her leg as she smashed against the hard ground. The pair collapsed in the wet dirt, their limbs a tangled jumble of elbows and knees.

"What the hell?" Jonah groaned. "Where did you come from?"

"Me? I was on a run. Why did you jump in front of me?"

Jonah rolled onto his side and tried to move his arm, but it was pinned beneath Avery's hip. "I was checking the trunks. Deer have been eating the bark and ruining the trees."

"And you had to choose this row to start on?" Avery shot back. She brought her injured leg to her chest and curled beneath him. Pain crackled in her ankle. She prayed it wasn't broken. If it was, her father would assume she did it on purpose.

"How was I supposed to know you would slam into me like a cannonball?" Jonah rested his head on the wet grass. Avery saw him grimace as the dew soaked his shirt. It would be drenched with sweat soon, anyway.

Jonah exhaled deeply. Avery's left leg hooked around his waist as they lay on their sides. He didn't seem hurt, except for his arm which was being crushed by most of her weight. He flexed his other hand where it rested against her ass and made a swatting motion. His palm connected with the soft flesh of her cheek.

"Hey!" Avery cried. "Did you just spank me?"

Jonah's eyes widened. "I didn't mean to. I'm trying to untangle myself."

Warmth bloomed in her cheeks as his touch sent a thrill of pleasure through her. She could feel the heat radiating off him. He avoided her gaze and lifted his free hand.

"I'm going to hold you up so I can pull my arm out, okay?"

Avery agreed and allowed Jonah to balance his rough palm on her shoulder. She leaned into his touch, letting her body slightly roll as he slid his arm out, but as he promised, he held her steady. Once freed, Jonah carefully lowered her upper body to the ground and pulled his legs out from beneath her hips. For a second, the movement aligned their groins. Involuntarily, her gaze flashed to his.

Jonah's hooded, hazel eyes burned intensely, and Avery emitted a small gasp. He didn't linger. Instead, he brushed her leg off his torso and climbed to his feet. She remained on the ground but sat up and gingerly examined her ankle.

Bending down, Jonah retrieved his fallen ball cap and slammed it back onto his head. "Seriously, Avery? What the hell was that? Why were you running so hard this way? The ground slopes. Even if I wasn't here to break your fall, you could have messed yourself up bad."

"Save me the lecture." She didn't look at him. Slowly, she rotated her ankle in a small circle as tears pricked the back of her eyes. It wasn't broken, but it was badly sprained.

"That's your problem. You don't listen to anyone but yourself."

"Okay, thanks for that."

Avery's apathetic attitude only infuriated the cowboy more. He crouched down in front of her and gripped her jaw, forcing her to look at him. "How am I supposed to trust you to operate farming equipment if you don't listen? Huh? It was a mistake for Stan to let you stay here." With a gentle jerk, he tossed her head to the side and straightened to look out over the brightening orchard.

Rage burned in Avery's veins. How dare he talk to her like an insolent child caught with her hand in the cookie jar when he was as much to blame?

"You don't know anything about me, but it hasn't stopped you from making assumptions and casting judgment since the moment I got out of the car."

He gestured wildly toward the utility barn. "So your unwillingness to be here excuses your dangerous behavior? You're lucky it's early. What if Stan had driven by in the tractor?"

Avery pursed her lips, ready with a sharp retort, but the image of colliding with the tractor's teeth made her pause. As much as it pained her to say, he had a point. "You're right. I should have asked where it was safe to jog."

"Exactly."

"You're still an asshole, though."

Jonah opened his mouth but abruptly closed it with a clack of his teeth. "Don't take it personally. I'm an asshole to everybody lately. I just . . . I didn't know what to expect. I thought you were going to be mean, stuck up, and entitled. It threw me when you turned out to be so . . . friendly."

Avery arched her eyebrows. "When I came on to you outside the showers, you mean?"

Color warmed the back of Jonah's neck. "Yeah, that was part of it." An awkward silence bloomed between them, growing larger the longer neither of them spoke.

Avery shrugged and balanced her elbow on her propped knee. "Whatever. It didn't mean anything. I was a little drunk and wasn't thinking clearly. I apologize if I made you uncomfortable. Trust me, it will never happen again."

Jonah raised his gaze to hers. "No. I'm the one who should apologize. It was completely inappropriate of me to . . . touch you when I had an—"

Avery waved her hands. "I said it's fine. You don't have to remind me how disgusted you were."

"Disgusted? Are you serious?"

"Yes." Avery leveled him with a hard stare. "You couldn't get out of there fast enough. I get it."

Jonah put his hands on the back of his head. "That's not even . . . Christ, you're infuriating."

Avery cocked her head and offered a tight smile. "One of my specialties."

Jonah growled and stalked a few steps toward the barn. "That's great, but now I need you to get your ass up. We have a lot of work to do with only half the time to do it because you're new and slow and have no idea what you're doing."

"You go. I'll catch up."

Jonah seethed through gritted teeth. "Stan made you my responsibility, now get up."

"No."

He took a step closer, and she couldn't help but notice the way his biceps bulged beneath his short sleeves.

"Are you always this combative? No wonder your dad was sick of you."

Avery's hands gripped the lush grass. Tiny pops sounded as she yanked dozens of blades from the clinging earth. "For your information, asshole, the relationship I have with my father goes far beyond a rebellious adolescent fit. And believe it or not, I'm not following your precious orders to fuck with you. When you threw your giant Neanderthal body in front of me, I fell on my ankle and injured it. So do me a favor and start your little chores without me so I can crawl my ass home in blissful silence."

The second the last word fell from her lips, Jonah's body language shifted. Gone was the malice in the firm set of his jaw and the agitated way he held himself. He turned his hat and knelt beside her.

"You're hurt?" He reached out as if to touch her ankle.

"Don't. I don't need your help."

"At least let me look at it. It could be broken."

"It's not broken, just twisted. I'm fine."

Jonah stood and extended his hand. "Come on. You can lean on me until we get up to the store. Carrie keeps bags of ice in there."

"I said I don't need your help. I'll rest it a few more minutes and it'll be good to go."

Jonah snickered. "You're being stupid."

"Don't call me that."

Jonah exhaled a steadying breath and slapped his palm on his thigh. "Fine. If you refuse to cooperate, I'll do it myself. Like you said, I have chores waiting, but I can't leave you here without medical attention, so . . ."

He didn't finish his sentence. Instead, before Avery could protest, Jonah scooped his arms beneath her ass and the back of her knees and hoisted her off the ground as easily as if she were a sack of potatoes.

Chapter 17: Jonah

Avery shrieked in his ear. "Let me go! Put me down right now. I did not give you permission to touch me!"

Jonah rolled his eyes and tightened his grip on his squirming passenger, caging her even closer to his body. "Consent is implied in an emergency situation."

Avery smacked his arm. "That only applies if the person you're manhandling is unconscious, you moron. And this isn't an emergency."

Jonah shrugged. The motion jostled Avery a bit and her breasts rubbed against his chest. He was suddenly aware of just how little clothing she wore and how much of her flesh was exposed.

"Your injury prevents you from walking on your own and creates an unsafe work environment for others. Who knows? If I left you there, I could have tripped over you and hurt myself."

Avery glowered. "Only because I would have kicked my other leg out and struck you in the back of the knee."

"See?" Jonah answered. "Unsafe work environment."

They walked a few more yards and passed the utility barn. The little general store sat on the top of the hill beyond the parking lot. Avery started squirming again, but his arms were as inescapable as steel bars. She groaned.

"This is ridiculous. You don't need to carry me. I'm sure I can walk now."

"Nope. Too risky. Wouldn't want you to further injure yourself by putting too much weight onto it."

"Oh? Too much weight, huh?"

Jonah sighed. "You know I didn't mean anything by that. You have an amazing body."

Avery snorted. "Funny, you didn't think so last night."

"I wasn't—" Jonah started but shut his mouth. It would do no good to argue with her again. She had a way of spinning his words to make him the bad guy. Last time he checked, not taking advantage of a woman he barely knew was considered morally sound, but perhaps things had changed in the last year since he'd shut himself away from the rest of society.

He reached the entrance to the store a minute later and rolled Avery onto his chest so he could pull open the door. Surprisingly, she wrapped her arms around his neck to secure herself, but in doing so, elevated her tits even closer to his face. Her nipples peeked through the thin spandex. An urge to bury his face in her soft mounds assailed him, but Jonah pushed the consuming thoughts down. They would only get him in trouble.

The small bell chimed to announce their arrival, and Jonah carried Avery across the threshold of the quiet store. He hadn't seen Stan or Carrie yet that morning, and the silence from the dusty shelves and back room confirmed they were alone.

Jonah shuffled forward a few more feet and set Avery down on the counter. His fingers brushed the rounded curve of her ass as she balanced on the narrow width. After a second of juggling, she propped herself up, her hands perched on the edge of the flat surface between her thighs.

Avery's cheeks still held a rosy glow from her early workout, and her glistening body left a patch of warmth against his chest. Jonah's breathing stalled. Avery pursed her lips and swung her uninjured leg. "So . . . is there ice in here or not?"

Jonah shook his head and stepped away from her spread thighs. "Yeah, back here. I'll grab it."

Avery nodded. "Yup. I thought that was kind of the point."

Jonah fixed her with a frown and moved around the display of candles to where the ice fridge was located. He grabbed a small bag and carried it back. The temperature did little to cool his rising desire. His thoughts flashed back to the night before where he lay in bed, picturing Avery riding his cock. She looked so hot perched there, and she didn't even realize.

He cleared his throat and joined her once again. Avery reached out for the bag, but Jonah shooed her hand away.

"I can do it," Avery insisted.

"Not sitting up there. You'll fall over trying to reach."

Avery pouted but sat back and allowed him to tend to her. Jonah moved between her legs again and gently took hold of her sore ankle. He cupped it in one hand and used his other to apply the bag of ice to the side. Her frown deepened at his proximity.

"Why don't you grab a chair? That way you wouldn't have to hold it."

Jonah shook his head while his thumb massaged small circles against her skin. "With a sprain like this, you need to keep your leg elevated."

Avery leaned in. Only a few inches separated them. "Then get me two chairs."

Again, Jonah shook his head. "I can't do that. As I said, you're my responsibility. I need to make sure you take time to rest and ice your ankle properly before throwing yourself into difficult labor."

"And what makes you think I won't just soak up this opportunity to lounge around all day?"

Jonah licked his lips. He could smell her coconut lotion, feel the heat from her breath. "Because you love proving people wrong, especially me it seems."

"Because you're so fun to tease. You make it too easy. I've never met anyone as serious as you."

"You don't know what I've been through." Jonah's fingers massaged her ankle deeper and inched higher up her leg, rubbing the full length of the muscle. He moved to the underside of her calf, but she didn't stop him. A low hum of pleasure rumbled in the back of her throat and went straight to his cock.

"Whose fault is that?"

A rare smirk cracked Jonah's stern façade. "Touché."

He kept pressure on the ice against her ankle as his other hand continued to explore higher up her leg. Squeezing her inner thigh, he massaged the soft skin. Avery sighed and closed her eyes. His pinky grazed the border of her shorts, and he licked his lower lip. His cock throbbed as he imagined peeking beneath the thin fabric and cupping her sweet pussy in his palm while his fingers stroked her clit. His dick grew hard, straining beneath the denim. Avery moaned again. She was putty in his hands, and he yearned to take her mouth in his and feel her groan against him.

It was impossible not to look at her thinly covered cunt. His touch hardened, and her eyelids lazily flickered open. Nerves kicked back in, and Jonah thrust his attention to the ice.

"Why didn't you tell me you were hurt before? Why did you make me believe you were being obstinate?" He moved his hand back down her leg as she studied his profile. Hopefully, she wouldn't notice the husky timbre his voice had taken on at the thought of tearing her shorts off.

Avery chuckled, low and deep. "What? And interrupt that verbal berating? Are you sure you don't have any kids because that seemed as if you'd practiced it once or twice."

"No kids. No family." Jonah replied, massaging a safe spot on the side of her calf. But who was he kidding? When it came to this woman, no area of exposed flesh was safe. Her body was so soft and supple. Would she break beneath him? Jonah smirked. He pictured her riding him, and the idea of her hips bucking as she took his cock made his palms sweat and his dick throb more than what he thought possible.

Avery's next words were soft, and she leaned even closer. With help from the counter, they were the same height. "Sometimes, it's easier to be alone." She regarded him with sad eyes, her cupid's bow lips begging to be kissed.

Jonah bent his neck and whispered into their shared space. "That's the scariest part." His fingers paused on her leg, and in tandem, they moved. Two magnets unable to fight the pull any longer. Yet before their lips could touch, the front door opened and Carrie strolled in, a carton of pears balanced on her hip.

Chapter 18: Jonah

"Well, well. Don't we look cozy in here?" Carrie's words were innocent, but her tone cut like a combine. "Jonah? I thought my husband asked you to show Avery the ropes around the orchard? She can't learn anything propped on my register now, can she?"

Jonah's cheeks flushed and he took a quick step away from the counter, still holding Avery's sore leg. "Avery was out for a run before work this morning and I startled her. She fell, and I wanted to get some ice on it before it started to swell." He gestured to the ice pack like a student brought under his teacher's brutal scrutiny for cheating on a test.

"Hurt your ankle, did ya?" Carrie parroted. "How does it feel now, Avery?"

Avery pulled her leg out of Jonah's grasp and rotated her foot. "Better. The ice really helped. It's probably fine. I'll get changed and meet you at the barn."

Carrie pursed her lips. "Well, look at that. You head back to your cabin and put on some decent working clothes. It's a miracle you've not been burned to a crisp wearing that skimpy thing."

Avery slid off the counter, careful to avoid Jonah's offered hand. "It's a sports bra, Aunt Carrie. They're literally meant to be worn without a shirt."

"Never mind that. You two have a long day ahead of you. Grab a piece of toast and some sausage from my house, then get to it."

"Yes, Aunt Carrie."

"Yes, ma'am."

Jonah hung back and allowed Avery to leave first. He watched as she gingerly applied pressure to her ankle, then walked normally when it became apparent she wouldn't fall. She tried to slip past Carrie, but her aunt touched her elbow and whispered something too low for him to hear. Avery's lips flattened to a thin line before she pulled the door open and rushed out. The high-pitched bell above swung wildly behind her.

Jonah bounced the melting bag of ice between his palms and stood awkwardly before the orchard's matriarch. "I'll dump this outside." Carrie didn't respond, only narrowed her eyes, and hiked the pears higher onto her hip. He hooked his thumb toward the side door behind the register. "I'll go this way."

Still, Carrie remained mute, but the threat in her gaze was clear.

Chapter 19: Avery

I thought I asked you to be a good girl.

Aunt Carrie's words wove through her mind like venom, but there was no stinger to rip out to dull the pain. Who did she think she was? Carrie wasn't her mother, yet for some reason, she refused to see her as anything more than a sex-fueled teenager incapable of making her own decisions. Avery had been on the pill since tenth grade. She could take care of herself.

Fury raged through Avery as she hobbled to her cabin. Maybe she could talk to Uncle Stan about his wife's meddling ways. Was Aunt Carrie truly worried she'd come across grumpy Jonah ravaging her niece against an apple tree?

Avery's first instinct was to wrinkle her nose in disgust, but then she remembered the way he'd touched her on the counter, his rough hands massaging her muscles. She reached her door and yanked it open. Once inside, she unleashed a heavy sigh. Alone at last.

Gripping the bottom of her bra, Avery pulled it over her head and dropped it on the floor. Her fingers slipped into the waistband of her joggers and let them fall as well. She stood in her panties. Nothing else covered her skin save for the warm sunlight. Extending her hands above her head, she arched into a stretch. She hadn't had a chance to complete her cool down after her run, and now— with Jonah waiting for her—she'd have to make do with the short time given.

Avery focused her breathing and moved her body into several practiced yoga poses. Her mind should have been clear, but she couldn't escape the feeling of Jonah's expert touch. A sly grin curled her lip. He'd thought he was so sneaky as he advanced up the length of her leg. He'd tried to make his touch seem casual, meandering, but it wasn't hard to guess his destination.

She had closed her eyes to allow him free reign, curious about his intentions and how he would behave when left unobserved. He didn't disappoint. Avery loved how small she'd felt in his hands, the coarse way he'd explored her as if he were losing control.

The vision of Jonah thrusting into her against the apple tree suddenly didn't seem so horrific, but she had no intention of letting the cowboy know that.

Five minutes later, Avery hustled back out into the increasing humidity and power-walked to the utility barn. Uncle Stan, down in the fields, waved from his pedestal atop the large tractor, and Aunt Carrie was fortunately nowhere to be seen. Up ahead, Jonah's broad shoulders were visible just outside the building's towering double doors.

Gravel crunched beneath her shoes as she slowed her pace and marched up the slight hill. "Hey."

Jonah nodded. "Hey. That was quick."

"Not much need for a beauty routine out here."

"Fair enough." Jonah ducked back inside the barn and

returned with two full paint cans and a pair of brushes clutched in his thumb. "You ready to paint?"

Avery scrunched her nose. "Paint? I thought by chores you meant picking apples and stuff like that."

Jonah pointed to some faraway destination past the side orchard. "It's only June. The fruit's not ready for harvest yet. Still lots to do in the meantime though."

Avery crossed her arms. "Like paint Aunt Carrie's kitchen?"

"No. We need to make sure all the new plantings are painted to prevent sunscald."

"Trees can get sunburned?"

"Yeah. If the young trees are exposed to too much sunlight, it damages the plant's outer layer. This leads to lesions that can spread to the leaves and result in rotten fruit."

Avery's eyebrows arched. "Wow. I had no idea there was so much that goes into farming."

Jonah twirled a screwdriver in his hand and fitted his hat snugly over his head. "It's a science like any other business."

"That makes sense." Avery bent down and hefted one of the paint cans off the ground. She stumbled, not expecting it to be so heavy. "Whoa. Are these baby trees close?" She scanned the tall copse nearby. All of them seemed too mature to be new plantings.

"Nah. They're on the other side of this section, near the pumpkins."

Avery's mouth fell. "Great. Let's get going then."

The clang of keys chimed. "I mean, you can walk if you want to, but driving might be faster."

A white golf cart sat off to the side of the barn. Avery hadn't noticed it. Her shoulders slumped forward. "Thank God. I never would have made it carrying this thing."

Jonah hoisted the can still on the ground into the little

flatbed on the back of the golf cart before grabbing two additional cans. Avery plopped hers in as well and wiped the sweat from her forehead.

"Should I grab some water? Looks like we're going to be down there all day."

Jonah shook his head. "There are spigots planted throughout the orchard. Long as you don't mind drinking from a hose, we'll be fine." His lips quirked as if daring her to protest.

Avery shrugged and hopped into the passenger seat. "Fine with me."

Jonah didn't say anything, only mirrored her movements and slid onto the plastic cushion beside her. He stuck the key in the ignition but hesitated. "You put on sunscreen, right?"

Avery rolled her eyes. "Yes, Dad. Geez. We have sun in the city, too."

Jonah held up his hands. "Just wanted to make sure. Carrie would have my head if I brought you back looking like a dried-out lobster."

Avery's mood soured at the mention of her aunt. She glanced away and pinched her lips. "I could really care less about what my aunt would say."

Tension claimed the moment. Jonah rested his hands on the steering wheel and drummed his thumb on the pleather cover. "I'm sorry for what happened back there in the store. I really was only trying to make your ankle feel better."

The memory of his large hand caressing her upper thigh disagreed, but if he regretted touching her that way, then so be it. Avery was used to being dismissed. Her father had given her plenty of practice.

"Whatever. It doesn't matter. Let's just go." Her tone was flippant and cool as she made eye contact with him. She was so tired of his dizzying actions. One minute he was practically pressing his erection against her, and in the next he was denying any attraction whatsoever.

Jonah continued to sit there and let the engine idle. Avery could see he wanted to say something else, but at this point, she had little interest in being the ping pong ball in his court of hot and cold emotions. She had her own shit to deal with. Besides, she'd promised to be a good girl.

Chapter 20: Jonah

The first week passed in a blur of paint, wire fencing, and backaches. He and Avery secured the indestructible mesh around the base of all the newly planted trees, painted their trunks to deflect harmful UV rays, and dug more irrigation canals in case the dry weather continued.

To his surprise, Avery was a quick study and was able to replicate his work after a simple instruction or demonstration. At first, he predicted the beauty queen would struggle or complain about the heat or buzzing insects, but once she had her materials, she left their shared area and set up a fair distance away to ensure conversation wouldn't be feasible.

Jonah liked to think they were too busy to chat, but ever since their heated encounter in the general store, their relationship had taken an icy turn. Whenever he tried to break the silence while they drove to their next location or took a break beneath the shade, Avery would respond with clipped, one-word answers that often deflected back to him. His one consolation was that he wasn't the only one she seemed angry with. Dinners with Stan and Carrie were a forced affair, and whenever her relatives asked a pointed question she couldn't avoid, Jonah observed in amazement as she gave a flawless answer while at the same time, divulging as little personal information as possible.

When Stan first told him his niece was going to help, he couldn't wait to burden her with a task and go about his day. Yet as the seventh day wound to a close, Jonah found he missed her snarky remarks, her snorts of laughter, and most of all, the tension that had sparked between them since the first day they'd met. It wasn't the sexual chemistry he craved—though there was plenty of that. It was simply the connection they had and the easy camaraderie she'd tried to foster, despite his cantankerous moods.

Jonah had lost touch with most of his other friends after what happened last year. It was too much work to try and brighten the rain cloud that seemed to have taken up permanent residence over his head. But Avery was different. She accepted his sour outlook as a challenge, and he didn't realize how influential she had been until she shut him out.

He paused his digging and rested his elbow on the worn wooden handle of his shovel. Jonah didn't need Avery to fall in love with him, but he couldn't work beside her every day knowing how much hatred she seemed to harbor toward him either.

They were working on the last irrigation canal. Avery crouched halfway down the row, shovel in hand and white air pods firmly buried in her ears. The need to hear her voice propelled Jonah to drop his tool. Bending down, he retrieved several hard green nuts that rolled under his sneakers.

Jonah bounced them in his palm, then lightly tossed the first in Avery's direction. It arched high into the air and landed on the ground a few feet away from where she stood with a solid thud. She didn't look up or pause her movements.

Jonah tossed another nut, this time aiming for the flat head of her shovel. Again, it soared through the sky but clattered off the steel plate. Avery jerked back and inspected the ground. Her head snapped in his direction, and she grimaced as he closed the intentional distance between them.

"What are you doing?" Avery ripped one of her air pods out and brandished her shovel like a barrier or a weapon.

Jonah pulled off his white sweat-soaked shirt and waved it like a flag of truce. "I just want to talk."

Avery's frown deepened. "Come to tell me I'm digging wrong?"

Jonah jogged the rest of the way and stopped, leaving a comfortable amount of space between them. The last thing he wanted was for her to feel trapped. He slung his soggy t-shirt over his pale shoulder, his farmer's tan on full display.

"No. Nothing like that."

Avery slammed her shovel so the lip bit into the ground and it stood on its own. She stuck her hands on her hips and regarded him with an exasperated expression while she waited for him to articulate the reason for the interruption.

"It's just . . . we didn't start off on the best foot, but this week we somehow drifted even farther south." She didn't agree or add any additional comments, only continued to stare at him and purse her lips. "If I've offended you in any way, I want to apologize. I lied when I said I didn't need to know you to work alongside you. I'd love to get to know you and hear your laugh again, and I guess, be your . . . friend."

Avery's chin sunk an inch lower. "My friend?"

"Yeah. If you're open to it. It'd make the days go by faster if we didn't try so hard to ignore one another."

"It's not hard for me." Avery's voice was strong, void of any wavering emotion.

Jonah clapped his hands. "Welp, this was a waste of time then. Sorry to bother you." He pivoted on the balls of his boots and started walking back toward his shovel.

"You really have no idea why I'm pissed at you?"

He paused and swung his head over his shoulder. "Uh, should I?"

Avery crossed her arms. "Yes."

Jonah retraced his steps and wrinkled his brow. "It wasn't the 'I don't care about who you are' quip?"

"No. It wasn't. I knew you were a jerk, but I didn't realize you were so manipulative."

Jonah's jaw dropped, and he touched a hand to his chest. "Manipulative? What are you talking about?" He marched closer, fighting to keep a level head.

Avery matched his stride until they were practically nose to nose. "Why do you keep messing with me?"

"With you? What the hell are you talking about?" Jonah growled, nearly losing control. Who was she to spit on his character?

Avery rolled her eyes. "Oh, please. That lame excuse that you were only interested in making my ankle feel better? You were nearly fingering me."

Jonah's anger morphed into shock. "You're mad I didn't touch your pussy? Is that it?"

"No, you fucking idiot. I'm angry you lied and used me when it was convenient for you."

"What?"

"You made me think you were interested in me, only to flake out and deny everything the second my aunt called your name."

Jonah's mouth gaped, at a loss for words. "I don't . . ." His sentence trailed off. His first instinct was to deny her accusations, but the last week floated behind his eyes. Staring at Avery on the back of his truck, nearly kissing her in the bathrooms, leaning into her touch when they'd walked into one another outside the cabins, and finally, the sensual way he'd rubbed her leg. Apparently, he hadn't been as subtle as he'd thought. "You're right. That was a shitty thing to do. I didn't mean to lead you on."

Avery's gaze hardened and she gripped her elbows as if she might shatter. He'd never seen her look so vulnerable. "Lead me on? Right."

Jonah's gut clenched. The sadness in her voice was an arrow straight to his heart. "It's not you. I'm just . . . not in a good place right now to start anything—"

Avery held up a hand. "I get it. I've heard the speech."

Jonah hung his head. "That didn't come out right. I'm sorry for being such a dick before. I'm trying to sort some shit out and I dragged you into the middle of it." He paused to gather his thoughts and took a steadying breath. "What I'm trying to say is I would love to start over and be friends."

She was quiet for a long minute, then she unwrapped her arms from their protective position and reached toward him. "I'm Avery. It's nice to meet you."

A relieved grin split Jonah's lips. He grasped her small hand in his and shook it once. "Jonah. It's a pleasure to have you here at Sterling Orchards."

He waited, still clasping her hand in his, until Avery could no longer fight the small smile that betrayed her unreadable expression. "That was so cheesy."

Jonah shrugged. "Well, that's how we should have met."

"Rednecks don't just insult your shoes and tell you to 'git in the truck'?"

"I never insulted your shoes."

"Maybe not out loud, but you definitely had money on me falling flat on my face."

Jonah nodded. "Yeah, that sounds familiar." They continued to hold hands, but neither one pulled away, too busy reveling in the first real laugh they'd shared.

At last, Avery made the first move and dropped her hand to her side. "Friends, huh? It might take me a bit to get used to that. I don't have too many back home."

"Same here. I thought I did, but when tragedy strikes, you learn real fast who's really there for you."

Avery cocked her head and looked at him. "Yeah. It's hard to trust other people."

"That might be the first thing we agree on."

Jonah grinned once more. The sensation felt odd, as if he was exposing too much of himself, but as he stared at Avery and witnessed the hard veneer melt away, he felt lighter than air. He hooked his thumb behind him.

"I should head back."

"Yeah, I'm not finishing this thing by myself."

"All right, then."

Jonah strolled to his spot. It warmed him to see Avery smiling again. That's why he didn't feel the need to apologize for lying to her again. Truth was, he ached to be so much more than friends, but first he needed to figure out what exactly that meant for the rest of his heart and the woman who already owned it.

This was enough. Enough for now.

Chapter 21: Jonah

The truce he and Avery forged was soon interrupted because the next day, the rest of the crew arrived. Jonah wasn't bothered. He had known Mac and Marissa for years, and their presence energized the orchard. Mac's endless supply of bad puns and Marissa's boisterous laughter took him back to the halls of junior high. But their arrival disrupted the private bubble he'd inhabited with Avery. Now it felt as if that space was shattered by new voices and constant activity that drew her away from him.

The rows and fields pulsed, and Avery absorbed the fresh vitality like a sponge. Her laugh grew louder and more carefree over the next two weeks. Often, Jonah would hear its ghostly remnants echo on the breeze from where he worked downhill. It made him smile and ache at the same time.

He was glad she seemed to be enjoying herself. She and Marissa clicked like two long-lost sisters. After their talk that day, his and Avery's relationship had improved, but it wasn't the same. Avery didn't let go or drop her guard like she did with the others. It was a subtle punishment reserved only for him, a sentence he feared he would never be able to overcome.

Avery's laughter flooded his eardrums and stirred him from his thoughts as Mac helped her uncoil the irrigation hoses.

He was a good guy, solid and kind, but the unfamiliar tug of jealousy sunk its teeth into Jonah as he watched Mac stand behind her and show her how to properly dislodge them from their steel spools. The young farmhand's arm brushed hers, and rage erupted in Jonah's stomach when Avery tripped and fell against Mac's torso. He didn't know if their interaction was anything more than accidental contact, but either way, he refused to stand there and pretend like he wasn't bothered by her casual smiles and the easy way she accepted Mac's hands on her waist.

Jonah dropped the bag of fertilizer he was pouring into the wheelbarrow and stormed out of the utility barn. Out of the corner of his eye, he caught the surprised look on Mac's face, but he couldn't read Avery's expression. It didn't matter anyway. He had turned her down, told her he wasn't ready for anything more than friendship. She had every right to seek affection from Mac. Still, the idea of some other guy holding and touching her body made him see red. He had absolutely no claim to her, but that didn't stop the territorial thoughts.

"Jonah? What's wrong, man?" Mac called out.

Jonah didn't answer and kept walking, grinding his boots into the small gravel path. Behind him he heard Avery respond.

"I wouldn't worry about it. He's always got a stick up his ass about something."

He was out of earshot before Mac could say anything more. His only goal was to put as much distance between himself and Avery as possible. Stalking out into the humid morning air, he chose a row at random and purposefully strode through it. He knew he was overreacting. He liked Mac real well, but he wanted to be the one who made Avery smile. Jonah swatted at a low-hanging branch and sent a hard, tiny apple skittering into the grass.

"Whoa, I guess I should have worn my hard hat today."

As if waking from a stupor, Jonah glanced around, searching for the disembodied voice. He spied Marissa's dark brown skin against the grass.

"Oh, shit. I'm sorry. I didn't see you there."

Marissa scoffed. "Obviously." Scooting backward, she straightened out of her crouch and rose to her feet. Yards of coiled wire fencing sat on the ground beside her.

Jonah jerked his thumb over his shoulder. "I have to spread some fertilizer on the Honey Crisps, but then I can help you mend those."

Marissa pursed her lips, her maple eyes fixed on him. "Thanks, but first you want to tell me what's got you all worked up?"

Jonah shook his head. "Nothing."

Marissa arched her brow and crossed her arms. "Really? Cause you just about took my head off with that apple." Jonah remained tight-lipped and didn't meet her eyes. "How long has it been since you slept with Avery?"

Jonah's jaw dropped. "What are you talking about?"

Marissa rolled her eyes. "Oh, please. I've only been here a couple of weeks, but I've seen the way you two look at each other."

Jonah put up his hand. "Wait, she's been looking at me?"

Marissa shook her head. "Let me guess, you slept with her but got cold feet the minute you got your pants back on, and now she won't talk to you."

Jonah frowned, remembering Avery in her towel as he held her in his arms. She took a big chance approaching him, and he'd shut her down flat. "Not quite, but you're on the right track. Did she tell you?"

"No, moron, but men are all the same." Marissa tugged off

her gloves and tucked them in her back pocket.

Jonah stepped closer and touched his hands to his chest. "Come on, you know I'm not that guy. It's just . . . after Laura . . . it's too soon."

Marissa gave Jonah's shoulder a gentle squeeze. "I understand, and I'll never know your pain, but do you think it's too soon because you're not ready or because you're worried people will judge you?"

Jonah opened his mouth but was unsure how to respond. "I mean, I felt a little guilty, but . . ."

Marissa interrupted. "Did you get hard? Have you jerked off to thoughts of her?"

Jonah laughed. "Geez, Marissa. I forgot how blunt you are."

"So, that's a yes," she continued. She popped her hip and balanced her hand on her waist. "Do you want my advice?"

"Not really, but it seems you can't be stopped."

"Give Avery a chance, even if it's just a fling. We all know how much you loved Laura, but it's okay to move on and be happy with someone else. Don't punish yourself. There's obviously a connection between you two. Focus on having fun."

At her words, a heavy weight lifted off Jonah's chest. He had spoken to counselors and therapists, of course, but he never anticipated falling for someone again. At first, he'd had no idea how to live without Laura. Their futures had been so entwined, then suddenly part of him was ripped away. Yet, there was something about Avery that stirred those long-dormant emotions he thought he'd lost back in that cold office.

"Thanks, Marissa. I really needed to hear that." Jonah smiled, then immediately grimaced. The motion still felt strange.

His friend nodded. "No worries. I'm glad I could help. Now hurry up with that fertilizer. I've got thirteen trunks to wrap.

The deer are awful this year."

Jonah leaned forward and planted a gentle kiss on Marissa's forehead. "You got it. Give me half an hour."

Marissa tugged her gloves back on and smiled at Jonah's enthusiasm. "Just be careful, all right?"

Jonah jogged backward and gave her a quick salute, but he didn't understand her concern. He pivoted and continued back up the row toward the utility barn.

Hope fluttered in his chest and the dark cloud that had smothered him for the past few days lightened. After listening to Marissa's advice, he felt good, ready to share small pieces of himself. She was right. He didn't have to forget Laura to find happiness with Avery. He only hoped he wasn't too late.

Jonah slowed his jog and pushed open the weathered door, but the scene within stopped him dead in his tracks and chased away his brief sliver of happiness. Avery stood in a slant of sunlight pooling in the middle of the floor, her chin tilted upward. Mac stood before her, his lips just shy of hers. Hearing his abrupt entrance, they jumped apart, and Avery's gaze locked on his.

Jonah's breath caught at the sight of the competing guilt and triumph he saw in Avery's eyes. He dropped his stare to the floor, grateful his hat covered the burn rising in his cheeks. "Sorry to interrupt."

"It's all good, man," Mac said casually. "We were just bringing out the hoses."

Jonah nodded and pointed to the wheelbarrow. "Mind if I get that out of your way?"

Avery took a step away from Mac's tall frame. "There's nothing to get in the way of. We're working."

Her tone was clipped as she strode past him. Jonah hid his surprise, and his gaze flickered back to Mac. He couldn't get a clear read on either of them. Avery sounded upset, though whether she was upset with him or with Mac, he wasn't sure.

"Okay, then," Jonah grumbled and brushed past her, slightly knocking her shoulder with his.

Avery didn't pause in her stride, but Jonah caught the way her knuckles whitened as she gripped the heavy hose tighter. Marissa's words echoed in the back of his mind. Now he understood.

Chapter 22: Avery

Who the hell did Mac think he was? And how dare he assume she wanted him to kiss her. They had been discussing when the orchard would open for tourists, and the next thing she knew, his lips were closing in. Another wave of anger deepened her fury. Of course that was the same moment Jonah chose to return after he stormed off like a toddler. And there she was, stuck in a testosterone meat pile with two dicks ready to butt heads over who gets to mount her.

Avery kicked the door further open and stepped into the sun's heat. A thin line of sweat already pooled beneath her breasts and in the crevices of her thighs. She was thankful for her cut-off jean shorts and thin green tank. At only 9 a.m., the temperature soared over ninety degrees, and a full list of chores awaited them.

She heaved the long hose down the gravel path and turned right when she reached row seven which was marked by a cute apple cutout that had faded to a pale yellow from years of sun exposure. Avery continued to mutter under her breath about male privilege as she dragged the hose into position. With a large exhale, she rolled the tubing and lined up the holes with the thin trunks.

Halfway down the length, a kink twisted the hose and

aimed the holes skyward. Avery cursed and dropped to her hands and knees, pushing it back into position. A flash of yellow caught her attention several rows away, and she smiled and waved at Marissa who was crouched in a similar pose as she worked on repairing the wildlife fences beneath the older trees.

Avery was glad the young woman was there. Their early friendship was a breath of fresh air compared to all the fake friends she'd had back home. Plus, Marissa offered her a safe space to escape her smothering thoughts of Jonah.

Avery's knees pressed into the dry earth, carving shallow depressions into the grass. Jonah's rejection stung, but what bothered her even more was her own behavior. Aunt Carrie warned her to stay away from him, yet she had charged headfirst after a guy she knew nothing about. She was so used to being in control, of wielding men's hearts with a flick of her wrist, but Jonah's seemed to be locked in a steel cage. When she approached him in the showers, she was only thinking about sating her own desire. Yet, she couldn't turn off the terrible feeling of vulnerability that lingered every time she saw him, an admission he would never be privy to.

Avery leaned back on her heels and wiped the gathering sweat from her brow with the strap of her tank. The hose now lay nice and straight. All she needed to do was turn on the water and start on the next row. She pushed off the ground and stood, pulling her shorts down to cover the swell of her ass. Around her, the lazy hum of bees and cheerful bird songs reminded her why she loved her uncle's farm. She didn't need a man's attention to feel good about herself, not when nature was there to provide all the serotonin she could want.

Inhaling the summer air, she headed to the utility barn. Avery glanced from left to right, but Jonah was out of sight.

Halfway up, Mac headed her way, his arms full of black, snake-like piping. Internally, she groaned as he smiled at her. Mac was cute in a boyish way, but he was young, only twenty-two, and was the type of guy who preferred the sound of his own voice. The irony wasn't lost on her. A few weeks ago, all she wanted was to lose herself in casual sex with Jonah, but the idea of the same scenario with Mac made her cringe.

Avery stepped to the right of the path to give Mac a wide berth. "Hey," she said as she passed him.

Mac's smile faltered and he paused mid-stride. "Hey, Avery? I just wanted to apologize for what happened in the barn. I shouldn't have tried to kiss you."

Avery stopped as well and nodded. "Yeah, that was dumb."

Mac grinned. "My Mama always said I was a few cards short of a full deck, but I'm sorry for pushing myself on you."

"Thanks, Mac. Let's just be friends this summer, okay?"

"Cool." Mac's smile widened and he tilted the crown of his head to her. "I'm going to lay these down in rows ten through thirteen. Can you grab fourteen and fifteen?"

"Sure thing. I'm about to turn on seven, then I'll be right down."

"Great. Stan mentioned weeding out the strawberry patch this afternoon too."

"Awesome." Avery chuckled with sarcasm. "I'll meet you there."

"Okay." Mac turned and continued down the gently sloping hill.

Avery relaxed, surprised and relieved by his apology. One problem down, one to go.

An hour later, Avery sat on a little foam mat at the edge of the strawberry patch. Thick gloves enveloped her hands and sweat gathered on her wrists. It was past midday, and the sun shone as if executing a personal vendetta. Two buckets full of weeds belching dark green tendrils over the sides stood beside her stooped frame. Uncle Stan had warned her weeding the patch was going to be sore work, but she'd never imagined the deep pain that would plague her arms and back.

A small laugh of disbelief fell from her lips. She was certainly soft from living in the city, but she knew without a shadow of a doubt she would never have made it as a pioneer in the old west. Avery looked to the right and waved to Mac fifty yards down, who was busy taming the weeds in another patch. He wasn't looking in her direction, and she let her hand drop, too sweaty to care. Lunch couldn't be far off, but then again, she had no idea how long she'd been out there. She pictured her phone back in the cabin on the corner of the little desk. It was uncomfortable to carry in her shallow pockets all day, but she'd give anything to know the time, to have a glimpse of hope as the passing moments brought her closer to her escape from the fiery twilight zone.

Resigned to purgatory until she received word from the others, Avery eased back onto her knees and bent in an awkward crouch, extending her arms to reach the thick weeds. She braced her weight with one hand while the other followed the serpentine train of green to the rich soil below. She burrowed her hand down to the base, wrapped her fist around the invasive vine, and yanked it with enough force to sever the stubborn roots. Victoriously, she rose, the weed clutched in her grasp, and tossed it behind her into the nearest bucket. She groaned with satisfaction and was wiping her brow when a dark shadow towered over her.

"You all right?"

Jonah's deep voice seemed to vibrate in Avery's chest when he spoke. She was annoyed by his appearance, but she was too hot to exert enough energy to do anything about it.

"Fine, just waging war against these weeds. Did my uncle glue them in here?"

Jonah chuckled. "Seems like it. They've been particularly brutal this year."

Avery turned away and pulled another weed. The need to eradicate all of them was becoming addictive.

"Well, I came by to let you know we're breaking for lunch up at the main house."

Avery groaned again as she ripped the next deep root out of the ground and showered her lap with soil. "Awesome. I was beginning to wonder what would kill me first, heat stroke or starvation." Once more, she tossed the evil weed into the bucket. This time, she pushed back onto the soles of her shoes into a downward-facing dog pose, desperate to stretch out the kinks in her leg muscles. She gritted her teeth as they cramped and burned from the strain.

A pained grunt resounded in her throat as she straightened to a standing position and rolled her neck to the left. "Ow. Is there a way to request a transfer?"

"Want me to rub that knot out?" Jonah asked hesitantly.

Avery's eyebrows shot up. "Really? I mean, you don't have to."

Jonah shrugged. "I've pulled those weeds before. That pain is no joke if you let it settle."

Avery scoffed but presented him with her back. "Kind of sounds like some bullshit line guys say to get a girl's guard down."

"Worked, didn't it?"

Avery shot him a pinched look over her shoulder, but it was without malice. Jonah's expression was unreadable as he rested his large hands atop her upper back. Squeezing with all his fingers, he rubbed from top to bottom, applying just enough pressure to make Avery grit her teeth from the pain. It hurt, but felt so good at the same time.

Jonah was right. Numerous knots had formed in the short time she'd worked. Avery sunk into the massage and relaxed her body. She didn't care that Jonah had rejected her, didn't care that he'd humiliated her. In that moment, the only thing that mattered was the magic his hands wove.

His fingers traveled further down her body, the tips grazing the sides of her breasts as he worked. He didn't loiter, but his touch sent a flash of heat to her sex as she remembered how he'd touched her before. An involuntary moan slipped out of her parted lips as his fingers rubbed deeper, easing the pain away with every stroke. Avery's head fell forward, and she closed her eyes.

"How about you just keep touching me like this all day." Avery laughed. She meant it as a joke, but once her wish was out in the open, Jonah's hands dropped to her waist and rested just above her low-rise shorts. He pulled her back against him, and a hard mound of heat pressed against her ass.

He leaned in close. His lips brushed her ear and tickled the fine hairs coating the back of her neck. "I haven't stopped thinking of you." Jonah's voice was gruff and thick with need.

Avery's sex pulsed as a thrill of desire gripped her. She arched her ass higher against Jonah's cock. His hands had felt so good all those weeks ago, and she recalled how wet he'd made her. While his hands skirted the edge of her shorts, he planted a gentle kiss below her earlobe. Jonah resumed rubbing her lower back, but this time, his fingers dipped below the material of her waistband and grazed the lacey panties she'd thrown on that morning.

Wetness gathered between her thighs as her need swelled, but she'd been burned by him before. She'd put herself out there, and he'd made it clear he wasn't interested. So now that he had worked through whatever was bothering him, she was supposed to leap into his arms and spread her legs with a smile on her face?

No. He wouldn't get her back that easily. He deserved to work for it. Avery cleared her throat and stepped out of his embrace. "Thanks for that. We should probably head up before Aunt Carrie sends out a search party."

Confusion flitted across Jonah's face for a moment, but he composed himself and fixed the front of his jeans just as Mac approached them.

"Hey guys, what's going on? Looked a little intense there for a minute." Mac quirked an eyebrow in Avery's direction.

"Jonah helped work a kink out of my neck. These strawberry fields should come with a warning. Picking may result in spinal injury." Avery chuckled, but Mac didn't look convinced.

Mac swiped the sweat off his forehead with his forearm and nodded to Jonah. "What's up?"
Jonah hooked his thumb over his shoulder. "Carrie's made lunch for us all."

"Sweet." Mac grinned. "I only had a few slices of old turkey left in my mini fridge. Did you tell Marissa yet?"

"Just did."

"Nice." The three of them stood there for an awkward moment, not wanting to be the first to leave.

Avery rolled her eyes and slapped the sides of her thighs. "Let's go then."

Her statement set the men in motion, and they quickly

fell into step. Avery took the lead. Their heavy feet thundered behind her as they fought to be the first to reach her side. With a slight frown, she realized Jonah lingered behind as Mac settled into place next to her.

"Are you going to the festival tonight?"

"What festival?"

Mac smiled. "The annual Waterfront Festival. They build and race cardboard boats across Seneca Lake."

"They what?"

"Yeah, it's a lot of fun to watch. Teams build boats out of big cardboard boxes and whoever can get across without sinking wins."

"But they're cardboard. Don't all of them just disintegrate?"

"That's why you need fast rowers."

Avery arched her eyebrows. "That does sound entertaining."

"You want to go?"

Mac's hopeful tone filled Avery with guilt. She didn't want to lead him on, but she had to admit she loved the weight of Jonah's bated breath as she withheld her answer.

"Sure. I'll ask Marissa to come, too." Avery tossed a casual look over her shoulder. "What about you? Up for some shoreline comedy?"

Jonah's lips twitched. "Why not? But you better take care not to stand too close. Wouldn't want you to get wet."

Heat pulsed to Avery's sex and she clenched her thighs. Jonah's face remained unreadable, but his steady gaze burned from beneath his worn baseball cap.

"Cool, yeah. A group thing. Awesome." Mac's enthusiasm faltered as the trio crested the hill and continued to the main house. He cleared his throat but kept his stride even with hers. "I didn't realize you were into stuff like this anymore, Jonah."

"I'm not really, but it'll be a nice change of pace, especially with berry season opening this week. Kick it off with a bang, I guess."

"Awesome, man. Just awesome."

The tension that radiated between the two men was tangible as they reached the main house, but the aroma of chili broke the stalemate.

Mac groaned. "Ah, Carrie! You know your chili is my favorite." He jogged ahead and wrapped her aunt in a big hug from behind as she ladled her signature dish into the awaiting bowls.

The few wrinkles framing Aunt Carrie's eyes smoothed as her face lit up with surprise when her feet left the ground. "Robert Macalister, you put me down this second." She scolded him with a shrill voice, but Avery could hear her joy. Mac set her aunt back on her feet, and she swatted his arm with the saucy spoon. "Sit down, you heathen."

Mac grinned boyishly, slipped his legs beneath the large picnic table, and claimed the bowl Aunt Carrie had just finished filling. Avery took the spot beside him and suppressed a sigh when his eyes lit up.

"Your real name is Robert?" Avery nodded in thanks as Aunt Carrie filled her bowl to the top. She didn't miss her aunt's approving smile.

"Afraid so. Robert Theodore Macalister. Didn't exactly help me become the babe magnet I was hoping to be, so when I was fifteen, I started introducing myself as Mac, and thankfully the nickname stuck."

"And the babe magnet goal?"

"I do pretty well."

"Lucky you."

Mac shoveled a large spoonful of chili into his mouth and shrugged. "It's fun, no doubt about that, but it'd be nice to find someone interested in something deeper, you know?"

Avery swallowed her first bite and licked the back of her spoon. Her gaze flickered to where Jonah sat opposite her. "Sure. Though casual sex has its perks, too."

"Avery." Aunt Carrie scolded as she set the large pot down on the cork trivet. "I don't want to hear about your scandalous escapades at the table."

"What? Mac brought it up."

Aunt Carrie sat down and fixed her with a weighted stare. "That's enough."

Silence settled over the meal but was thankfully broken by Marissa's arrival. She sidled in and sat beside Jonah, tucking her work gloves into the large back pocket of her overalls.

"Sorry, I'm late. What'd I miss?" Marissa quirked an eyebrow.

"Just Aunt Carrie's purity speech and double standards for women."

"Oh? Good stuff."

Aunt Carrie huffed and marched inside. Avery didn't watch her go.

Marissa pulled the last bowl to her and plunged her spoon into the thick concoction. "I've been on the other end of that before. She about stopped breathing when I introduced her to my girlfriend last year."

Mac shrugged. "She's part of that traditional generation."

Jonah pushed his empty bowl away and the spoon rattled against the ceramic sides with a metallic chatter. "Doesn't mean she's entitled to make people feel bad about their choices."

"I'm not saying that," Mac argued.

Jonah put up his hands and stood. "Well, I'm a firm believer in women's rights. If a woman wants to use me, I'm not going to say no."

Marissa threw a roll at him and scrunched her nose with laughter. "You're a pig."

Jonah snagged it before it hit the ground and ripped into the soft bread with his teeth. He'd said it casually, but the image it painted in Avery's mind sent a pulse of warmth to her pussy. His message was loud and clear, but she wasn't going to use him until she was good and ready.

Chapter 23: Jonah

Jonah snagged his empty bowl and deposited it in the large plastic dirty dish bin. Part of him wanted to stay behind and talk to Avery, but he opted to quit while he was ahead. He'd learned with Laura that women demanded you walk a fine line. They didn't want to be smothered with attention, but their desire to be pursued was strong. He hoped he'd made his intentions clear without going over the top, but Avery was so hard to read.

Down in the fields, he couldn't believe she'd agreed to the impromptu massage. Her body was soft beneath his touch as she gave into him, trusting him to provide her with pleasure. He hadn't anticipated it would turn sexual, but the moment he'd heard her moan, all his reserve and honorable intentions had fled.

Involuntarily, his touch had become possessive. All he'd wanted was Avery's body against his, a desire that was further heightened by her carnal response. Even now, he felt himself thicken, remembering how the curves of her ass had framed his cock. He couldn't stop imagining hooking her panties with his thumbs and sliding them to the ground. Avery would never have agreed to it, but that hadn't stopped him from fantasizing about bending her over and taking her right there in the field. Then Mac had reared his ugly mug and sauntered over, dispelling Jonah's daydreams, along with any possibility of asking her if she was open to giving him another chance.

Jonah wasn't pleased Avery had agreed to go to the festival, but his jealousy had calmed when she immediately mentioned Marissa. Then she'd extended an invitation to him. He didn't know if she was being polite or if she actually wanted him there, but he intended to find out.

He gripped the wheelbarrow's worn, wooden handles. After he dumped the collected weeds, he needed to rope off the back half of the blueberry and raspberry patches to ensure overexcited tourists wouldn't tear through the entire crop to fill their buckets. Berry season wasn't nearly as popular as apple season though, and with the festival in town, Stan would probably dismiss everyone early for the day.

As tempting as it was to corner Avery and hash out whatever they had—or what he wished it might evolve into—it was better to keep his distance. He'd made the first move, now the ball was in her court. Jonah just hoped his decision to play it cool wouldn't blow up in his face.

Chapter 24: Jonah

Country music blasted out of garbled speakers as the group wandered down the main strip. Dusk was still a few hours away, and the sun's searing gaze had yet to relent. As predicted, once Stan had heard of their plans, he'd let them cut out an hour early, confident the orchard was equipped to handle the influx of families and first dates berry season invited.

Jonah took a deep breath and inhaled the greasy scent of fried dough, churros, and buttery, pretzel-crusted Philly cheese steaks. No matter how many fairs or festivals he'd attended as a kid, there was always some new mash-up or fried concoction to try. He had typically never enjoyed events like this because of the crowds, the lines, and the screaming kids, but Laura thrived on that energy and had pulled him onto every ride and inside every white tent that offered goat's milk soaps and vibrant dream catchers. He'd put his hands in his pockets and she'd slide her arm into his, and while she marveled at the lambs and piglets, he'd watch her face light up with joy. The stench of livestock was absent at the Waterfront Festival, but the pang of Laura's absence hit him harder than he'd expected.

Everywhere he looked, he saw the ghost of her smile and heard the painful echo of her laugh. He'd thought he would be okay, but maybe it was a mistake to come tonight.

"Do you want one?"

A sharp elbow caught Jonah in the chest, bringing him back to the present. He blinked away the memories. "Ow."

Marissa stuck out her tongue and raised her eyebrows. "Do you want one?"

"Want what?"

"A beer. I'm buying the first round."

"Oh, uh . . . Yeah, sure. Thanks."

Marissa ordered four cups of golden liquid and handed the vendor two twenties.

"Nice. At things like this, the beer is usually half-foam," Avery said as she brought the plastic cup to her lips.

"Welcome to the Finger Lakes," Marissa replied, taking a sip of her own. "So how much longer until they launch?"

Mac pulled his phone out of his back pocket and checked the time. "Twenty minutes. If we head over to Captain Bill's, we should be able to watch the regatta from the docks."

"Great! Which way do we go?" Avery asked, spinning in a tight circle.

Mac pointed to a tall white building behind them. "That way."

Avery grinned and marched in the appointed direction. She reminded Jonah of a little kid leading a treasure hunt. Her excitement was infectious, but it could only do so much to buoy his mood. Everyone filed behind Avery, and he brought up the rear. Part of him yearned to head back to his truck. The festival was just a few miles from the orchard. They'd be able to hitch a ride back, but he'd spent the last seven months isolating himself from anything and anyone that might remind him of Laura. He had to stop running at some point.

Marissa turned to glance over her shoulder at him and furrowed her brow. "You okay?"

Jonah nodded. "Just a lot of people is all."

Marissa laid a comforting hand on his forearm. "I miss her too, but she'd want you to have fun."

Jonah scoffed. Marissa was aware of his limited tolerance for heavily crowded spaces, but she'd also been one of the only people to see him at his lowest point and knew how easy it would be for him to succumb to those dark thoughts once more.

"Besides, how do you plan to win the girl from way back here? Romeo is on the move, man."

Jonah glimpsed the writhing crowd in front of them. Avery's bleached blond ponytail swung side to side with Mac's flannel-clad shoulders right behind. Sure enough, his friend's hand rested on the narrow stretch of exposed skin just above Avery's frayed denim skirt. A sudden desire to break the cocky bastard's fingers surprised Jonah. Avery wasn't his, but the sight of another guy running his hands along her body unleashed a swell of fury he hadn't felt in a long time.

"Thank you."

Marissa ran a hand through her afro blow-out. "Anytime. Laura would love her, by the way."

"Yeah?"

Marissa nodded, her smile bright. "It's okay to fall again, you know." Jonah quirked his lips and tapped his nail against the side of his cup. "Don't feel guilty. You loved Laura and she knew it, but that's the amazing thing about the heart. There's always room for more."

Jonah gave her arm a gentle squeeze and offered a weak grin. "How do you know exactly what to say every time?"

Marissa shrugged and took a sip. "It's my gift. Now, come on. I want to get a good seat this year."

"Ladies first."

Marissa spun around and cut a path through the revelers in line for fried dough and apple dumplings, leading Jonah to the docks. All the private yachts and large tour boats had been cleared away and the teams were just arriving with their haphazard-looking vessels.

Jonah scanned the throng of spectators in search of Mac and Avery and found a pair of tanned legs wearing a familiar pair of sandals. His heart warmed as he pictured Avery's expression when he'd picked them out at the store. It was like she'd never been on the receiving end of such a gesture.

Rounding a larger woman with a Gaelic cross tattooed on her left arm, he edged closer to where Avery sat. Several yards down, her legs dangled off the dock. Jealousy flared in his gut once more. Mac was beside her, his leg brushing against hers. An idea sparked in Jonah's mind, simple, yet effective.

He strode over to where Avery and Mac sat and rested his beer on the slanted wooden post to Mac's right. Marissa sipped hers and stood behind the two of them, but instinctually gave them a wide berth. She couldn't have known what he had planned, but the glint in Jonah's eye no doubt spoke of brewing trouble.

"Do you know anyone racing today?" Jonah asked Marissa.

"Not personally, but I think Jasmine mentioned her brother's friend was a part of it."

Avery turned and looked over her shoulder. Jonah's ego inflated just a tad at the thought that she might have been waiting for him. "Hey, what took you so long?"

"Got caught up a bit back there, but I'm glad we found you," Jonah answered.

Mac raised his beer. "Too bad. You snooze you lose, man. We got the best seats in the house."

Jonah shrugged. "I'm not worried about it."

With a casual twist, Jonah swung his shoulder and knocked into the side of his cup. The amber liquid sloshed over the edge, and the disturbed weight was too much for the thin plastic container. The cup tipped over, and half the contents poured onto Mac's head.

"Oh, shit!" Jonah fumbled for the cup and managed to right it, but the beer had already soaked Mac's hat and slid down his collar.

"What the hell?" Mac hunched beneath the cold onslaught and swatted his cap off his head. His arms pinwheeled to defend himself against the unknown attacker. Jonah stifled a laugh. Another few inches of squirming and Mac would fall into the lake.

"Sorry, man," Jonah said. "I didn't realize this thing wasn't flat." He glanced at Marissa and saw her suppress her own giggle.

Mac groaned and yanked off his beer-soaked shirt, depositing it in a damp heap at Jonah's feet. "No worries. It was an accident. I was getting hot, anyway."

"Want me to go to Captain Bill's and buy you a new shirt? I need to grab another beer."

Mac shook his head and beat his hat against the worn planks, trying to dry it. "Nah, but I'll take a beer."

"Sure thing. Anyone else going to need another?"

Marissa raised her half-empty cup. "Me."

Jonah nodded and his gaze flickered to Avery, but before he could ask, she pushed herself to her feet.

"I'll come with you. You'll need help carrying them all." Avery looped her thumb into the top of her skirt, and the denim dipped below her hip bone. Jonah didn't miss the glimmer of soft skin.

Mac turned abruptly. "But you're going to miss the start."

"We'll be quick." Avery shot Mac a smile. Jonah loved the way her nose crinkled with the movement, but he wasn't thrilled she was trying to soothe Mac's worries.

Stepping past the farmhand, Avery slipped her hand into Jonah's. He hid his surprise as a wave of victory washed over him. "See ya in a few."

Jonah caught Marissa flashing him a knowing look over the rim of her cup but didn't spare Mac another glance.

Together, they wove back toward the line of vendors. The crowd had grown now that the race was about to begin. Avery clutched Jonah's hand and molded her body close to his back. Her floral perfume wrapped him in a pleasant cloud, turning his thoughts carnal. He yearned to bury himself in the scent of her sweet center and nestle his tongue between her legs, but he still had to riddle her out. Was she trying to decide between him and Mac or just playing hard to get? The way she pressed her breasts against him in that moment made him think she'd chosen him, but he wouldn't want to assume and drive her away . . . again.

"Thanks for coming with me," Jonah said.

Avery cuddled closer as they passed a dad with an infant strapped to his chest. "Like I said, you can't carry them all."

"I could have gotten three."

"Then you wouldn't have anything to drink."

Jonah smirked. "Oh, I would have had a beer."

Avery narrowed her eyes and scrunched her nose. "You spilled your drink on purpose."

"Was it that obvious?"

"Nah. You played it pretty cool, but why?"

Jonah shrugged. "It wasn't really planned. I saw him next to you and didn't like it."

Avery arched her eyebrows. "Oh really? Jealous, huh?"

"A little bit."

Avery smiled. "How'd you know I'd come with you?"

"I didn't." Jonah shook his head. "It just felt good to bring his ego down a few pegs. Your company is a prize I wasn't sure I'd ever win again."

"I'm a prize?" Avery danced away but kept her grip on him.

Jonah pulled her in and spun her, making her fall against him. "Only if you want to be." He leaned down to capture her lips with his, but Avery turned her head and stepped out of his embrace.

"Come on, yo-yo. Let's grab those beers."

Chapter 25: Avery

"Yo-yo? What does that mean?" Jonah asked, following behind as she slunk through the congregation of people in line for the Coors truck.

Avery rolled her eyes. "Because I can never tell what's going on with you. One minute I'm on your lap, the next you push me away, and now you're trying to kiss me. Whiplash much?"

Jonah squeezed her hand, slid his other along her hip, and pulled her toward him. Avery's heart raced. His hand felt so good. "Yeah. I'm dealing with some personal things. I know I should stay away until I figure it all out, but I meant what I said earlier. I can't stop thinking about you."

Jonah caught her gaze and time seemed to stop. The raucous music and rowdy laughter muted and the hundreds of bodies milling around them faded to nothing but insubstantial shadows. The only thing Avery sensed was Jonah's proximity and the warmth radiating from his husky timbre.

Her sex pulsed under the weight of his hand. She couldn't deny her attraction, but did he deserve a second chance? What if he rejected her again? She hated being made a fool. "I've thought about you, too."

Avery's voice was gravelly and raw. She hadn't meant to unleash so much emotion. She knew rejection. Her whole life, her father never had time for her and pushed her away. Over the years, she'd built a wall. Brick by brick, she'd encased her heart and told herself it didn't hurt. His barbs would simply bounce off her thick shield and puddle at her feet.

Sometimes, she'd step over them and allow time to wash the discarded feelings away, but others, she'd take a running start and stomp as hard as she could in the hopes that each drop would splatter across her father's perfect world. Sleeping with all his prospective new executives seemed to rile him the most.

But Jonah wasn't part of her father's world. He had no motive to hurt her. For the short time she'd known him, he'd presented himself as sturdy and honest. Everyone had demons to overcome, herself included.

Avery cleared her throat. "Come on, they're probably wondering where we are." Jonah's face fell a little, but he didn't push further. She kept her hand tucked in his and sauntered toward the beer trucks. On their right, a small white tent selling baubles and rings appeared. She slowed her pace and scoured the velvet trays from afar. Multi-colored dresses hung from plastic mannequins, large hibiscus petals rippling in the slight breeze.

"Do you want to look?" Jonah asked, leaning in close to her ear.

"Oh, um, no. It's okay. We don't have to. The jewelry would turn my fingers green anyway."

Jonah rolled his eyes and tugged her toward the vendor. "Come on, darlin'."

Avery resisted at first, but once they slipped under the tent's cover, her excitement blossomed. Having grown up in the city, she was accustomed to flea markets and street vendors, but her father had never let her stop, proclaiming they hawked cheap goods that would tarnish within the day. But dear Daddy wasn't there to spoil her appetite for the gaudy costume jewelry, and she pored over the cluttered collection with zealous energy. Butterfly clips, bedazzled bangles, and mood rings brought her back to sixth grade. A white daisy ring with a painted yellow center caught her eye. She pushed it over the knuckle of her right-hand ring finger and held it out to Jonah.

"What do you think?"

Jonah tore his eyes away from the bucket hats that twirled on the rafter and clasped her fingers. He rubbed the dainty petals with the pad of his thumb and glanced up. "It suits you."

"Yeah?"

Jonah nodded. "Cute but tough."

Avery pursed her lips. "I'm going to try one of these on." She lifted a short black dress with fun splotches of red flowers from its place on the rack. "Excuse me? Do you have a dressing area?"

The woman nodded and pointed to the corner where two tent flaps met to create a makeshift dressing room. "There's a small stool in there for your clothes, too."

"Thank you." Avery bounded over to the alcove. For the most part, it covered her, save for an inch-wide gap that ran vertically from the top of the tent to the pavement. "Jonah, it doesn't close all the way. Can you stand guard?"

"Sure." Jonah positioned himself directly in front of her and shielded her body with his.

Avery crossed her arms. "Turn around, dummy."

A crooked smile pulled at Jonah's lips as he reluctantly followed her order.

She poked him hard in the ribs. "No peeking."

Chapter 26: Jonah

A soft whoosh of air accompanied Jonah's laugh as he held his sore rib. "You're so bossy. And in case you've forgotten, I don't need to look. I've already seen you naked." Another hard poke to his other side made Jonah's torso buckle slightly forward. "Quit it."

"No. You've *almost* seen me naked. You're not curious to see me *without* the towel?" Behind him, Jonah heard the rustle of soft fabric as Avery stripped out of her shirt.

His cock twitched as her skirt followed. He wondered what color the panties were that he'd felt by the strawberries. Jonah licked his lips and shifted to the right. Across from him he saw a flash of blond hair and was startled for a second, thinking Avery may have snuck by, but he felt her movements as she picked up her fallen clothes. That's when he realized a circular mirror stood opposite him with a perfect view of the scene over his shoulder.

Jonah crossed his arms in front of his jeans and lowered his head, attempting to appear nonchalant to onlookers. His hazel eyes fixated on the mirror, and his breath caught. A lacy pink bra was wrapped around Avery's chest and cradled her soft breasts. Smooth skin peeked over the top of the satin fabric. He stifled a groan. With each of her movements, her breasts gave the slightest bounce. All he wanted to do was press his lips against them, to find her nipples with his mouth and feel them harden beneath his tongue.

As if sensing his stare, Avery twisted away while she searched for the bottom of the dress. Jonah didn't mind. Now her perfect ass was on display, and his cock grew rigid as he remembered how firm it'd felt beneath his hands when she'd arched into him. He bit his lower lip. She wore a black thong.

Jonah's cock pressed uncomfortably against the zipper of his jeans. The urge to spin around and pin Avery against the wall was overwhelming as the memory of caressing her thigh drove him wild.

His gaze slid down to her cheeks, following the thin fabric as it disappeared, only for the lace to wink back at him where it covered her pussy. He dreamed of running his fingers along her slit and feeling her wetness soak the delicate material. He'd pull it to the side, rub the head of his cock along her warm center, and urge the tip between her folds. Would she like that? Would she push back and demand he fill her with his hard length?

The image of Avery bent over, grabbing the wobbly stool as she looked back at him over her shoulder, was everything. He'd grip her hips, his thumbs rubbing her ass in small circles as he slowly thrust into her, eliciting little gasps and moans from her lips as she tried to keep quiet. Her breasts would sway back and forth as he fucked her, threatening to spill out of the cups. He pictured releasing those beautiful rose buds and pulling them between his fingers until she groaned. He'd try to go slow, withdrawing his cock to the tip, only to succumb and slam back into her. The urge to take her rough and fast made his dick throb.

As the scene played out before him, a warm hand slid

around his waist, stopping dangerously close to the front of his jeans. Jonah's head tilted back. He was so hard, so lost in the dream.

"Do you think it fits?" Avery asked.

"Don't worry, I'll make it fit," Jonah muttered under his breath.

There was a long pause, then Avery laughed. "No, I meant the dress."

Jonah's eyes sprung open, and he twisted around to face her. "Oh, yeah. I did, too. Sorry. I was a little lost in thought." He looked Avery up and down, blown away by how well the flowy dress hugged her curves. "You look great."

A cheeky look sparkled in Avery's eyes, and she pursed her lips. "Thank you." She twirled, the loose fabric kicking up, Marilyn Monroe style. Jonah suppressed another groan as her panties flashed once more. She danced, and he took an involuntary step closer to the dressing room. "What were you thinking about?"

The fabric swished across her thighs and settled. It would be so easy to lift the dress, pick Avery up, and slide her onto his cock. Jonah cleared his throat and shook his head. "Nothing much."

"Oh." Avery's inquisitive expression softened into a slight frown, and she ran her hand across the front of Jonah's jeans, unable to miss the hard length fighting against the seam. "I'd hoped you might have been thinking about me."

Jonah hissed through his teeth. Her fingers traced the outline of his cock, and she pressed the heel of her palm against him, rubbing intently.

"Does that feel good?" Avery asked.

"You have no idea."

Avery sidled closer and pressed her breasts against his chest as she tipped her chin up and batted her lashes. "What do you want, Jonah?"

Jonah slid his hand along the small of Avery's back, balling the thin material in his fist to subtly expose the tops of her thighs. "I want—"

"No sex in the dressing room." A stern voice called.

Jonah looked away from Avery, startled. "What?"

"No sex. Dressing rooms are for trying on merchandise only." The vendor crossed her arms over her chest and fixed them with a sour expression.

The tips of Jonah's ears flared red as he stepped away from Avery and tried to hide his obvious erection. "Sorry."

Avery slammed her hand over her mouth, her eyes sparkling mischievously. Without a word, she slunk back inside the dressing room, leaving Jonah alone to contend with the shopkeeper's angry stare. Thankfully, she changed much faster the second time, and soon emerged, diffusing the awkward tension.

"How much for the dress and the ring?" Avery asked, holding up her adorned finger.

The woman furrowed her eyebrows. "Thirty-five dollars."

Avery dug in her purse and fumbled for the correct bills. Jonah cleared his throat and withdrew his wallet. He fished out a fifty-dollar bill and handed it to the vendor. "There you go. Keep the change. Sorry for the, uh . . . moment."

The vendor snatched the large bill, and her expression softened a touch. "Thank you. I hope you enjoy it elsewhere."

Jonah nodded as the vendor's stiff posture relaxed. Avery offered a small wave and tucked the dress over her arm. Together, they disappeared into the crowd. Jonah was careful to keep his hand on her lower back, unwilling to let her go for even a few minutes. Once the tent was a fair distance away,

Avery spun around and placed her hand on his chest.

"Can you believe that?" Avery erupted in a fit of giggles, amusement snorting out of her nose. "I feel fifteen again, like I just got busted by my friend's parents."

"That was pretty humbling." Jonah slid both arms around Avery's waist and pulled her so close that she was almost dancing on his feet.

Avery flicked the faded brim of his hat. "My aunt was wrong about you."

"Hmm? How so?"

"She made you out to be this wounded lamb, but it turns out you're the big bad wolf—rubbing me by the strawberries and trying to have your way with me in public? Do you do this to all the new farmhands? Pretend to be this mysterious broken man to draw unsuspecting lovers to your bed?"

Jonah shrugged. "Mac took some convincing."

Avery gasped and smacked his arm. "You're incorrigible."

"I'm just kidding. Carrie looks out for me, but sometimes she goes too far."

They fell into an easy canter and headed back to the shore. While they were in the tent, the race had begun and drew a fair share of festivalgoers to the dock. They strolled easily through the street while cheers and enthusiastic cries crescendoed.

In the water, five teams fought to stay afloat, their oars chopping and displacing the waves with fierce urgency. Mac was right. It did look entertaining, but they were in no hurry to return to the sidelines. "What do you mean?"

Jonah rested his arm along Avery's shoulders. He liked the way she fit against him.

"Nothing. Just something I went through last year."

Avery cuddled closer. "You can tell me."

Jonah rubbed her arm. "Thanks, I know."

Jonah saw hope flare in her eyes. He bit the inside of his cheek. He wanted to tell her about Laura, but he'd grown to hate the look of pity everyone regarded him with once they knew. He couldn't bear to have Avery look at him like that, as if they could no longer see him, only the ghost of his loss.

His past danced on his tongue, but part of him continued to resist. He wanted to tell her, wanted to share the many memories of Laura with Avery, but not here. Not in a mass of strangers where he'd have to yell to be heard.

"Maybe some other time."

Avery's chest fell, but she didn't pry further. Relief washed over him. How had he ever thought her immature? She led him toward the nearest beer truck and grinned.

"Freshman year, I did a keg stand, but fell and chipped my tooth."

"Did you really?" Jonah winced and cradled her against him. "I'm not gonna lie, it's hard to picture you being graceful at anything."

"Hey!" Avery swatted his chest. "I'll have you know, I used to do ballet."

"Did you play the tree in the recital?"

"No! I was good, you jerk."

Jonah snickered playfully and tucked her arm in tighter, content with her easy smile. "Tell me how you broke your tooth, then."

Avery launched into the embarrassing anecdote. She seemed fine with the subject change, and for the first time, the thought of sharing his true feelings—and one of the biggest pieces of himself—with another person didn't terrify him.

Chapter 27: Avery

June surrendered to July in the blink of an eye. Gone were the occasional clouds that rolled lazily in front of the sun. Midsummer descended hot and sticky, relentless in its onslaught during the day and offering little reprieve even after the moon crested the rolling hills. Each night, Avery laid awake atop the covers, clad in nothing but a cami and panties with droplets of sweat dotting her skin. The cabins weren't equipped with AC, and the mini fan that sat on the desk only succeeded in blowing the humid air around in a stale eddy.

Avery had hoped to find solace in the showers, yet no matter what time of day she ventured under the hiccupping stream, lukewarm water drizzled from the showerhead in unsatisfying bursts. With the rain still holding out, Uncle Stan diverted every drop he could to the crops. Summer was usually her favorite season, but that was when she was playing the familiar role of socialite in Manhattan, enjoying the heat from exclusive hotel pool decks and climate-controlled luxury cars.

At the orchard, sweat was her constant companion, and even under a heavy layer of sunscreen, her skin blistered and crisped until she resembled an old brick patio. Her sunhat became a stable fixture on her head. Uncle Stan pushed all of them from dawn to dusk, and especially with the drought, there was no time for casual, sexy outfits. Her worn flannel accompanied every tank top, along with new knee-length shorts that protected against the endless movement and chaffing, not to mention the biting insects.

Living in the city, bugs were never something Avery had to consider. Butterflies graced the gardens surrounding Bryant Park, and the occasional fly ventured inside conference rooms, but nothing could have prepared her for the onslaught these winged pests waged each and every day.

Bumble bees and wasps lurked in the apple trees or hopped from flower to flower underfoot, stingers at the ready. Crickets hurled themselves through the tall grass and provided an inescapable melody while she worked and slept. But the gnats were the worst. They were like teeny missiles that congregated in thrumming clouds, each one attempting to burrow into her ears, nostrils, and wet corners of her eyes.

The first time she'd dug a little black body out of her eye, she'd screamed, but the practice was so commonplace now that she barely felt it until she looked in the mirror after dinner and found several knotted clumps collected in the corners.

Never had Avery been so exhausted. She was used to putting in fifty or sixty hours a week, but corporate life was nothing like manual labor. Work in the orchard may have been less mentally taxing, but it was also one of the most isolating jobs she'd ever encountered, and her muscles ached with bone-deep fatigue.

The orchard spanned twelve acres. With all the different crops and only a handful of farmhands to work the land, everyone was stretched to separate corners to ensure nothing was missed. After a quick banana or bowl of oatmeal, it was rare that Avery would encounter anyone else until they met up at their cabins at sundown, and by then, everyone was far too tired to do anything other than shower and sleep.

Avery tried to recall how many weeks it'd been since the festival. Two? Three? The days flew by when she didn't have her phone in her back pocket, reminding her of the hour. Was Jonah thinking of her? Every few days, she imagined sneaking into his cabin and continuing their conversation. It had ended on a cliffhanger by the docks, but by the time his light turned off and he settled in, it was far too laborious to keep her eyes open. Whatever haunted him was painful. Aunt Carrie had stressed that at the beginning of the summer, but sometimes letting someone new in acted as an unexpected balm to a broken heart. Not that she wanted him to fall in love with her, but if her company could crack his stony façade, maybe it would help dull the shattered pieces he kept buried.

Avery wiped her sweaty brow with a black handkerchief, an item she'd started tucking in her back pocket at Uncle Stan's suggestion. The thin material was already limp and damp from previous use, but at least it erased the wet, tickling sensation as beads of perspiration slid along her collarbone and neck. She returned the bandana to its place and angled her pruning shears. Yellow Jackets buzzed around her as she reached into the thick foliage to trim the fruit in the middle. Uncle Stan had assigned her to the dozen or so rows of Crimson Crisps today, and their tart aroma flavored the thick breeze.

She stretched onto her tiptoes and swiftly cut the long stems that held the bright red apples. At first, she hadn't understood the need for trimming. What was the point of cutting half the apples off the tree and leaving them to rot on the ground?

Marissa had explained. Similar to a stylist shearing off dead ends, thinning the branches was a crucial step to help the tree and its healthier fruits make it to maturity. They also left the fallen fruit because it encouraged wildlife to eat it instead of the remaining apples, and their scat became a natural fertilizer. Avery had wrinkled her nose at the thought, but it made sense and cut down on the need for harmful pesticides.

She tossed her hair off her neck and cast away the distracting thoughts along with it. *Snip. Plop. Snip. Plop.* Avery lost herself in the easy melody as she inspected the fruit for rot or damage. If one didn't pass the test, *snip.* If a bushel grew too close together, *snip snip.* She carved the fruit from the branch, careful to maintain a space of about five inches between each so the chosen ones had plenty of room to grow.

Previously cultivated fruit squished under her sneakers as she rounded the narrow trunk to reach the other side. Soon enough, she had trimmed the lowest hanging branches and turned to look for the step stool, but the ladder wasn't in its usual place.

Avery groaned and swatted a party of gnats away from her mouth. Closing her pruning shears, she rested her hands on her head and glanced toward the utility barn at the top of the hill. She was in the front orchard, a five-minute walk. Unable to continue without the stool, she trudged along the path she'd worn through the tall, dry grass and mumbled under her breath.

If only her father could see her now, sunburned, and drained but strong. Not once had he called or checked in, not that she expected him to, but it would have been nice.

Her steps transitioned from grass to gravel, and the scruff of her sneakers kept a steady rhythm as she climbed to the top. Hoping to break up the monotony of her thoughts, she scanned the area left to right, but nothing aside from the scratchy swell of cicadas greeted her.

Avery grabbed the metal handle, thankful the front of the barn was steeped in shade, and stepped inside the dusty structure. Uncle Stan's large tractor was missing, along with several irrigation hoses, but the step ladder she sought rested behind the old metal wagons guests used to carry their spoils. She rolled her eyes, annoyed that whoever put it away was so diligent in its placement. The barn was stuffy, and moving all those wagons back and forth would be more time-consuming than she'd anticipated. Voices drifted in from outside, and Avery's spirits soared, but the subject of their conversation quickly doused her enthusiasm.

"You can't be serious." Mac's tenor boomed. A touch of incredulity colored his tone.

"Why not? You've seen the way he looks at her." Marissa retorted.

"Yeah, as a piece of ass. It's not like he's in love with her or anything. How can he be? She's a sorority girl living off Daddy's dime."

"You're just jealous because she didn't want to sleep with you."

Mac scoffed. "Please, you can't stand there and tell me you don't see it, too. Laura was so gentle and classy. Av's got the mouth of a trucker and never misses a chance to show off."

Avery sucked in a sharp breath and her cheeks flushed scarlet. They were talking about her. She wedged herself into the dark corner, pressed her back against the wooden slats, and prayed they had no reason to enter the barn. Marissa's shadow fell across the concrete floor as she stepped in front of the open doorway. Her voice softened, but Avery could still make out her words.

"Of course she's different than Laura. No one could ever compete with that girl. Jonah looked at her as if she were the sun, but I don't get why you're so upset that he's interested in Avery. The guy is allowed to move on. He's practically been a hermit since it happened. He's entitled to some fun."

Mac clucked his tongue and kicked the gravel. Several of the small pebbles hit the side of the barn, and Avery flinched.

"I guess. He's just one of my best friends. I don't want him to fall for this girl and then get his heart broken at the end of the summer when she flees this shithole for her fancy life in the city."

"Aww, look at you, all sentimental. You know, if you treated women with this much sensitivity, you might be able to keep a girl."

"Shut up," Mac said without malice, and the two shared a laugh.

Marissa opened the door, expanding the swatch of sunlight that painted the floor. "Don't worry about Jonah. He's a big boy. Let him get his dick wet, clear his head, and then at the end of the summer when she leaves, he'll be ready to start a real relationship with someone who cares about him."

The pair strode into the utility barn, dragging hoses behind them. Avery swallowed the thickening lump in her throat and stepped forward.

"Oh, shit!" Marissa exclaimed, clutching her chest. "I didn't see you there."

"I figured," Avery said without inflection.

An awkward silence broiled the stale air. Marissa wrung the hose in her hands and bit her lower lip as Mac stood behind her, an unreadable expression on his face.

"Listen, if you heard all that, it's just . . . We've known Jonah a long time, and . . . we want what's best for him," Marissa said. Her hesitant words hung in the dead space, swirling to the hay-covered floor with the dust motes and dried fly corpses.

Avery nodded. Despite the heat, the guilt in their eyes sent chills rippling down her body. "And clearly that's not me."

She exhaled a steadying breath and raised her chin higher. "Because you know all about me, right? I'm a princess waiting for Daddy's helicopter to swoop down and save me from this place."

"That's not—"

"Let me finish," Avery said, cutting off Marissa before she could bullshit an excuse to save face. "All my life, I've endured people's opinions of me. Swallowed my pride and stayed silent because I knew one day I would prove everyone wrong. You have no idea what motivates me or about the relationship I have with my father because you've never asked. The moment you saw me, you both invented a backstory based on my appearance and had no interest in confirming those ideas. I'm sorry if my presence has thrown a wrench into your summer. Believe me, it was not my choice to come here. Talk all the trash you want about me, but don't you dare think for one second that you're better than me. I am working just as hard as you, and I do it without saying cruel things behind your back."

Avery's voice wavered. She turned and lifted the ladder over the tower of wagons. Mac made a move to help her, but she shot him a dirty look. "I don't need your help, and I don't need your friendship. I'm glad I heard your true opinions of me. Now we don't need to pretend anymore."

She wielded the ladder like a shield and stormed out of the barn. Marissa and Mac jumped back to avoid the hard edges of the legs, their mouths frozen in shock. Bright sunlight kissed Avery's face. She tilted her chin to the sky as a solitary tear rolled down her cheek.

Rejection was a familiar landscape. Growing up and attending private schools, gossip was ingested and regurgitated at a breakneck pace. Being the daughter of one of the wealthier patrons of the school, Avery was no stranger to fake smiles and backstabbing rumors. She'd learned long ago to keep friends at arm's length because self-preservation and image were worth far more than loyalty.

As she marched back down to the front orchard, her biceps burned from dehydration and strain under the unforgiving weight, but she refused to crumble because of their cruel words. If there was one thing she'd learned from her father, it was that she would never be enough for anyone, so she'd carved out a comfortable bubble to which she could retreat. She could love herself, and that was enough.

Chapter 28: Jonah

The ladder swayed beneath Jonah's feet as a strong breeze kicked up. He pocketed his pruning shears and wove his hands through the full branches to grip the solid trunk in the center. With a slight twist of his hips, he shifted the top rung of the ladder and nestled it closer to the trunk, anchoring it amongst the lower brambles. Satisfied the metal scaffold wouldn't budge again, he retrieved his shears and continued trimming the smaller Red Delicious from the high bundles at the top.

From his vantage point, he could see the whole of the side orchard, everything from the first few rows of Macintosh to the Jonagolds at the far end. When he first started working at the orchard, he'd wondered about his qualifications. Did it matter that he had a background in landscape irrigation, or was Stan just some weird romantic who enjoyed poetic symmetry across all avenues of his life? Hell, the old man probably gave Mac his nickname.

Jonah wiped the gathered sweat off his brow and adjusted his damp ballcap. He knew it was futile to search for Avery amidst the treetops, but it didn't keep him from trying. A flash of her darkening ponytail or her red shirt, flitting like a cardinal through the branches, would help get him through his shift until he caught up with her later by the cabins.

With Mid-July around the corner, Stan's casual management had ended. Now, each farmhand worked from the crest of dawn until twilight dimmed the night sky. The jovial group meals and proverbial vespers by the fire were over. Lunches were staggered and cut, a quick sandwich and an apple of choice. The meticulous schedule didn't bother Jonah after five years of working for Stan. He was no stranger to the orchard's strict demands. If his boss didn't tighten the schedule, they wouldn't have enough crops to ship to their partner grocers or satisfactory inventory left for the hordes of tourists that descended every September.

No, the long days didn't bother Jonah, but each day he couldn't help feeling some resentment as he watched Avery walk in the opposite direction, away from his assignment. A few weeks ago at the festival, they had teetered on the edge of starting something real, but the orchard came first. Once again, it seemed as if all the progress they'd made had disintegrated like sand, and he was helpless to watch as more of her trust slipped through his fingers with every passing day.

Jonah trimmed the last apple at the top and carved out a large gap for the healthier fruit to grow. As he descended the ladder, his thoughts swam back to something Avery'd said a while back. He knew Carrie was protective of him, but would she really forbid Avery from getting close to him? He wasn't brittle. Yes, his heart had been gutted, but did that mean he deserved to be alone and unloved for the rest of his life? Warmed only by the ghost of his past love? Marissa and Mac had been paired several times now to irrigate the rows, yet he and Avery remained separated. Was Stan oblivious to the division, or was Carrie whispering in his ear, pulling the strings behind the scenes?

Jonah's bladder felt uncomfortably full. Usually, he would

relieve himself next to one of the trees, but his water bottle was nearly empty, and the bathrooms were close to the front orchard where Avery was stationed. What a happy accident it would be if he ran into her. He made note of which row he was in and started the long march back to the common area.

Cicadas hummed, and plump carpenter bees droned along in languid breezes, dutiful workers bounding from flower to flower. Up ahead, the gravel path curved, and the hulking silhouette of the utility barn loomed. Still one hundred yards away, the double doors flew open, and Avery stormed forward like a tornado hell-bent on destruction. She made it about a dozen yards when a painful sob racked her chest. Without slowing her stride, she dropped the ladder she carried, veered left, and disappeared into the trees, her destination the main house.

"Avery!" Jonah called out. "Avery!" He cupped his hands around his mouth and hollered to no avail. Either she didn't hear him, lost in her own thoughts, or she purposefully ignored his cries. He jogged to catch up but slowed when he rounded the side of the barn and caught sight of Marissa and Mac standing inside, guilt etched onto their features. "What happened? What's wrong with Avery?"

Mac reached up and scratched the back of his neck while Marissa bit her lower lip. "She may have heard us talking," she admitted.

Jonah furrowed his brow. "About what? What's going on?"

"We didn't mean for her to hear," Mac said. "We were just shooting the shit."

"What did you say?"

Marissa stepped forward. Worry creased the skin around her lips. "We didn't know she was in the barn. I was riding Mac because at last there was a girl he couldn't charm, and then

Laura came up and we might have mentioned how Avery was nothing like Laura and that the only reason you were showing interest in her was because she might be a good rebound to help you get back on your feet."

"An easy way to get his dick wet is what you said," Mac added.

Marissa smacked his arm. "Shut up. It was just locker room talk. I swear I didn't know she was there, Jonah."

Jonah ran a hand over his mouth as rage boiled in his gut. "Wow, and here I thought I knew you guys." Marissa frowned and wrung her hands while Mac crossed his arms over his chest. "When did it become okay for you to comment on my life, huh? For you to pass judgment about who is good enough for me? Did you forget you didn't even like Laura when we first got together? You called her a snob and said she was stuck up. Now Avery is trash? Why? Because she didn't fall to her knees and suck your dick like all the girls you brag about banging?"

"It's not like that—" Mac protested, but Jonah waved his hand.

"And you." He turned his attention to Marissa. "Were you just yanking my chain at the festival? I thought you told me to give it a real shot with her."

"I did, but I thought it was just sex. You don't know this girl, Jonah."

"Yeah, and neither do you. You say you were looking out for me? It feels more like a stab in the back. Who I sleep with is none of your concern. I expected a lot more from you guys, especially you." Jonah pointed at Marissa and hung his head as he pivoted atop the gravel. He resumed his pace and followed the same path Avery had disappeared down.

"Jonah?" Marissa called, but he didn't stop, didn't turn around. He was so sick of playing by society's rules and withholding his own feelings for fear of others' judgment. In the grand scheme, what did it matter? Just because he was falling for someone new didn't diminish the love he felt for Laura. It didn't make her or their relationship any less real and for his friends to throw Avery under the bus to defend his honor was inexcusable.

Jonah's arms pumped as his boots slammed against the gravel, his pace creeping from a jog to a sprint. Unless Avery had ran the whole way, he should be able to catch up. He leaped from the manicured path onto the well-trodden earth. For a moment, he was torn. Would she have retreated to her cabin, or had she needed Stan's jovial reassurance?

Taking a chance, he veered left and headed toward the main house. He passed through pools of cool shadows as thick clouds gathered above. The sweet tang of Honey Crisps flavored the humid afternoon. After two minutes of hard running, he emerged from the sentinel of trees and slowed as he approached the large back deck.

Jonah fought to catch his breath as it fell in shallow gasps. He wasn't out of shape, but maintaining the orchard rarely called for an all-out sprint in near one-hundred-degree heat. He propped his hands on his hips and climbed the shallow steps. His heavy boots ominously thundered across the wooden planks. He hoped it wasn't a sign of what was to come.

With one last deliberate exhale, Jonah slid open the sliding glass door and stepped into the air-conditioned home. The sight of Avery momentarily eased the tension constricting his heart, but his relief didn't last long. His eyes traveled up her long, slightly sunburned calves, to her backside where a pair of masculine hands rested just above her ass. But that wasn't the worst part. His gaze hardened as he watched Avery throw her arms around the man's neck and bury her face in the crook of his shoulder, holding him close.

Chapter 29: Avery

Uncle Stan and Aunt Carrie weren't alone. Jovial laughter echoed throughout the first floor as Avery rushed into the cool house. The sound disarmed her. Jonah couldn't have beaten her there, and besides, this laugh was different. It was too deep, too rich compared to the quiet breathy chuckles she'd been able to pull from him. This was a jarring burst of happiness, one that grated against the raw emotions crashing like furious waves within her.

Inside, a man stood with his back to her. Golden blond hair lay in gentle curls on the nape of his neck. Avery's feet stuttered when she took in his broad shoulders and tapered waist. The stranger turned his head, and his profile caught the graying light streaming in through one of the skylights. The tightness in Avery's chest relaxed, and the sharp edges softened enough to dismiss her heartache for the present moment. Her body reacted before her mind could and before she knew it, she was racing to the living room. The man spun, a large grin lighting his goofy face.

"Jesse!" Avery cried as she ran into his waiting arms.

"Avs! It's so good to see you!" Jesse wrapped his arms around her lower back and lifted her off the floor. He spun her once before setting her soles back on the ground and looked her up and down. "Geez, I barely recognize you."

"Well, I would hope so after sixteen years. And look at this hair! You look like a surfer."

Jesse tossed his sun-kissed locks dramatically. "I had to fit in with all the handsome Aussies somehow."

Avery ran her fingers through his waves and stepped out of his embrace, planting her hands on her hips. "Speaking of, why are you back so soon?"

Jesse jerked his thumb over his shoulder toward his parents. "I was just telling them. My girlfriend couldn't take the bugs anymore."

"What?" Avery's jaw dropped.

Jesse put up his hands and laughed. "From the jumping ants to the locusts, she was done. But what really sent her over the edge was the night last week when a huntsman spider got into the apartment."

"A what kind of spider?" Aunt Carrie asked.

Jesse angled his neck and gestured for Avery to join them on the couch. The whoosh of the sliding door echoed, and movement on the other side made her pause. Jonah stalked across the deck, his fingers interlocked behind his head. Her chest constricted once more. Part of her was relieved he'd left, but she was also infuriated. She wanted to confront him and scream, to demand he explain his past and why his friends were so quick to agree she wasn't good enough to be in his future.

Avery envisioned running after him, but to what avail? If she caused a scene, it would cement Mac and Marissa's opinion of her, and she refused to give them the satisfaction. So what if Jonah only viewed her as a fuck buddy? Hadn't that been her early intention, too? But then he'd fought to win her back, sought her out and apologized. She had allowed herself to imagine the possibility of a real relationship with him, not one born out of spite for her father or as a simple way to pass the time. If she was honest, she liked thinking of him. She loved the days when their paths crossed for a moment and she caught glimpses of his rugged frame flickering between the narrow trunks and spreading foliage. But the reality was he didn't view her in the same light. As Marissa said, she was simply summer practice so Jonah would eventually be ready for a girl worth his time.

Avery ground the fleshy pulp of her cheeks between her molars, unaware that she had been lingering by the door.

"You okay, Avery?" Uncle Stan asked.

She shook her head. Loose wisps of hair tickled her face as she swallowed her frustration and adopted an easy smile. "Yeah, I was looking at those clouds. Do you think we might get some rain today?"

Uncle Stan cleared his throat, and Avery turned her back on the slider. Outside, Jonah retreated. "Nah, the weatherman said there's a chance of a thunderstorm, but with my luck, those clouds will dissipate within the hour. It's just too damn hot. No moisture to evaporate. My water bill will be through the roof trying to keep up with it all."

The armchair cushion hissed as Avery plunked down, taking the seat opposite Jesse on the loveseat. "It's a good thing Australia was too buggy for Wendy. Another hand will make a huge difference around here."

Jesse scoffed. "Look at you, talking like a seasoned vet. I'm happy to be home, and it's perfect timing because Wendy's going to her family's summer house down in Virginia Beach next week, so I'll have some free time."

"Lost without her, huh?" Avery teased.

Jesse shrugged. "Pretty much. I enjoy hanging with the guys

and doing my own thing, but I love being with Wendy more."

Tears pricked the corner of Avery's eyes. How was it that her younger cousin knew more about love than her? No doubt she'd had more lovers, but they'd all been shallow flings for personal gain. She'd never given her heart away. Why should she? Too many times, her father had shown her how little her affection was worth. Why would anyone else think differently?

Avery's thoughts flashed to Jonah. One day, she knew she would be ready to share that vulnerable part of herself, but now was not the time. So, it didn't matter what Jonah's friends thought of her. She hadn't come here for love or friendship. At the end of the summer, she would return to the city, and she would do it without a backward glance.

Aunt Carrie shot a curious look in Avery's direction and leaned forward to balance her chin in her hand, her eyes bright. "Tell us more about that spider, honey. What was it called?"

Jesse threw his arm over the back of the loveseat. "A huntsman. Completely harmless but the size of a dinner plate. They get into houses sometimes and chill in doorways. Wendy flipped when she saw it and demanded I get it out, but if I knocked it down, it would have fallen onto the floor, and this thing was as big as a cat."

They fell into easy conversation as Jesse recounted the interesting fauna they'd encountered and his girlfriend's comical reactions. After half an hour had passed, Avery's palms itched to return to the endless rows of apple trees, and she excused herself from the cozy group.

"I still have half a dozen rows to trim before the sun sets. Can't spend all day reminiscing with the scholar." Avery stood, gave Jesse's foot a light kick, and strode toward the door.

"Make sure you grab another bottle of water on the way out," Uncle Stan called. "I'll be along to inspect the summer apples. Next week, we gotta start picking and packaging them to ship out."

Avery saluted her uncle and wove down the hall into the kitchen. "Aye aye, Captain."

Laughter bubbled behind her as she tugged open the heavy stainless-steel fridge. Inside, bottles of chilled water lined the middle of the door. Avery hooked her thumb and forefinger around the squat top and withdrew one from the lineup. The fridge shut with a dull click, and Avery flinched at the swatch of unexpected color waiting behind the metal curtain.

"Aunt Carrie, you scared me."

"Sorry, dear. I wanted to catch you before you went back out."

"Oh?"

Aunt Carrie placed a cool palm on Avery's forearm. "I wanted to tell you how proud I am of you. We see how hard you've been working, how many hours you've spent learning the ropes. It's not always easy being the new gal, especially coming into a group that's been together for so long, but please know your dad would be proud of all the effort you've given too, and that's all that matters."

Avery stood before her aunt, speechless. Had she heard Mac and Marissa or was their disdain for her that obvious? She cleared her throat and tapped her nail against the plastic cap. "That's sweet of you to say, Aunt Carrie. It's a nice thought."

Her aunt offered her a reassuring squeeze and a fond silence spread between them. Avery was overwhelmed with the sense that Aunt Carrie wanted to say more, but for some reason she held her tongue. Her dark brown eyes shone with a watery sheen, and her signature chestnut braid rested over her shoulder. Seeing her surrounded by the familiar rosemary-scented kitchen and the panoramic windows overlooking the flourishing orchard beyond, Avery was struck by a swell of homesickness, not for the city and its concrete giants that battled the sky for dominance, but for this woman and the unassuming green fields.

Joyful memories of staying with her cousin's family when she was young assailed her. This place was so different from her sterile home, and she reveled in the easy camaraderie and love that filled their every day. Why had she run from this? Chasing success had only made her miserable, but at the time, following in her father's footsteps had seemed like the only option, the only way to make him see her. Yet, standing before Aunt Carrie and hearing her words of affirmation filled Avery with warmth and love that radiated like a physical flood, buoying her serotonin and self-esteem.

Avery's breathing hitched, and her chin wobbled. All these years, she'd fought to carve out a place for herself, had been manipulated to believe her achievements were the building blocks to love. Yet, she'd been blind to the fact that there was a soft nest right here, awaiting the day she was ready to come home. This woman had always been there for her, a loving mother who'd never asked for any validation in return.

Hiccupping sobs fell from Avery's lips and tears blurred her vision. Aunt Carrie was there in an instant, enveloping her in a tight embrace.

"It's all right, sweet girl. Let it out."

Her aunt's soothing words wrought cathartic magic, and Avery's cries deepened. She hadn't realized how taut she'd been, how punishing her internal standards had become. Salty drops coursed down her cheeks. Some slid down her neck and soaked her collar while others littered the floorboards.

She cried for everything: her absent mother, her cold father, the loving family she'd spurned, years of empty friendships she'd let wither and rot, the seemingly endless parade of men she'd shared her body with, thinking she could enact a twisted sense of control; the cruel words Mac and Marissa tossed into the air without care for who they wounded, the impossible hope of exploring her growing feelings for Jonah. Lastly, she cried for herself, for the loving upbringing she could have had.

Avery didn't know how long she stood there cocooned in Aunt Carrie's arms, but her aunt didn't rush her or step away. After a while, her tears slowed and her breaths evened out. A newfound sense of calm settled over her. It had been years since she'd allowed herself to let go like that, and the release was profound.

Avery's aunt squeezed her arms one last time. When she finally released her niece, she crossed to the sink and wet a washcloth with cool water, then passed it to her. "Press this against your face, honey."

"Thank you." Avery's voice was gravelly and raw. She hadn't expected seeking sanctuary would lead to an epiphany beside her aunt's fridge. The cool washcloth lapped up her tears, not erasing the pain, but soothing it. A shy smile tugged on her lips. "I better get back to work. I still have lots of rows to tackle."

Aunt Carrie reached for the terrycloth. "I'll take care of that, sweetheart." She didn't say anything more, but she didn't have to. The love in her gaze was tangible.

"Thank you for . . . thank you."

Her aunt nodded and busied herself with the silverware drawer, but she threw a quick wink over her shoulder. Avery's smile widened as she headed toward the door. The tart rows of Crimson Crisps called.

Chapter 30: Jonah

Propelled by a cocktail of testosterone, guilt, and a sliver of relief, Jonah fled the boisterous living room. He didn't know how to behave as his emotions flared. The desire to rip Avery out of Jesse's arms was strong, but Carrie would never forgive him if he caused a scene and ruined their happy family reunion. Escaping outside, he bounded down the deck toward the latrine. He may have been helpless to comfort Avery, but at least he could relieve himself and eliminate one stressor.

Reaching the building a few minutes later, he yanked open the door and strode toward the solitary urinal. He alleviated his heavy bladder, but his gut continued to roil. He could only imagine what Avery thought of him. She had every right to be upset. He knew how Mac and Marissa could talk.

He zipped his fly and washed his hands. The water slightly cooled his ire, but his thoughts couldn't settle. Did Avery want space or should he return to the house and wait until she emerged? He knew her well enough now that she'd probably push him away, but this time he wouldn't let her. She needed to hear him out.

Resigned to catch her after she was finished welcoming home Stan's world-traveling son, Jonah left the bathrooms and retraced his path back to the big house. Distant thunder rumbled and darkening clouds dominated the sky. He mumbled under his breath as a gust of wind kicked up and blew his cap off his head.

"Shit." Jonah raced after it as the breeze carried it down the hill toward the swaying apple trees. At last, it released its hold and dropped the hat. He bent down and swiped it from the parched earth, but a metallic skeleton caught his eye, lying on its side in the middle of the row of Honey Crisps. Curiosity piqued, he wandered closer and discovered the steel stepladder he had seen Avery clutching as she ran from the utility barn. He didn't know when she would leave Stan's or if she would even remember to collect it at all after what she'd heard.

Jonah leaned down, slung the ladder over his shoulder, and walked toward the front orchard as a new idea formed. If Avery needed the stool, it should be easy enough to deduce which trees she'd already trimmed. Hopefully once she was ready, she'd return and he'd be able to apologize for his friends' misguided musings.

Twenty minutes later, an uneven tempo of solid plunks sounded as discarded apples hit the earth. Jonah trimmed the fruit at the very top and inhaled the sharp fragrance as the heavy apples plunged to the dry grass below while he ruminated on how to approach the subject without further alienating Avery.

Plop. Plop. Plop. Sweat trickled down his shoulder blades. Would she ever speak to him again? Would she leave the orchard? *Plop. Plop.* Would she believe him?

"I don't need your help."

Avery's curt voice cut like a scythe, and Jonah wobbled as his imaginings suddenly became real. Overhead, the sky boomed as the storm approached. Slate gray clouds smothered the last of the white cumulus as if the weather was influenced by her mood.

"Avery, hey." Jonah pocketed the shears and jumped down from the middle rung. He wiped his chapped hands on the front of his jeans and adjusted his ball cap. She didn't flinch and stared at him without an ounce of expression. "I found the ladder you dropped and brought it over. I thought I'd tackle a few trees while I waited."

Avery crossed her arms. "Waited for what? The bitch to calm down?"

"No. Not at all. I followed you to the house, but then I saw Jesse. I didn't want to barge in after you, but I need to apologize for what Mac and Marissa said."

A deafening crack shook the orchard as thunder roared above them. The storm was rolling in, fast and angry. Clouds stretched like charcoal ribbons, threatening to release the first heavy rain of the summer. The offering elated Jonah, but the loud, guttural rumbles forced him to shout.

"Don't apologize if that's how you feel."

Jonah closed the distance between them, desperate to hold her but scared to encroach when she was already so vulnerable. Her crossed arms were a cage, forcing him out and her eyes shone with hurt.

"That's not how I feel. They're wrong. I never said those things."

Avery reached down and scooped up a few of the discarded apples. Her steps were deliberate as her features hardened. "I. Don't. Want. To. Hear. Your. Excuses." Every word was punctuated with fury, and she wound her arm back.

Before Jonah could connect the dots, Avery started chucking her arsenal of apples at him. The first one missed, but her aim quickly improved. A small, hard one caught him in the stomach, while another that must have fallen on its own accord a few days before, exploded in a mushy splat against his arm.

He batted most of them away, but one more caught him on the shoulder and left a trail of brown slime across his shirt. "Stop. I'm trying to explain."

Avery's lips pursed tightly, and she threw the last apple with all her might. "No matter what you say, they'll still be right. I can't compare to your ex. Like they said, I'm not sophisticated or classy. I barely have my shit together. I have no illusions about myself, okay? I know I have daddy issues, trust issues, and wield my body like currency. But I never pretended to be anything else!"

Jonah wiped the apple guts off his chest as another crash of thunder shook the field. A flash of lightning split the sky, illuminating the intimidating swell of the storm. "Avery, please. They both knew and loved Laura. We were together for three years."

Avery stopped a few feet away. Her amber eyes were hardened chips of fury that matched the skies. "Then why did you leave her? What drew you apart if she was so perfect?"

Jonah's expression darkened. "Cancer. We were engaged when she received the diagnosis. The doctors told us she had a year left, but she died within three months."

Avery's hand flew to her mouth. "Why didn't you tell me?"

Jonah hung his head. "Because of that reaction, right there. No matter where I went, the second anyone heard about Laura, they'd give me that look and pigeonhole me as a grieving widower. They made me feel like the only acceptable emotion was misery. My friends and family stopped talking to me because they wanted to give me space, and anytime I found some distance from my grief, someone was always there to remind me how much Laura would have loved it, or they would spear my happiness by asking if I missed her. Of course, I miss her. I love her, but she's gone. I've grieved her and will always remember our relationship, but I need space to grow and start a new life without her, too."

Avery was quiet as she digested his words. Another clap of thunder exploded overhead, the loudest one yet. She jumped and let her arms fall to her sides. "I can understand that. It sucks being forced to live your life based on others' expectations of you."

Fat rain drops haphazardly peppered the landscape, the final warning to take shelter before the heavens erupted. A large drip landed on Avery's cheek, forming a heavy tear. Jonah frowned. The desire to curl her into his chest and wipe it away was overwhelming.

She sawed her lower lip between her teeth. "It still doesn't change your opinion of me, though. Your friends wouldn't have said those things unless you gave voice to them yourself. I don't know what has been happening between us, but I'm done. I don't want to play anymore. I'm going to help my uncle and finish out the summer, then I'm gone. Back to the city or wherever, I don't care. Let's just stay out of each other's way until October."

"Avery, that's not what I want." Jonah took a step closer, but Avery threw up her hands.

"Don't you get it? I don't care what you want. All my life, I've done what other people wanted, thinking it would bring me love or friendship, but it only brought disappointment. I'm sick of being used. I'm not a marionette, and I refuse to dance for you or anyone else any longer. From now on, I'm only going to surround myself with people who love me, and I'm done wondering if that might include you."

As soon as Avery finished speaking, the clouds released their burden, drenching the parched ground beneath like the rain was a symbolic cleansing that echoed her powerful statement. Jonah ducked and shielded his head with his arms as the water fell in sheets. He looked up, but Avery was running, the backs of her legs kicking atop the dry earth.

"Avery! Avery, wait!" A sense of déjà vu assailed him. Twice in one afternoon, he was pleading for her to come back to him, but this time he didn't intend on letting her get away.

Chapter 31: Avery

Raindrops pelted her bare arms and neck hard enough to leave a trail of bruises. Avery was glad she would have an excuse when asked about the root of her sobs. Her face was slick with wetness, tears indistinguishable from the punishing rain.

She was a fool. A fool for thinking she could last at the orchard. A fool for thinking she had formed true friendships. A fool for thinking she was worthy of a guy like Jonah. And now, a fool for running in the wrong damn direction in the middle of the fiercest thunderstorm she'd ever encountered.

The wind howled like preying wolves as the afternoon transformed into an unrecognizable force. All around her, the apple trees writhed and bucked from side to side, their low branches nearly sweeping the ground as their narrow trunks arched like possessed spines, relinquishing all control to the savage gales.

Avery cupped her hands around her eyes. The front orchard was too far from the utility barn or her cabin to make a run for shelter, and the apple trees were too skinny, their leaves too narrow to offer adequate protection. She raced to the end of the row, battling the wind as if it were a malevolent foe intent on pushing her backward. In the distance, a towering maple tree loomed. If she could make it, she'd be able to ride out the storm beneath its wide canopy.

She'd taken another step when a large hand wrapped around her wrist. Avery whipped her head to the side, and her saturated ponytail slapped her cheek. Jonah's angry gaze burned into hers. "God dammit woman, would you listen to me? I'm trying to talk to you."

Avery shook her head and fought to pry Jonah's unyielding grip from her arm. "I don't care!" A deep reverberation shook Avery's chest as more thunder bellowed.

"Avery, please. Just listen. I need to tell you—"

"Leave me alone!"

The rain eased beneath Jonah's fist and broke his hold. Avery spun and sprinted ahead toward the maple, her salvation. She could hear Jonah's labored breaths as he chased behind her. A low growl—loud enough that she heard it over the pounding rain—sounded in his throat, and even though rage drove her, the thrill of being chased made her ache.

Gritting her teeth, Avery pushed her legs harder as she dismissed her pursuer, along with the sweet warmth building in her center at the idea of being hunted. It was a simple, primal reaction. It meant nothing. He meant nothing.

Another flash of lightning careened through the sky, spidering off in bolts of white-hot energy. The fact that she was racing toward a tree in the middle of a lightning storm didn't escape her notice. Just another item to add to the list of foolish acts, but she had nowhere else to go.

"Avery." Jonah's gruff voice sounded even closer behind. Was he gaining on her? Her pussy clenched as her name filled his mouth. She tried to convince herself it was a reaction to the friction from running, but her excuses were growing thin. "Avery, stop!"

His command was rough. Involuntarily, her pace slowed as

she reached the outer edge of the tree's expanse. She paused her stride, her lungs burning with strain. Slowly, she looked back at him through the curtain of rain.

"What, Jonah? What do you want?"

Jonah advanced and reached up. He tore off his baseball cap and flung it onto the ground, revealing an unkempt mop of dark brown hair. It had grown so much since that first night they might have been together in the showers. The rain attacked the dry strands immediately, and in seconds, a trail of water ran from the flattened edges. His eyes blazed as rain drizzled down his face, but he remained silent.

Avery threw up her hands. Her shirt, plastered to her body, pulled up with the movement, exposing her midriff. Cold drops traced the swell of her breasts as the material bunched, but she didn't right it. Better to let Jonah hash out whatever energy was driving him first. Then he could leave her to shatter in peace.

"Tell me! Tell me so you can leave me alone."

The roar of the storm quelled for a moment, and the only sounds were their shared breaths mingling in the narrow space separating them. Still, he stood silent.

"What do you want, Jonah?"

"You. You're all I've ever wanted from the minute you got out of that car, and I'm tired of pretending I don't."

In one swift motion, Jonah slammed his body against hers. He cradled the back of her head with one hand while the other encircled her waist and pressed her against his length. His lips crushed hers, stealing her breath as his tongue wrestled apart her lips. He tasted of rain and the sweet tang of apples. Avery responded without hesitation.

Her hands gripped Jonah's hips as she kissed him back, matching his passion. The rain continued to pour, making their skin slippery to the touch as they melded together. His shirt clung to his stomach, and with every haggard breath he took—his mouth never leaving hers as if he couldn't get enough—his hard abs contracted.

Avery pushed her hands beneath the wet fabric and yanked it over his head. Jonah's chiseled form met her appreciative gaze for only a moment before their lips tangled once more, and they quickly returned to drowning in one another. Warm hands moved to her waist and dipped under the band of her shorts. She unlatched the button, and Jonah tugged at the fabric as she wriggled out of the sticking denim, freeing her thighs at last before tossing them to the side. The skirmish left her panties hanging low on her hips, nearly halfway down her ass.

Without pause, he gathered the thin material between his fingers and gently pulled up, creating delicious friction against her clit. He tugged several more times and groaned low in his throat. Avery smiled around his mouth and directed her fingers toward his jeans and the thick belt that held them in place. Metal clattered as she manipulated the leather, bending and pulling the belt as Jonah rained kisses from her earlobe to her collarbone and back up again.

At last, the belt released, and the front of his jeans soon followed. Her fingers danced atop the stiff bulge that strained against the damp fabric. Avery flushed, remembering how he'd squeezed her thighs before. Her hips rolled at the thought, her pussy begging for his touch. Jonah hooked his thumbs into the waistband and yanked his jeans down over his hips. His cock sprung free, smacking Avery in the stomach, a spear of warmth.

Fighting to free herself from her own wardrobe, Avery shrugged out of her flannel, crossed her arms and pinched the bottom of her tank between her fingers, and rolled it up and over her head. Her breasts bounced in her bra, and she loved the way Jonah's eyes widened at the sight.

Abandoning her neck, Jonah's mouth sought her tits. Avery moaned when his tongue delved beneath the satin cup and caught her nipple. Using his thumb, he pushed the bra away to allow her breast to spill out into the palm of his hand. His tongue flicked the hard peak before sucking it between his lips, squeezing and kneading as he devoured her.

Her pussy ached with need. Jonah cupped her sex in his other hand and slipped two fingers inside her drenched panties. He tapped her pussy and slid into her wetness.

"Is this for me?" Jonah asked, his voice a husky rasp.

Avery unclipped her bra and shrugged off the straps. A small shiver traced her spine as the rain kissed the newly sensitive flesh where his mouth had been. She shook her head.

"It's from the rain."

Jonah cocked his head and eased his fingers into the warm pool between her legs as his thumb circled her clit. "Don't lie to me." He pumped his fingers inside her, withdrawing them to the first knuckle only to plunge back in.

Avery's eyes bulged with pleasure. "I'm not lying," she said in a breathless whisper.

"Really?" Jonah's lips pulled in a crooked grin and his pace increased until he was frantically fucking her pussy with his hand, never letting up his onslaught of her clit.

"Jonah." His name fell in a flushed moan as she stretched onto her tiptoes to escape his incessant touch, but that only brought her breasts back into focus. His hungry mouth claimed the other one as he nipped and bit the swollen skin.

Avery's head fell back as the cool rain continued to fall, dappling her skin and setting it even more aflame. Thunder ricocheted above, fueling their passion. She reached down and wrapped her hand around his thick cock, pumping it. A strained groan erupted in her ear as Jonah's head tipped back.

He inhaled through gritted teeth and grabbed her ass, arching her body closer to his. Still at the mercy of the rain, her nipples brushed his chest. The hard drops teased the rosy buds, drawing more pleasure. It was as if a dozen hands were ravaging her, hungry mouths licking and biting every inch of her naked flesh.

Avery increased her pace and delighted in the way the skin around Jonah's stiff shaft glided beneath her touch. She ran the pad of her thumb along the narrow slit, and a dewdrop of his arousal glistened on her fingertip. His eyes burned as she raised it to her mouth and flicked her tongue over the shining orb.

"You taste good." Avery smiled and replaced her hand, loving how his cock strained. She dropped to her knees and captured the crown of his dick between her lips, but Jonah pulled her back to her feet before she could swallow his full length.

He shook his head. A wide halo of water droplets flew from the ends of his hair. Avery's hips rolled. He was so sexy. "I'm not done with that pussy yet."

Before Avery could utter a clever response, Jonah withdrew his tantalizing fingers from her cunt and hooked his arm beneath her ass, lifting her clear off the ground. The motion dragged his length up so it perched on the inside of her thigh, dangerously close to her slit.

Jonah carried her beneath the full canopy of leaves, out of the pelting droplets. Rain continued to reach them inside, but it had lost its sharp bite and softened to a more sensual touch. Though the weather may have grown less demanding, the same could not be said for the lovers trapped in its embrace.

As Jonah walked, Avery jostled in his arms and wriggled her thighs out of his hold, wrapping them around his waist. She gasped as his warm cock slid against her. Weaving her hands behind his neck, she arched her ass, positioning her opening directly above the crown. Carefully, she held herself up and rubbed the head of his dick along the outside of her pussy, then she started to bounce. Easing her body down a fraction of an inch, she took the tip of his cock and rolled her hips as slowly as she could, hoping to tease.

Shivers climbed her spine, and her head fell back with delayed pleasure. She wanted more, so much more. The desire to claim all of him drove her wild with need. Jonah's grip on her ass intensified, and he dug his fingers into her cheeks to keep control. Avery pulled up again, releasing the tip, ready to slam all the way down, but Jonah was waiting.

"Not yet, darlin'. I need to taste you first."

Avery moaned. His words invoked another ripple of pleasure that seized her cunt. Jonah propped her up, stealing the luscious pressure she craved. He pressed his lips to hers, devouring her with savage ferocity. Her back crashed against the rough bark of the maple tree as Jonah pinned her in place against it. From her position, her feet were unable to touch the grass, her body held hostage to his deviant whims.

Jonah spread her legs, baring her carnal treasure while he kneeled before her, a stoic knight eager to service his queen. Yet, Avery was under no illusion. She didn't want the mild-mannered kisses of a serf forced into her bed. She'd rather them be equals, two servants rolling around hard and fast in the barn before the stable master sought them out.

Avery slid her hands into Jonah's hair and gently pulled the roots, drawing him closer. "Please," she gasped.

Jonah glanced up at her and smiled wickedly. Without

breaking eye contact, he leaned forward and bared his tongue. He pressed it against her slick and ran the wide, wet length from the bottom to the top, lapping her wetness like a starving man. Pleasure built like a cresting wave, sending Avery closer and closer to the edge.

She arched into the coarse bark at her back, loving the punishing texture. Jonah's tongue twirled around her sensitive bundle of nerves, again and again, subjecting her to grueling pleasure. Part of her wished to escape, desperate for a moment to breathe, but his skillful tongue made her thighs clench and her pussy yearn for more torture, for him to never stop until he pushed her over the precipice, and she flew.

His slow, languid licks gave way to an invasion. His tongue darted inside, curling and twisting as he held her aloft. Arduous play held her thoughts captive. Gone were Marissa's words. Gone were her insecurities. All Avery could think about was how exceptional his mouth felt sucking her clit.

Her nails gripped the side of Jonah's head harder as she pulled him and his clever tongue deeper. He circled the tiny nub faster and faster, adjusting to the intense rhythm as she guided. She closed her eyes, lost in her cresting climax. An unexpected hand cupped her breast and squeezed, bringing her back to the delirious moment. Jonah balanced her weight on one arm and massaged her right breast with the other, tugging her nipple until he was rewarded with her soft mewl.

"Jonah," Avery rasped. She was desperate to touch him, to be filled to the hilt with his thick cock. His tongue wasn't enough, couldn't provide the friction she demanded. "Please." Her plea was hoarse with need as her hips rolled. Her swollen clit brushed the rough stubble of his upper lip, sending a new swell of bliss directly to her core.

Avery gripped the trunk behind her and arched again, a

slave to the abrasive sensation. Jonah didn't say anything, didn't stop her, only stared with unbridled lust as she rode his face. Her orgasm rippled through her abdomen as her fingers sliced into the bark.

"Yes. Yes! Jonah, that feels so fucking good."

He moved his hand to her other breast and kneaded the soft mound before turning his attention to her nipple. He rolled the peak between his thumb and forefinger, tugging and pinching, sending electric shocks of pleasure radiating down her body to the tips of her toes.

"Fuck, Jonah. I'm coming. I'm coming!"

Jonah remained silent and flattened his tongue against her pulsing slit. Her orgasm ascended impossibly higher, yielding a feeling of weightlessness as her desire imploded. Avery's eyes closed and her lips froze in a silent scream as her climax matched the storm's undulating power. Over and over her pussy clenched, rocking back and forth, riding out the glorious release Jonah cultivated.

Avery's breath fell in ragged gasps as her body slowed at last. She was no stranger to sex, but that was the first true orgasm she hadn't orchestrated herself. Why on earth had she put up with bad sex in the past? A warm afterglow thrummed between her thighs. She was addicted, already craving her next rush.

Jonah used the back of his hand to wipe the remnants of her essence from his chin and licked his skin clean. He dropped his supporting arm and helped her slide to the grass, but he didn't let her go. Once her feet hit the ground, he tossed his hair and fixed her with a dangerous look that foretold dark deeds to come. The hand that cupped her breast dragged up her chest and settled against her neck. His long fingers spanned her throat, and he tested his hold with a light squeeze.

"My turn."

Chapter 32: Jonah

Confusion alighted in Avery's stare as his eyes raked over her naked frame. He felt her pulse race beneath his touch, loved the way her excited breaths caused her tits to heave before him. Her lean arms propped her weight slightly off the trunk, and her pliable hourglass torso meandered down to wide hips, the nude apex of her thighs shining from the come still painting her pussy.

"What do you want me to do?" Avery asked, swallowing around his fist.

Jonah maintained his stoic nature. He didn't growl, didn't praise her incredible body. He only stared beneath hooded lids and licked his lower lip. Her sweet flavor overwhelmed him and gave his hard cock yet another reason to throb as he remembered the feeling of her warm mouth. Yes, he wanted his dick between her pretty lips. He wanted to watch her take him, to hear her choke on his girth as he thrust down her throat, but he knew once her first groan around his cock reached his ears, he'd never be able to last, to fuck her in the manner she deserved.

Jonah closed the distance between them, gripped the center of his cock and pumped it slow three times. He moved the hand around Avery's throat up with deliberate rigidity until he held either side of her jaw. He increased his strength and tilted her head upward, forcing a small cry from her lips.

"Nothing. Like I said, it's my turn. The only thing I need you to do is not break before I'm finished."

Fear leaped to Avery's eyes, but her hips rolled, her pussy practically salivating. Jonah leaned forward and ran his lips along her cheekbone, trailed to her earlobe, and then rounded the soft edge of her jaw. She was so delicate, so fragile beneath his touch. He would show her what happens to wild mares that needed to be broken. He would be the one to tame her at last.

A soft whimper spoke of Avery's need, her desire flaring once more. She spread her legs, inviting him back to her warm center. Jonah grinned wickedly. As far as he knew, she'd only ever fucked prissy city boys in lavish suites where she was in control. Not out here where the rain pelted their sweating skin and the dirt churned to mud beneath their feet. Out here, they were no different than the animals who coupled in the long grass. His gaze took in her soft brown eyes and the pouty set of her bruised lips. She stared at him from under wet, clumpy lashes, as if daring him to show her how rough he could be. He didn't aim to disappoint.

Jonah swooped down and grabbed Avery's ankle, wrenching her right leg up to rest it on his shoulder. She grimaced from the pain of her stretching tendons, her teeth gnawing at her lower lip, but he didn't stop. Her calf rested on his shoulder, her slit now at the perfect height. There were no tender caresses, no gentle easing. Grasping her leg, Jonah thrust his throbbing cock into her tight little pussy, forcing her sweet center to accommodate his thickness.

Avery took him with a strained gasp as he buried his cock to the hilt. The sound drove him wild, a primal response from his unexpected entrance. Jonah growled low in his throat as she welcomed him and pulsed around his dick. He pumped in and out, careful not to withdraw completely, only to plunge back in, over and over. Her cunt gripped his length, and the friction forced his eyes to roll into the back of his head.

Avery cried as he pushed her harder against the trunk and craned her leg higher, increasing the pressure as he slammed into her.

Jonah her in place, his grip on her jaw sure to leave a mark. The thought propelled his hips even faster. Evidence of his fingers on her skin, marking her as his, was unlike anything. Never again would anyone question if she were good enough. He chose her. He glanced down and groaned as Avery's tits bounced, her pebbled nipples brushing his chest. Unable to resist, he bent his neck and suckled one of the rosy buds, his tongue teasing the peak and then biting it, just hard enough to leave a bruise. His. She was his.

The finality of that thought spurned delicious shivers of pleasure along his back and groin. The ghost of Laura was gone. Avery was who he lived his life for now, and his own self-acceptance heightened his pleasure as he claimed his new partner.

Avery inhaled sharply as his teeth came down around her nipple, but she pushed her hips forward and rolled them in time with his thrusts, taking him in even deeper. Jonah pulled out, leaving the head of his cock just inside her slit and marveled at the thick white come that swirled along his length. Avery's pleasure. They'd beaten down the wall between them at last.

Avery rolled her hips again, trying to claim his cock once more. "Please, Jonah . . . Make me come again." Jonah waited another few seconds, then slammed into her slick pussy. Avery threw her head back from the power of his thrust and moaned. "Fuck, yes. Harder."

Jonah pulled out, paused his thrusts, and speared her slit again with deliberate jabs. Avery melted to the side, her eyes closed in ecstasy. The desire to come was unstoppable as he stared at her, a languid pile of molten limbs, desperate for his touch. But he wasn't ready yet. For so many weeks he'd envisioned another chance to be with her, and now that his cock was buried in her cunt, her exaltations begging for more, he refused to let her down again.

"Yes, Jonah. Fuck. Make me come on your big cock."

"Not like this, darlin'."

"What?"

Avery's eyes snapped open, and her brows lifted quizzically. Without explanation, Jonah pulled out of her warmth, aching to return, but first, he let her leg drop unceremoniously to the wet grass below.

"Oh." Avery's breathless sigh was a live wire directly to his dick, making him impossibly harder.

She stumbled from shifting positions and tumbled to the left. Acting on instinct, her hands reached out to cradle her fall and her nails dug into Jonah's hips, her mouth perfectly aligned with his glistening crown. Before Jonah could rotate her body into the next position, she dropped to her knees and wrapped her beautiful lips around his cock, filling her throat with his length.

"Jesus, fuck," Jonah sighed and inhaled through gritted teeth. He hadn't planned that, but the feeling of moving from her pussy to her mouth was intoxicating and kinkier than he imagined. He let out a strangled exhale, trying to last through the unrelenting pleasure her tongue yielded. His hands threaded through her hair and gathered the tresses away from her face.

Avery's amber eyes found his as her mouth stroked his cock.

Her come lingered on the length, but she didn't stop. Locking eyes with him, she arched her head and took him deeper, her cheeks hollowing as they coddled his girth. The sight of her cleaning her own pleasure off his dick was so arousing.

Involuntarily, Jonah's hips pumped faster while her tongue lapped the underside of his shaft. His fist clenched harder around the roots of her hair as he guided her head. Her hand slipped from his hip to his balls. Gently, she cupped each one while her other hand played with her clit. The sound of her finger exploring her own body was too much.

"Shit." Jonah hissed as a new thrill of pleasure seized him. He couldn't last any longer. Her mouth felt too fucking good, too fucking warm, as he slid across her tongue.

Acting on instinct, he held either side of her head and drove his shaft into the back of her throat as his orgasm exploded. Vaguely, he heard Avery choke as he covered her tongue, but she didn't relent, only pulled him closer as she swallowed everything he had to give.

"Ah!" Jonah groaned as his climax spilled between her lips. She gazed up at him, smiling around his cock. That simple connection was so erotic.

Slowly, he pulled out of her mouth and took a step back. His dick glistened with Avery's saliva. Rough hands pushed him down, and he laid on his back against the cool earth. Still fingering herself, Avery sat astride him and gripped the base of his softening erection. She didn't push it into her slit. Instead, she rubbed the slick crown along the outside of her pussy while she circled her clit with two fingers, tapping and teasing the small pearl with expert finesse.

Jonah watched with hooded lids and cupped the swells of her breasts, tugging her nipples and rolling the beads between his fingers to enhance her climax. Faster, Avery wielded his cock against her pulsing core. She threw her head back as her hips stalled, the orgasm rippling through her.

"Fuck, fuck, fuck." Avery moaned in a high-pitched surrender as her body crested over the great height. Warmth spread over Jonah's cock as she came, sliding down his thighs to pool on the damp grass beneath them.

Sated, Avery collapsed forward and nuzzled her face into his neck. Together they lay there, equally spent. Their joined bodies molded together perfectly, her soft curves fitting against his hardened angles like long-lost jigsaw pieces.

Jonah ran his fingers through the soft tendrils of hair that kissed his cheek. "I love you, Avery."

She didn't say anything, but it didn't matter. Avery snuggled closer to his warm frame as the rain provided a soothing lullaby.

Chapter 33: Avery

They lay entwined, naked and content, time the least of their concerns. The heat from their coupling waned as their breaths grew lazy and languid. Avery's flushed skin had long since cooled, but between the humid summer air and Jonah's furnace-like body heat, only the whisper of chills graced her nude flesh.

Avery stirred against the rugged man beneath her. She wasn't cold, but she wouldn't object to a blanket either, plus she had to pee. Jonah stopped tracing loopy patterns on the back of her arm, and his eyelids fluttered open.

"Hey." He grinned and the adoring look in his gaze made Avery's heart melt.

"Hey, yourself."

Avery pushed off Jonah's chest and sat up straight. The skin beneath her thighs pulled slightly as she separated herself. The evidence of their passionate romp made her cheeks burn. Sure, it was sexy in the moment, but how would Jonah feel after the fact with her dried arousal caked to his stomach?

She dismounted and kicked her leg over his body. Her bare toes pushed off the squishy dirt as she rose to her feet, angling her body away to shield her nudity. Jonah sighed, a sweet hum catching in his throat as he followed her retreating form.

"It's cold without you." Jonah's eyes crinkled around the corners. This was the most relaxed Avery had ever seen the grumpy farmhand, and his genuine smile transformed his usually severe expression.

Avery wiggled her ass and pursed her lips. "I have an idea how to warm you back up."

Jonah smirked and pushed himself onto his elbows. Wet grass clung to his back, but she didn't laugh. He looked ethereal, a satyr come to frolic amongst mortals. She glanced up at their leafy sanctuary. It was hard to believe life outside their small haven existed. They were Adam and Eve, encased in beautiful solace and pleasure within the Garden of Eden.

Jonah climbed to his feet and shook his head. "I wish I could rebound that fast." He pressed his forehead against hers and brushed a light kiss across her lips.

Avery snuggled into him, and her fleeting insecurities vanished as her mind wandered back to the logistics of what came next. Peering at the ground as the driving squalls gave way to a misty drizzle, she found where they had flung their clothes in their desperate dash to free their bodies from the caging cloth. Her denim shorts were rolled in a tight ball on the outskirts of the canopy, saturated with rainwater. Her bra stretched several yards away, the inverted cups hosting shallow pools while her shirts were almost unrecognizable heaps. Her panties were nowhere to be found.

"Umm, how are we going to get back?"

"Oh." Jonah scanned the dripping trees.

"Everyone probably hunkered down in their cabins or the main house, and my clothes are too wet to put back on."

"Huh. Good point. What about mine?"

Avery rolled her eyes and crossed her arms over her chest to ward off the chill. Now that the storm had calmed, the wind kicked up and unleashed cool air from the north. "Yours are going to be just as wet as mine."

Jonah chuckled under his breath and nodded. "True, but my clothes aren't as itty bitty as yours."

Avery cocked an eyebrow. "What are you implying, sir?"

"That you'll be glad my shirt will cover every delicious part of you."

Avery wrinkled her nose playfully. "But what will you wear?"

"I'll be fine in my boxers. We'll throw them on and hit the showers. The warm water will stave off any colds."

"Aw, what a good mom you are."

Jonah threw a wide grin her way. "Careful with that tone, young lady or I'll have to spank you."

Avery sashayed over to her heavy clothing and bent at the waist to display her curvy ass as well as the soft mound tucked between her legs. "My tongue always did get me in trouble."

Jonah groaned as he swiped his clothes, too. "Oh, I know exactly the kind of trouble your tongue is capable of." He flung his boxers and jeans over his shoulder while he twisted the sodden shirt. A slew of rainwater trickled out, but it was far from dry. He flapped it a few times to ease out the wrinkles and fitted it over her head. It hung comically off Avery's narrow frame.

"Perfect." She laughed and shivered under the wet garment's kiss.

"You'll only have to wear it for a few minutes while we walk to the showers." Jonah traced her jaw with his fingertip, and his voice grew husky. "Then I can take it off you."

Avery's eyes sparkled with mischief. She pressed her body against Jonah's firm length. "I thought you needed time to recover?"

Jonah shrugged and dropped his hand to the smooth column of her throat. His fingers continued down to the gentle swell of her breasts where the damp shirt clung, leaving little to the imagination. Avery sucked in a sharp breath as her nipples hardened beneath the heavy fabric.

"Usually, I do, but seeing you in my shirt is a real turn-on."

Avery arched her brow and slid her hand along the hard planes of Jonah's abdomen. His growing cock twitched against her thigh. Her pussy ached at the thought of a second round, but the once warm summer rain had turned bitter, and the wind whipped the wet shirt against the top of her thighs. It wasn't exactly a romantic atmosphere. She wrapped her hand around the base of his shaft and brushed a lingering kiss atop his lips.

"Fuck me in the showers. Where we first started."

Jonah groaned but nodded in agreement. He stepped back and slid on his boxers. His thickening erection was even more pronounced against the gray material.

Avery took his hand. "Come on, we can sneak over this way." She pulled him toward the rows of gala apples.

Jonah frowned and dug in his heels. "We don't need to sneak. Let's just take the path."

Avery bit her lip and blinked the accumulating mist off her lashes. "But the others will see."

"So? We're decent now. No way was I going to risk Mac seeing you naked."

Avery shook her head. "No. They'll see me wearing your shirt and know we were together. I don't . . . I don't want them to say anything."

Jonah's confused expression softened. He tucked an errant strand of hair behind her ear and cradled her face in his hand. Shifting the drooping neck of his shirt below her collarbone, he exposed a dark mark his mouth had left behind.

Bending, he planted a soft kiss on the bruise. Chills ran over Avery's arms. He sunk to his knees and rolled the bottom of the shirt up to reveal her naked flesh and the half dozen bites he'd marked her with. Avery gasped at the map on her skin. Everywhere Jonah had pleasured her, claimed her.

One by one, he kissed each of the marks. A trail of fire ignited deep in the pit of her stomach with every brush of his lips. Avery wove her fingers through his hair, guiding him along. At last, Jonah pressed his face against her warm center and her body couldn't help reacting to the flash of heat his mouth ignited.

Avery's hips rolled and wetness began to pool between her thighs. Jonah stood and pressed his forehead to hers. "I don't care what they think, Avery. All I want is for you to be mine. As long as you know that, nothing else matters. Before you, I was dead. You woke me up. I meant it when I said I love you. You're all I want."

Heat colored Avery's cheeks, both from the magic Jonah's lips cast and his statement. Twice. Twice he'd said he loved her, but she'd never known love. Was that what made her heart race each time she saw him, or was that simply old-fashioned lust?

Jonah must have seen the way her face crinkled. He put up his hands. "That wasn't an ultimatum or anything. It's okay if you don't feel that way, too. I've spent far too much of my life not saying the important things, and from now on, I'm going to voice how I feel, including how I feel about you, to anyone who will listen or needs a reminder." He chuckled as he teased her and kissed her once more. "Does that help ease any worries?"

Avery fought the small smile that tugged at the corner of her lip. "It's hard not to feel reassured when you put it like that."

She rolled her eyes, then fixed him with a gentle stare. "Thank you."

Jonah kissed her forehead while the wind tossed the ends of her hair into his face. "All right, let's get to the showers. I think Mother Nature is tired of watching us fornicate."

Avery leaned in and gave his shaft one last squeeze, then she pushed off his shoulder with her other hand and sent him stumbling backward. "I'll race you!"

Jonah growled. "That's not fair. I can't run with this thing."

"Guess I'll have the shower all to myself, then." Avery laughed over her shoulder as her bare feet trudged up the hill. She avoided the gravel path but followed the serpentine movement atop the grass. In only one minute, she was already two hundred yards ahead. A thrill rippled through her and urged her legs to go faster. For so long she'd been the hunter, pursuing whichever unsuspecting males would wound her father most. Yet, as Jonah's breaths drew nearer, desire flooded her swaying tits and made her pussy clench at the thought of being his prey.

Would he scoop her up and spank her bare ass right there next to the wheelbarrow? Or bend her over and tease her again with his glorious tongue? Avery stretched her legs longer, conscious that the movement forced the edge of the shirt to ride up and expose the curve of her ass.

"Too fast for you, cowboy?" Her words were light, but the path behind her was empty. "Jonah?" Avery glanced left and right. Only dark trees met her gaze. "Jonah?"

Two hands grabbed her waist and hoisted her off the ground as Jonah charged from the side. A surprised cry rent the air as her feet left the ground and Jonah flipped her backward. His deep baritone laugh filled the space between them as he wrapped her legs around his hips and gripped the underside of her thighs, dangerously close to her pussy.

"Where did you come from, you goof?" Avery squealed and lightly punched his bicep.

"I had to get you back for cheating."

"That wasn't cheating. That was taking advantage of your poor equilibrium."

"Yeah, okay." Jonah scoffed and situated her closer as her body began to slip. Coincidentally, her new position brought her slit level with his cock. She hadn't bothered to put her panties back on, and only his boxers separated them. He was soft—for now.

Avery wrapped her hands around the back of his head and arched her back. She smiled while the rain kissed her face. Her pussy pressed into his groin. "What's your prize for capturing me?"

Jonah nipped at her neck, and his hands squeezed her glutes, his fingers edging ever closer to her opening. "I'm sure I can think of something."

He crested the top of the hill. The cabins emerged into view, along with the shower and latrine behind them. Jonah continued walking past the utility barn and set Avery on the ground. He pulled the hem of her shirt down, fully covering her ass.

"Worried?" Avery teased. She linked her arm through Jonah's and leaned against him.

"Only about Mac looking out his window and catching a glimpse." He gave her ass a light smack. "Mine."

Avery kissed him, and they hurried their pace as the rain picked up again. Goose bumps prickled her skin, the shirt doing little to keep her warm. Golden light gleamed in two of the four cabins. They rounded the back of the first small lodging. The exterior light above the bathroom door burned, signaling their oasis. Jonah reached for the handle, but the door swung outward.

"Oops. Hey." Marissa's expression morphed from neutral to surprised. Jonah stiffened at Avery's side and clasped their joined hands tighter. The other farmhand's gaze trailed up from their bare feet, but she blushed and glanced away when she reached their visible thighs. Marissa cleared her throat. "You two look like a pair of drowned rats."

"We were working down in the front orchard when the storm hit. Stranded us under the big maple," Jonah explained.

Marissa cocked her brow. "And you obviously discovered a way to pass the time." The jab was lighthearted but caused Avery's gut to twist and her pulse to quicken.

Avery heard the click of Jonah's jaw. "It's none of your business, Marissa."

She threw up her hands and had the decency to look ashamed. "No. I'm sorry. That came out wrong. I was looking for you . . . both of you."

"Why?" Jonah asked.

"To apologize again, and Avery, to apologize to you properly. We were stupid and rude. *I was stupid and rude.* You're right. I don't know anything about your life and shouldn't have assumed negative things about your character. I enjoy working with you. You've been a real asset to this orchard. I can be a bitch and let my mouth run, especially if it gets some laughs."

Avery frowned and her mouth hardened.

Marissa flinched. "But that doesn't mean it was okay for me to say those things about you. I told Jonah at the festival. I've noticed such a change in him. Laura, and everything that happened to her aside, you make him bright and challenge him in a way she never did. I was a fool, and I hope you can both forgive me."

Jonah's severe countenance softened. He leaned in and wrapped Marissa in a one-armed hug. "Thank you, Riss."

Marissa's light brown eyes shone wetly. "Thanks, big guy." She didn't say anything as her gaze drifted away from him and silently waited for Avery to either accept or spurn her apology.

Avery withdrew her hand from Jonah's. She didn't want a crutch. She needed to stand on her own. Rolling her shoulders back, she lifted her chin. The fact that she was only clad in a sopping-wet oversized tee did little to impact her confidence. She recalled the way Jonah had kissed each mark he'd branded her with, and her thoughts flashed back to when she first met him. Marissa was right. He had changed immensely from the grumpy, closed-off country boy he was. And if Marissa's observations were to be believed, Avery had been the catalyst.

"I appreciate your apology. I know how hard it can be to admit when you're wrong." Avery let out a small laugh, breaking the tension. Marissa's tense shoulders relaxed. "I think it's sweet that you care about Jonah enough to look out for his well-being. I wish I had friends like that. But just because I'm offering you forgiveness doesn't mean I will tolerate further comments about my proposed inadequacies or supposed vile intentions. If my relationship with Jonah fails, it will be because of our combined shortcomings, not because of false accusations you've hissed in his ear. Is that understood?"

Marissa's jaw dropped, and a surge of power inundated Avery's stance. "Yeah . . . I mean, I understand."

Avery offered a curt nod and slipped her hand into Jonah's once more. "Good. Then we're cool."

Marissa wrapped Avery in a tight hug and shook her head. Her new, long braids tickled Avery's wrists. "Girl! That was incredible. Even my own mama never made me feel that low."

A sad smile pinched Avery's lips. "Well, she should talk to

my dad for pointers."

Marissa clucked her tongue and tilted her head. "Have you ever stood up to him like that?"

Avery scoffed. "No way."

"Maybe you should. Bullies only respond to strength. It might put him in his place and show him you're not a kid anymore."

The image of her father fumbling for words in her presence was encouraging, yet as she stood there in the rain with mud squishing between her toes, that reality seemed as unreachable as the clouds.

"Yeah, you might be right."

Marissa touched her nose stud, not fooled by her response. "Think about it, okay?" She exhaled and clapped her hands. "Well, now that I've found you, I am heading back to my cabin for an early night. With all this rain, I'm sure Stan will haul us out before dawn to capitalize on 'nature's blessing.'"

Jonah laughed. "True. After a nice, hot shower, we're going to do the same."

Marissa winked and snuck passed them, landing a playful slap on Avery's ass. A low cackle followed. "Have fun, kids."

Avery pulled her shirt down, previously unaware it had ridden up, as the pink in her cheeks cooled. Jonah laughed and shook his head.

"Are you okay? I have to say, I didn't know you had that in you."

Avery ducked through the door and held it open for Jonah. The bathroom was empty. Immediately, she gripped the edge of her shirt and pulled the clinging material off. A cool breeze drifted down her body, but it felt so much better to be out from under the shirt's damp confines. She spun on the balls of her feet and threw the garment against the wall where it landed on the bench with a loud smack. Tossing her hair out of her face, Avery stood before Jonah with her hands on her hips.

"To be honest, I didn't know I did, either. It felt good to stand up for myself. What about you?"

Jonah's hooded eyes appreciated her body but connected with her gaze shortly after. He pulled the door shut behind him. "I think her apology was genuine, and I hope she's happy for us, but I also think she's right."

Though Avery's face fell, Jonah kept speaking before her doubts could dig in.

"You should say something like that to your dad." He crossed the tile floor and wrapped his arms around her lower back, caging her in.

Avery relaxed and chewed on her bottom lip. "He wouldn't listen."

"Then make him. You're smart and resourceful, Av. You don't need his approval."

"I know, but . . . it'd still be nice."

Jonah planted a long kiss on her forehead. "Come on. Let's get in the shower and let the hot water wash it all away for now."

Avery nodded, glad she didn't need to have an answer right then. She turned and cranked the handle, and a stream of icy water spurted until the water warmed. She opened the glass door and fluttered her lashes. "You going to join me?"

Jonah's eyes widened, and his fingers thrust into the waistband of his boxers. "Definitely."

"Wait!" Avery threw up a hand. "We don't have any towels."

Jonah's head fell forward. He pulled the band back up and straightened. "I'll grab some from my cabin. Hop in and get warm. I'll be right back." He gave her a quick kiss and dashed back out into the rain.

Heeding his advice, Avery tested the temperature and stepped beneath the now scalding stream. A guttural sigh heaved from her lips as the water drizzled down her shoulder blades. She gritted her teeth. The heat hurt, but in the best way, especially after having been exposed to Mother Nature's fury.

She let her head drop back. The steady flow massaged her scalp, drumming her hairline with an expert touch. Her whole body warmed from the inside out, chasing the shivers away at last. Avery squirted a dollop of shampoo into her palm and lathered every strand. She soon got lost in the languid rhythm and jumped when a frigid hand slid across her stomach.

"Sorry. Didn't mean to startle you." Jonah's deep voice whispered in her ear as he crowded into the stall. "Oh, wow. This feels so nice."

Avery spun and presented him with her ass while the water washed the suds from her hair. "Mhm. I feel like a whole new person."

Jonah palmed her curves and dragged her backward to press against his groin. "One who enjoys shower sex, I hope."

Avery laughed, poured her body wash onto a loofa, and bent at the waist to soap up her calves. Behind her, Jonah groaned, and his stiff cock nudged her. "Well, we'll have to see how good you are before I can judge if I enjoyed it, won't we?"

Jonah licked his fingers and cupped her sex from the back. Avery gasped at the unexpected intrusion but sank into his touch. Without further warning, he spread her pussy and sunk into her warmth. She welcomed him back. His large hand forced her to remain folded over. Pumping his hips, he began to drive his cock deeper and deeper, hitting the delicious spot within. She braced her hands against the wall as he thrust harder.

"Then take notes, darlin', because I aim for a perfect score."

Chapter 34: Avery

The weeks rolled by, as subtle and silent as the grass. One morning the fields were groomed and manicured with precise lines and the next they were nearly knee-high with beautiful wildflowers sprinkled throughout. A whole new cycle of flora born and matured amidst their blissful oblivion.

The end of August reared its golden-crested head as hazy afternoons bowed to crisp mornings. The summer was slipping away, each dusk swallowing the sun faster than the day before. Strawberry season was long over, and the bypassed fruit withered on the vine, but the apples flourished. Juicy red ornaments hung proudly, nestled among emerald leaves. The last of the transport trucks pulled out the day before, carrying most of the orchard's stock to packinghouses. There, the harvest bins would be emptied, and the best fruit washed, sized, and sorted before being sent to the grocery stores Uncle Stan partnered with.

Avery was astounded to learn just how many apples remained for the "U-Pick" season. Fifteen percent of the perfect apples still adorned the trees, luscious jewels suspended on narrow limbs. She'd thought after the main harvest was complete, they'd get a break from the incessant schedule, but with the impending rush of tourists primed to descend at the start of

September, the list of chores had only increased.

She didn't mind the labor, though. With Jesse's return, an extra pair of hands offered relief, and now that most of the rows had been harvested, their tasks were centralized to prepare the main hub of the orchard for the next phase. Although her responsibilities didn't usually align with Jonah's, Avery didn't complain, for their nights belonged solely to them.

When Jesse returned, Avery had offered him her cabin. There was nothing wrong with his childhood bedroom, but having his own space to retreat to, one that didn't share a wall with his parents, made it less awkward for everyone when his girlfriend joined him.

Aunt Carrie wasn't pleased when Avery moved in with Jonah, but the elder woman held her tongue and simply gave her a knowing look. She was an adult, after all, perfectly capable of throwing herself into a passionate relationship that may very well end in heartbreak once summer bled into autumn. Three weeks remained. There was no point in worrying about goodbyes yet.

"Are you done with the white paint?" Mac asked.

Avery glanced down at the plywood shark cutout she was painting. She'd seen videos of families and teens sticking their heads through these silly photo ops but she'd never participated before. She inclined her head toward the open paint can.

"Yup. I'm all done with the teeth. Just finishing the water and then updating the year. Are you doing the fence?"

Mac sighed. The main fence extended from the road, all the way up to the zinnia fields lining the parking lot. Avery didn't even want to guess how many hours it was going to take him to refresh it.

"Yeah, I definitely drew the short straw on this one."

They shared an easy laugh. He retrieved the bucket and

loaded it, along with his supplies, into the golf cart. He offered her a light smile before he pulled away down the dusty drive. Mac hadn't apologized as sincerely as Marissa after the incident in the utility barn, but he had backed off and treated her respectfully ever since. It was a good enough arrangement for Avery, and they'd developed an easy friendship. The orchard was too small to hold a grudge.

Avery added the final stroke of paint and massaged her neck. The famous, giant Adirondack chair loomed out of the corner of her eye. Marissa rounded the corner of the children's playhouse and threw herself down at one of the picnic tables. She shed her work gloves and wiped the sweat off her forehead.

"Gravel is spread. I underestimated how many neck muscles would cramp up from holding that position for so long." Marissa groaned and rotated her right arm, pressing the tips of her fingers into a pressure point. "How's the painting coming?"

"I think I'm in the same boat." Avery huffed. "I did the kids' double mural this morning and just finished the shark. Do people really take pictures with these things?"

Marissa snorted and fanned her gloves in front of her face. "Not so much now. You have two kinds of parents, the ones who sit on their phones and let their kids climb all over everything and the helicopter moms who need eight pictures of their family against every single backdrop and demand a nice smile because they're having so much fun."

Avery frowned. "Both sound miserable."

Marissa shrugged. "It's comical, actually. How's Jonah?"

Avery straightened and leaned the photo board against the playhouse to dry. She carried the bucket of red paint over to the Adirondack chair and dunked the large brush into the crimson color. "Good. He's harvesting pumpkins and gourds today. I'm shocked people buy pumpkins this early."

"Girl, just you wait. Fall around here is a whole vibe. Folks make it their entire personality from September first to December. Don't people in the city decorate?"

"Not really. If you're lucky enough to live in a brownstone, some of the stoops will be decorated, but the dressings get vandalized or stolen."

"Another reason to stay."

Marissa said it jokingly, but Avery felt as if she'd been pricked with a needle. "What do you mean?"

"Oh, come on. After everything with Jonah, you're going to leave him to go back to a life you hate?"

"Uh . . ." Avery was speechless. "We haven't really discussed anything yet. I don't even know where he lives when he's not working at the orchard."

Marissa waved her hand. "He's close. He's got a small house in Geneva, but that's not the point. You love him, right?"

Avery pulled the brush out of the thick paint and dragged it along the two-by-four. "Are you always this direct?"

Marissa leaned forward, and her long braids fell across her chest. "Yeah, but don't change the subject. I already know he loves you. It's written plain as day on his face."

A small chuckle warmed Avery as she turned away from the other woman. "He told me he loved me, but I haven't said it back. We've only known each other for a couple of months. People don't fall in love that fast."

Marissa wrinkled her brow. "I thought you were a reader?"

Avery rolled her eyes. "Well yeah, but those are stories, not real life. Jonah and I . . . we're too different to be long-term."

"You don't want to be with him after this?" Marissa gestured with her hand at the magic of the orchard.

Avery paused her brushstroke and fixed Marissa with a long stare. "Of course I do, but my whole life is in New York. I can't throw away everything I've worked for because I met a hot cowboy."

Marissa held her hands up in surrender, her gloves pinched between her fingers. "I get that. History is full of women who sacrificed their own careers to follow a man. You do you. So . . . how is he? He know how to use his dick?"

"Marissa!" Avery squealed and pressed the back of her hand to her lips.

"What? I'm just making conversation." Marissa laughed and stuck out her tongue.

Avery resumed her task and laughed along with her. "As a matter of fact, he does. He tries to be gentle and go slow, but once he picks up the pace and grabs my hips, he loses it and gets rough. But that's the way I like it."

Marissa shook her head. "Ya'll make me miss my girlfriend. Lucky for me the season's almost up, then I can go back to Buffalo and be with her."

"Why do you work way out here?"

Marissa slipped her gloves back on and stood. "The money's good, plus, she goes on archeological digs all around the country every summer, so she's gone for weeks at a time with her students. I miss her, but I'm glad she's able to do what makes her happy."

"Wow, you guys have a strong relationship. I can't imagine being away from someone I love that long."

"I thought you weren't in love."

Avery's eyes widened. "That's not . . . I didn't mean. It's not the same with Jonah and me."

Marissa hiked up her shorts and winked. "Sure, honey. Just make sure your heart knows that before you leave."

Chapter 35: Jonah

The wheelbarrow's wooden handles barely registered against Jonah's callouses. His muscles burned as he pushed the cart over the uneven terrain to the front of Carrie's general store. The freshly- laid gravel bit into the tire and slowed his pace as he navigated over the sharp edges and into the small patch of grass reserved for the pumpkins. Gourds and squash weren't a large source of revenue, but they were an easy add-on for the average guest. Plus, the pumpkins didn't need the same maintenance as the other crops. They could grow practically anywhere.

Jonah expelled a heavy sigh and dumped the wheelbarrow's contents onto the grassy knoll. He'd been transporting pumpkins for the last day and a half and had a sufficient supply for the upcoming weekend's demands.

It was all hands on deck as the orchard prepped for opening weekend. Stan didn't advertise or market the "U-Pick" season aside from a few local signs staked into the ground for a few miles around the farm, but customers religiously flocked for the inaugural weekend each year.

Everyone who worked at the orchard referred to the first Saturday as "Armageddon." Hordes from the city drove up Friday night and breached the entrance as soon as Stan opened the gate. Honey Crisps were always the first to go. Row upon row of the crunchy, delicious apples disappeared by sundown as wealthy Manhattaners emptied trees in search of the perfect ingredients for pies.

Jonah didn't know if the urbanites baked the pies themselves. He imagined they bought a bushel to post on social media and left them to rot in the hallway of their posh apartments, but maybe he was being too hard on them. After all, Avery was from the city, and he had been wrong about her.

He heaved the metal wheelbarrow back onto its tire and headed back to the utility barn. Passing by the covered pavilion where guests would weigh their pickings, a flash of bright color caught his eye. Avery's cheerful murals brought a smile to his face. Even the oversized chair had been given a refreshing face-lift and appeared warm and inviting rather than rundown and forgotten.

The whole orchard breathed with new life. From the meadow of vibrant zinnias and hearty mums to the new picnic tables awaiting joyful families at the top of the hill, Jonah couldn't believe another summer had already come and gone. Yet unlike last year, this September would hopefully bring a new adventure rather than a painful ending.

He felt like one of the hundreds of apple trees he tended to. Last year, the fruit he bore was neglected, forced to fall and rot atop the earth. It wasn't anyone's fault, but Laura's tree required everything the farmhands could give. All their love and attention. His branches had shied away from the sun, anticipating whatever fruit he bore in her absence would be small and sour. But he hadn't expected to be brought back to life. Not by the sun, or everyone's constant pity, but by a woman whose soul was as rich as the earth and whose carefree attitude was as nourishing as a thunderstorm in a drought.

Jonah tugged, and the large double doors of the utility barn swayed open with a protesting grumble. Brown paint chips flaked off beneath his harsh command. He prayed he wasn't around when Stan decided it was time to sand and repaint the ancient structure. Jonah set the wheelbarrow down along the left wall and grabbed his fixed blade from the wooden shelf. He fit it in his belt sheath and picked up the bottom of his shirt. Using the dirt-covered fabric, he wiped the sweat off his forehead but left behind a trail of grit at the same time. He couldn't wait to shower. Hopefully, Avery would be up for one, too.

Jonah shut the barn door and meandered back out to the main house. When he'd spoken to Avery at lunch, she'd said she was going to help Carrie prepare the dough for their signature cinnamon doughnuts. The line for the sweet treats was always a mile long, and last year, they had reached a two-hour wait. They'd tried to supplement the supply with popcorn and caramel apples, but the other snacks hadn't doused the doughnut craze. This year, if they were able to make enough dough to get ahead of the rush, it would cut down on the massive lines and ultimately create a better experience. Yelp reviews hadn't been kind to the orchard lately, and Jonah knew Stan was doing his best to cope with the mounting pressure.

Jesse dumped wood chips from the bucket of a small front loader next to the picnic tables and waved. They didn't serve much purpose, but it was a great play feature for kids, especially once they added in a few toy trucks. Jonah smiled and hope ballooned in his chest. All their hard work was coming to fruition, and he looked forward to a cool evening of relaxation with Avery. She still hadn't said she loved him, but words didn't matter. Thoughts of what she would do at the end of the season however, made his breathing stutter.

He'd practiced asking her to stay and move in with him once the orchard closed, but each time he'd tried to voice his desire aloud, he'd lost his nerve. He knew she longed to return to the city. He didn't want to interfere, but the thought of watching her drive away in that fancy car physically hurt. His pulse raced. He needed to know what her plans were. Tonight, he'd double down and hash it out with her, even if she tried to avoid it.

Summer was nearly over. As much as he wanted to enjoy the rest of their time together and not rock the boat, he wasn't a dewy-eyed schoolboy. They were both adults and should be able to talk about their feelings and intentions without angering one another. At least, he hoped.

Jonah knocked on the back door of the main house and slid the slider open. The scent of flour, sugar, and warm butter flavored the air, and Avery's laughter melted his resolve. "Hello?"

He was careful not to brush up against the cream-colored walls as he entered the kitchen. Avery stood beside her aunt, her elbows dusted in sparkling grains of granulated sugar and cinnamon. His cock stirred as he envisioned licking every single one off her soft skin, but he pushed the enticing fantasy away as Carrie walked over from the fridge with a large tray.

"Hey there, Jonah," Carrie greeted him.

"Afternoon. I brought all the pumpkins and gourds up from the patch. Do you want them arranged any special way?"

Carrie balanced the tray in the one free spot on the counter and waved her hand. "Oh, thanks honey, but I'll head down later tonight and move them around if need be."

"No problem, ma'am."

"Again with the ma'am. I'm sick of that nonsense." Carrie scoffed and picked up the formed dough, then set it on the tray.

Jonah shrugged and removed his ball cap. "Sorry, Carrie. Won't happen again."

Carrie clucked her tongue and bustled around the island. Once the tray was full, she toddled back to the fridge and slid it onto a shelf. At least six other steel platters had replaced the usual jugs of juice and consistent leftovers, all burdened with more than three dozen mini-doughnuts each. To anyone else, it would seem like an overwhelming amount, but Jonah knew they'd sell out in minutes. He wouldn't be surprised if Carrie recruited Avery to roll dough for the next three days.

"I should hope not," Carrie teased. "I was just telling Avery I'll make a batch for all of you tonight."

Jonah smiled. "Sweet. Have you ever had one before?"

"A doughnut? Of course." Avery tilted her head and rubbed her nose, leaving a streak of flour across her cheek.

Jonah's heart warmed at the sight. He wished they were alone, wished he could wrap her in his arms and sit her on the counter amidst the powder and cinnamon and kiss her until her skin glowed fresh and clean and her pussy rocked against him.

He shook his head. "Naw. Dunkin doesn't count. These little babies will change your life." Jonah tucked the brim of his hat into his back pocket and skirted the granite edge of the island.

Avery raised her eyebrows. "Is that so? What about Levain or Magnolia Bakery? Those are some of the best in the world." She swiveled her hips a fraction to align her body with his, two magnets straining to unite.

Jonah placed the palm of his hand on her lower back. His index finger sought the narrow strip of exposed skin between Avery's shirt and black shorts and rubbed sensual circles along the dimples of her back. With his other hand, he traced a swirl through a small sprinkle of cinnamon near the carton of eggs.

The tiny grains stuck to his fingertip, and he raised his hand to her mouth.

Instinctually, Avery's lips parted as she stared at him with innocent, wide eyes. His length throbbed. Her baby-pink tongue slipped between her lips, awaiting his touch. He complied and sprinkled the cinnamon sand atop her taste buds.

"Those big corporate chains all taste the same. Homegrown and homemade, that's why the city folk drive hours to come here. These doughnuts are magic and melt in your mouth if you make 'em right."

Avery's tongue flickered over the pad of Jonah's finger. She held his stare as if it were a challenge. He pressed his body against her hip as a ragged breath fell from his lips. The memory of watching her lick something else with her soft tongue made the already warm kitchen nearly unbearable.

The fridge closed with a dull thud, and Carrie spun around and dusted her hands on the front of her apron. "All right, I won't be having any of that in my kitchen. Jonah, your hands are filthy. Take your nasty self out of here and stop contaminating my dough." Her commands were sharp, but Jonah knew at this point, it was more for show.

Once Avery had moved into his cabin, Carrie had rested her case and abandoned her quest to keep them apart. Jonah appreciated it and knew her aunt's blessing meant a lot to Avery. But even though Carrie had accepted their relationship, it didn't mean she was comfortable with their intimacy, especially near her newly formed treats.

Jonah backed away from Avery and held his hands in the air. "Yes, Carrie. Sorry to interrupt."

Carrie answered with a firm nod and picked up a ball of dough that sat on the cutting board. She started kneading and pulling it apart into smaller pieces, manipulating and forming it into mini rings. "And I don't want to see you back here, do I make myself clear? We've got work to do. If you're running out of chores, you can meet Stan behind the pavilion. He could use a hand setting up those Port-a-Johns."

Avery scrunched her face and chuckled. Bowing her head, she focused on the mixing bowl in her hands. Jonah narrowed his eyes at her playfully. *Little traitor.*

"Got it. I'll head over and help take care of that. Have a lovely rest of your day, ladies."

Avery laughed and said something under her breath while Carrie clucked like a bustling chicken shooing a cock out of the hen house. Jonah stepped out into the golden afternoon and pointed his shoes in the direction of the main pavilion while his heart stayed behind, safe and content.

Chapter 36: Avery

Opening day bloomed early, welcoming the coming excitement amidst dawn's silky tendrils. Jonah roused Avery with a gentle shake and a hushed whisper, drawing her from slumber.

"Good morning, sleepy. It's time to get up."

Avery sighed and burrowed deeper into the nest of shared blankets, but her dream began to disintegrate. The once vibrant scenes became wispy and translucent, her mind unable to preserve the mystical existence between reality and her subconscious universe.

"I don't want to," Avery grumbled from beneath the comforter.

Jonah ran his hand along the length of her curled body and pulled the bottom of her nightgown slowly up the ridge of her thigh to expose the curve of her ass and her cotton panties. He toyed with the waistband and walked his fingers up the front to cup the heat between her thighs. Avery arched into his touch.

"We told Stan we'd meet him before sunrise. It's almost six."

"You go. I'll catch up." She refused to open her eyes.

Jonah sighed and dipped his fingers inside her panties. Beneath his touch she stiffened, but if the sun wasn't awake yet, she didn't see any reason why she should be. He stroked her slit and the pad of his thumb pressed her clit, arousing the sensitive pearl.

"I told him we'd both be there. Carrie is counting on you to fry the doughnuts, remember?"

Jonah's deep, soothing voice, coupled with his tantalizing touch, made her pussy ache. Without warning, he slipped two fingers into her and flexed his hand, pumping fast. Avery's hips rolled. With her eyes still closed, she gathered the soft fabric of her nightgown in her fists and yanked it up over her navel.

"Fuck me first. Pretend I'm Sleeping Beauty, but a kiss won't wake me. Only an orgasm bestowed by a prince will break the curse."

A soft laugh answered her request. "I don't think that's how the story goes."

Avery moaned as Jonah's fingers curled inside her and drove deeper. "Well, Perrault got it wrong. This is the only acceptable way to wake a woman."

Jonah's mouth captured her own and he licked her lips. A thrill of pleasure soared through her, enhancing her need. He added a third finger and spread her wider before adding more pressure to her clit. Avery mewled and her palms slapped the fitted sheet as her orgasm began to build. She held on and let her mind go blank, lost to the pleasure.

The next moment, Jonah withdrew his hand and sat up, removing the delicious friction. Avery's eyes popped open.

"Too bad I'm not a pampered prince who can lounge about all day. Village life starts early for farmhands and stable boys, but at least the breakfast is a plus." Jonah stuck his fingers in his mouth and licked them clean.

Avery rolled over onto her stomach, aware of how inviting her ass looked against the messy sheets. "That's so unfair. You can't leave me like this."

Jonah snickered and pressed his mouth to hers. Then he swung his legs off the side of the mattress and pulled a clean t-shirt over his head. "You should have woken up earlier."

Avery wrinkled her nose and feigned a gasp. "You're playing a dangerous game, sir."

"And you're going to be late. Come on." He flicked his wrist and gave her ass two little love taps.

Avery dropped her head back onto the pillow but slid her body over until her feet met the floor. "Oh, we'll see about that."

Five hours later, Avery was in the thick of it. Burns from the hissing and spitting devil fryer covered her forearms. Aunt Carrie hadn't exaggerated. Over the last few days, they'd prepared over one thousand mini-doughnuts, but selling them by the dozen diminished their supply a lot faster than she'd anticipated.

Aunt Carrie left to make more dough while Marissa manned the register and Avery battled the temperamental fryer. The seasoned hands had tried to tell her, but coming from the city, she had thought she knew crowds. She was a frequent participant in the Black Friday shoe-deal-mad-dash at Lord and Taylor, but this was beyond compare.

By eight in the morning, a line of Mercedes and Land Rovers perched along the dirt road outside the orchard, fancy engines growling as they waited for the gate to open. Uncle Stan decided to invite them in half an hour early, and the cars leaped to attention.

Jesse acted as a parking assistant, ensuring guests stayed on the gravel. A few tried to weave through the coned-off barricade and park on Uncle Stan's front lawn, but he was quick to reprimand and redirect.

At first, the store was quiet. The general mass of people poured onto the grassy area beside the pavilion, scavenged for red-painted wagons, and grabbed their complimentary loot bags. It wasn't until about ten-thirty that people began checking out.

They streamed inside the tiny country store like a stampede, "oohing" and "awing" over the organic soaps and homemade apple butter. The women—trying to dress the part and "rough it" for a day in the country—flooded the store in new hiking boots and tight tank tops, wrapped in stiff flannels with designer sunglasses and push-up bras.

Avery had snorted behind her hand at first, but then a wave of humility hit her. Was this what Jonah had first seen when he looked at her? Did she still come across as snotty as the other women did?

Most of the men hung back and pitched camp outside by the makeshift pumpkin patch. Numerous bags of apples littered their feet, along with bumpy, ugly gourds. They were all the rage. Each of them stood with their feet apart, expensive sneakers half-buried in bags of Honey Crisps. Their khaki shorts hung neatly off their meticulous frames, and their collared shirts belonged on the back nine of a golf course rather than in the earthen orchard. Some sported Ray Ban shades while others squinted at their phones, but all of them possessed the same casual smirk that bespoke the truth: they were too sophisticated to enjoy themselves. The arrogance was revolting, and rather than feel a kinship toward the wealthy guests, Avery was stifled by their presence. She couldn't wait for their eco-friendly cars to crawl back down the long drive.

A new mob rushed through the front door, the high-pitched bell chiming chaotically as it swung back and forth. Avery adopted a fixed smile and greeted the customers. "Good morning. May I interest you in some snacks or beverages? For drinks, we have apple cider, lemonade, or bottled water, and for food, we serve, fresh popcorn, candied or caramel apples, and our signature doughnuts."

A tall brunette pushed with her elbows and fought to secure her position at the front of the line. "We'll take two dozen doughnuts, one popcorn, and two cups of cider."

"Sure. Would you like plain or cinnamon sugared?"

The brunette wrinkled her nose and glanced to her left. "Babe! Baby!"

"What?" A somewhat annoyed voice called from the arrangement of maple syrup bottles.

"Come over here. I don't want to yell across the store."

The brunette's Brooklyn accent brought an amused smile to Avery's lips. The man skirted a large group of teens busy smothering their hands with bottles of locally produced chamomile body butter and eventually reached his partner's side. In the meantime, Avery had busied herself collecting the narrow sleeve of popcorn and two cups of chilled cider.

"What's up?" the man asked.

Avery presented the brunette with the other half of her order, bouncing anxiously on her feet as she waited for the guy's decision. The other customers' weighty stares sent her stress into overdrive.

"She wants to know if you want all the doughnuts to be covered in cinnamon or if you want any plain."

The man shrugged. "I don't care. Cinnamon is fine with—"

His gaze swung to Avery and the rest of his sentence evaporated. Avery glanced toward the woman, uncomfortable with the intensity of her boyfriend's stare. "So . . . all cinnamon then?"

The brunette nodded. "Yes. What is wrong with you?" Her question was directed at her dark-haired partner, who had yet to recover from his momentary lapse.

The man shook off his stupor at last and cleared his throat. "I'll go put the apples in the car."

The brunette rolled her eyes and balanced the rest of her purchases in her arms. Avery flipped the metal wire basket into the bubbling oil. She looked up, still slightly uncomfortable because of the strange encounter. Why had that guy looked at her like that? Almost as if he knew her?

"These will be ready in two minutes."

"Thanks." The brunette busied herself with her phone.

"Can I help you?" Avery tended to the next few people in line and scooped the fried doughnuts out after the timer buzzed. She gave them a minute to cool, sprinkled extra cinnamon sugar on top, poured them into the wax paper bag, and handed them to the woman with a smile, the odd instance already fading from her mind. It was too busy to dwell on the habits of strangers. "Have a great day."

The woman flashed a perfect smile and melted into the teeming crowd, heading in the direction of the register.

Aunt Carrie arrived half an hour later, a pile of stacked trays in her hands. "How you are doing, honey?"

Avery handed three bags of doughnuts to a man holding a gurgling baby with cherub cheeks. "Enjoy. Have a great day." The father nodded in thanks, and another took his place. "Swell," she responded with a sarcastic arch of her brows and greeted the next guest. "How may I help you, sir?"

Aunt Carrie patted her arm and gestured toward the door.

"Go take a break. You've been working nonstop since dawn." Her aunt scooched past Avery and settled in front of the next customer. "Hello. Have you tried our famous fritters?"

"We wait for them every year." The man chuckled, his grin just visible beneath his bushy beard.

Aunt Carrie leaned forward. "Well, you're in luck because this is a fresh batch. I just finished forming them myself."

"Oh great. I'll take two dozen please."

Warmth settled over Avery as she witnessed the caring way Aunt Carrie interacted with the guests, like they were beloved relatives. She touched her aunt's elbow. "Thank you. I'll be back in a little bit."

"Okay. Oh, can you bring more plastic bags down to the boys at the pavilion? They're in the back room beside the extra picnic tables."

"Yeah, sure." Avery excused herself from the teeming throng of people and escaped out the back door.

Musty air, scented with flavors of sun-dried wood and years of stored apples, lingered in the dim storage area. Avery's dirty sneakers slapped against the hay-strewn concrete floor. A cardboard box balanced on one of the folding tables to the left. Shiny plastic bags were visible through the gaping flaps.

Digging her hand halfway into the contents, she pulled out a sizeable amount. If it wasn't enough, she could always trot back and grab some more. Avery whistled a nonsensical tune and exited the dry storage. The noon sun and heavy humidity greeted her like a bear hug and sweat dampened her underarms before she had even completed the short walk to the pavilion.

"Hey, guys." Avery sighed. She set the stack of clear bags on a crate near the scale and brushed back the little flyaways that curled around her hairline. "Carrie said you needed more bags."

Jonah smiled and planted a swift kiss on her cheek. At his feet, a ruddy-faced toddler sat in a wagon while his older brother yanked the handle back and forth.

"We pick apples!" the toddler cried.

"Apples? I don't know if we have any of those. This is an orange orchard," Jonah said.

"No, it's not." The older brother shot back. His small hands slammed against his bony hips. "My Mommy said we're here to pick apples."

Jonah grinned at the woman standing behind them. "Oh, she did? Well, you can check but I'm pretty sure I only saw oranges on those trees. Do you need a bag for all the oranges you're going to pick?"

Avery chuckled and passed him one of the bags. Jonah crouched down and offered it to the excited child. The older brother yanked it from his hands and tossed it to the little boy in the wagon.

"Hey, what do you say?" The mother scolded.

"Thank you," the boys chimed.

Jonah tipped his hat. "You're welcome. You have fun picking those oranges. Come show me how many you find okay?"

"We're picking apples!" the older boy yelled, a huge grin on his face.

Jonah shrugged. "I don't know. You'll have to look hard, okay?"

"Okay!" The older boy grabbed the wagon's handle tighter and raced away, pulling his little brother behind him.

"Thank you." The woman smiled gratefully and followed her sons.

Avery took a step closer to Jonah as the sweet family meandered away. A vision of Jonah teasing their own child assailed her and left her nearly speechless. She'd never put much stock into having a family of her own. Executives, especially women, didn't usually reach the pinnacle of success with a demanding family life, but the idea of a happy child with her eyes and Jonah's smile skipping off on an apple scavenger hunt warmed her heart far more than she'd ever thought possible.

"That was really cute," Avery whispered. Jonah wrapped his arms around her waist and pulled her in. She emitted a squeal of delight when he lifted her feet off the ground.

"It's nice to view the orchard through a child's eyes. It's an adventure."

Avery nodded and kissed him while her hand cupped his scruffy jawline. In that moment, suspended in his arms while images of a possible future danced through her head, she'd never felt such hope. "A grand adventure, indeed."

"Yo, Jonah," Mac called. "The other line's backing up. Can you weigh their apples?"

"Oh, shoot. Sorry." Jonah's arms slipped away, and the soles of her shoes touched back down to reality. "I'll see you later."

"Sure. Have fun."

"I love you," Jonah said. He winked and turned to the slightly disgruntled guest, then took the giant bag of apples out of his crumpled fingers. "Good morning, sir. Let's get those weighed for you. Looks like you found some big ones."

Avery drifted several steps away from the bustling hub and watched as the visitor's perturbed frown transformed into an easy grin while Jonah joked and talked. He had such a way of putting people at ease.

She slid her hands into her back pockets and shot Jonah one last glance. He had said he loved her several times now, but each time he'd spoken it without ceremony. He wasn't looking for validation or to have his ego stroked. He simply voiced his emotions. Avery knew she'd told Marissa she wasn't interested in a long-term relationship, but she was surprised to discover that she had to bite her tongue to keep herself from saying it back.

224

Chapter 37: Avery

Thick bees droned from flower to flower and filled the air with their hypnotic hum. Avery wove around the pumpkin patch on her way to the main house and smiled as children sat on the squat fruits. The once pristine rows now rolled helter-skelter down the small hill, but she'd learned it didn't have to be perfect for the guests. Perfection was far too rigid and demanding. Allowing room for mistakes and giggles fostered growth and shining memories.

Avery hopped over an upside-down pumpkin as her stomach growled. There hadn't been time for breakfast, and she was growing desperate for the sandwiches Aunt Carrie left all of them in the fridge. Her thoughts had wandered to ham and cheese when a familiar voice stopped her.

"Excuse me, Miss?"

The same man from earlier called to her from behind. Avery scanned the pumpkins for the brunette or perhaps a small child he might be chasing around, but he stood separate from the rest of the families.

"Yes?" Unease gripped her as the man advanced.

"I was wondering if you could tell me where the restrooms are?"

Relief washed over her. He wasn't a threat. He just needed to pee. "Oh, sure. There is a row of Port-a-Johns around the store by the tree line."

"Thanks so much." The man smiled, his dimples deep craters. Why couldn't she shake the feeling they'd met before?

"No problem." Avery hiked up the rest of the hill and exhaled a pent-up breath once she reached the porch. Maybe all the activity was making her paranoid. Her hand closed around the handle of the sliding glass door when the man spoke again.

"Do you think I could use your bathroom? Port-a-potties freak me out." He laughed. His words were casual, yet his body language was predatory, and his shoulders rolled like a stalking feline.

Avery's nerves prickled with alarm and her skin paled. His earlier odd behavior, compounded by his following her, wasn't normal. Fear spiked in her gut. She crossed her arms and raised her chin. It was important that she mask her growing panic. "This is a private residence and is off-limits to guests."

The man jogged up the few stairs and casually closed the distance between them. Avery swallowed the thickening lump in her throat but matched his stride. The last thing she wanted was to be pinned against the door with this guy blocking her path. She scanned the busy fields over his shoulder. They were too far away for anyone to hear them, but hopefully, a shrill scream would garner attention. She had to keep him confined to the porch. If he managed to get her inside . . .

Her gaze swept toward the pavilion. She could make out Mac's and Jonah's faint outlines, but they were too busy to notice her.

"Come on, Avery. Can't an old friend ask a favor?"

"Old friend? Where do I—" Avery paused as the man's statement sunk in. "How do you know my name?"

The man clutched his chest as if he'd been wounded. "Ouch.

I know you only used me for a quick lay, but I thought I'd made a better impression than that."

Avery's pulse raced, and she took a step to the left, careful to angle her body toward the steps. "I'm new to the area. Perhaps you have me confused with someone else."

The man shook his head and toyed with the expensive cuff on his watch. "Avery Sterling. I know who you are. Though, I guess we didn't spend a lot of time talking. Maybe if I licked that sweet pussy again, it'd jog your memory." He took two large steps and backed her against the waist-high railing. His eyes zeroed in on the front of her shorts, then flickered up, staring beneath his lashes.

Avery gasped as the details of her final morning in the city sparked in the back of her mind. *Fucking Todd.*

"Todd? Wow. I didn't recognize you." The sun-bleached wood dented beneath Avery's nails. "What are you doing up here?"

Todd curled his lip. "When my girlfriend mentioned she wished we could find a spot in the city to go apple picking, I suggested your uncle's hokey dump to give her that redneck experience she was searching for."

Avery frowned. "How did you know this is my uncle's orchard?"

Todd replied with an irritated scoff. "There's this new thing called the internet, Avery. I understand you've fully embraced living off the grid out here, but many people find it quite handy. A Google search can tell you practically anything, business records, genealogy, even local news announcements about your dear cousin's invitation to teach abroad."

Avery balked as he vomited information. "Have you been stalking me?"

"*Stalk* is a strong word." Todd braced his hands on the rail, caging her in. "Tracking is more apropos."

"What do you want with my family?"

Todd raised his chin and gestured to the frivolity below. "I could care less about your backwoods family."

Avery clenched her teeth and slid her feet further apart to brace herself. She only had one option and needed the proper leverage.

"Then what do you want, Todd?" Her voice was cold and serrated.

He leaned in closer, and the scent of his aftershave turned Avery's stomach. "To humiliate you."

"What?"

"You heard me, you little skank. I lost everything because of you. Do you know how many times I interviewed for your father's company? Six. Six fucking times I sat across from him and practically begged him to give me a chance. Finally, he offered me the position, and I went out to celebrate. And who do I run into? You. Dressed in some slinky red dress with your "fuck me" eyes."

Avery turned her head and cast a sideways glance toward the parking lot, but Jesse's reflector vest was nowhere to be seen.

"So I went home with you and took advantage of the easy lay, but it wasn't until your father waltzed in that I realized you had set me up. He fired me before I even had a chance to put my dick back in my pants. I lost my apartment and any security I thought I might have for my future, all because Daddy's little whore didn't get what she wanted and threw a tantrum."

"You don't know the first thing about me," Avery hissed. Anger flared and propelled her body off the railing, straight at Todd.

He didn't back down. They were nearly nose to nose,

snarling cats poised on a hairpin trigger. "Don't I? I know Daddy doesn't trust you enough to even give you a position in the mailroom. I know he forced you up here because he was tired of your shitty distractions. And I know you're about to lose everything good in your pathetic life."

Todd's hands darted to her hips and his breathing shook with anticipation. Avery leaped back and collided with the rail. "Don't touch me."

"Relax. I have no interest in fucking you again. Despite what your mountain man down there thinks, your pussy wasn't that good. But I am going to ensure you're the center of a scandalous scene."

Avery bared her teeth. "Get away from me."

"Not until you feel as humiliated as I did. How does becoming a sexual predator and exposing yourself to children sound? They won't let you within a thousand yards of this family-friendly orchard again. Not to mention that pesky charge that will never be expunged from your record."

"You're sick."

Todd shook his head, his perfectly coiffed hair unmoving. "No. I'm vengeful. There's a difference."

Avery's lip curled in disgust. "What's your plan? Strip me down and parade me through the orchard?"

"Something like that." Without warning, Todd's hands shifted up and fisted around the thin material of her flannel. The few buttons went flying as he forced her shirt open and exposed her black bra beneath.

"Don't touch me!" Avery screamed and punched him, landing a hard uppercut to his jaw.

Todd stumbled back but struck again. His fingers hooked around her bra strap and yanked down. A cool rush of air brushed Avery's skin, but she didn't look down. Instead, she brought her knee up and smashed it as hard as she could into the apex of his thighs.

A painful groan rumbled low in Todd's throat as he doubled over and released his hold. Avery didn't hesitate. She gripped the rail and kicked her legs, using the momentum to flip herself backward. The deck was only a few feet off the ground, and she caught her weight with her hands before she tumbled to the grass.

Hurried footsteps clambered across the wooden planks. "Run, little bitch," Todd growled. He reached the first step, still cradling his sore groin.

Avery swept her fallen strap back onto her shoulder and twisted to the left toward the cabins and latrine, away from the guest-populated areas, but also away from Jonah. In the distance, she could see smiling children piling into their cars, mouths sticky from caramel apples and candy. She scanned the gravel road for Jesse again, but he was too far down the lane.

Avery pumped her arms, sprinting as hard as she could. If she could reach her cabin, she could lock herself in and hopefully call for help. Her sneakers churned the dirt. She didn't look behind her, just kept running. Her cabin appeared on the other side of a large pine tree, and relief bloomed in her chest. She was almost there.

A sizzling sound sparked to life behind her, followed by Todd's laborious breaths. Avery chanced a look over her shoulder and was terrified at how quickly he'd caught up. His blue eyes resembled those of a hellhound intent on its prey, and in his hand, he held a small black device with two tapered prongs bent out like steel fangs. It sizzled again, mandibles clicking hungrily. Her heart plummeted as she recognized the object.

Avery swung her head forward and pushed her body harder, but she knew her chance of escape was dwindling, especially with the taser's reach.

Behind her, she heard a sharp snap, then two needle-like darts pierced her naked back. Avery collapsed. Pain consumed her as her body spasmed, held hostage by the bolts of electricity thrumming through her frame.

Todd loomed above her, a sinister smile on his face.

Chapter 38: Jonah

"There you go. Twenty-five pounds. That's a good haul." Jonah handed the half-full bag of Macintosh apples back to a rowdy guy in his early twenties, along with a receipt for the total owed. "Just head inside that building there and Marissa will check you out."

"Thanks, man." The kid accepted both and joined his friends around the side of the pavilion where they were all climbing onto the large Adirondack chair for obligatory photos. The girls in their group shrieked as the guys piled on playfully.

Another scream ricocheted through the orchard, but this one was void of the same jovial tone. It sounded scared, really scared. Jonah watched the excitable group. None of them seemed concerned. Easy smiles decorated each of their faces. With a frown, he scanned the children running up and down the mound of wood chips just to be safe, even though the scream had sounded too adult to have come from a child.

No one else appeared to have noticed the noise. Had he imagined it? A flicker of agitated movement flashed in the distance. A swatch of red snapped like a matador flag on the edge of Stan's porch. Jonah didn't recognize the man, but the familiar blond ponytail and denim shorts set off a warning bell deep in his gut.

"Avery?"

Jonah watched as she flipped back over the railing and sprinted away while the guy gave chase. The scene didn't look friendly or flirty, and instinctually, he knew the scream he'd heard had been hers.

"Mac! Avery's in trouble."

Jonah pushed through the line of guests waiting to weigh their apples and took off running. Avery disappeared around the front of the main house as if she were heading for the cabins. Behind him, he heard Mac apologize.

"Folks, I'm so sorry. We'll be right back."

Mac's long strides caught up in a few seconds and together they raced across the parking lot and over the pumpkin patch. Two minutes later, they veered down the slight slope where he had last seen Avery fleeing from the stranger. Jonah's chest burned with strain, but he didn't slow down. They rounded the large pine tree, and the sight awaiting them was something out of his worst nightmares.

Avery lay crumpled in the long grass, her body seizing and twitching unnaturally. Whimpers of pain accompanied a chorus of electric snaps. The same guy he saw on the porch crouched over her, yet from the dark gleam in his eye, Jonah knew he wasn't trying to help. He was the one causing her pain.

Rage swelled within Jonah. He didn't slow as he lowered his head and charged. The guy glanced up, a look of surprise twisting his features. He straightened out of his hunched position but couldn't react in time.

Jonah rammed his torso like a linebacker and drilled his shoulders into the attacker's stomach. The hit sent the guy flying back off his feet. A loud whoosh escaped from the man's lungs as his shoulder blades smacked into the ground. A black handheld device fell from his palm, and the energized clicks quieted, but Jonah didn't stop there.

Taking advantage of his opponent's momentarily stunned state, Jonah reared back and sat astride the guy's waist, pinning him down. He pulled his right arm back and delivered a hard blow to the attacker's cheek. Once, twice, three times. A red bruise blossomed across his face and his eyes rolled wildly, but he was too dazed to defend himself.

"Jonah," Mac called. "The bastard tased her."

A taser. That's what he'd heard when he came upon them. Jonah's vision burned scarlet. The asshole could have killed her if he'd held the trigger long enough.

Fisting his hands in the guy's expensive polo shirt, Jonah lifted the man's upper body off the ground and shook him until his teeth clacked together. Blood from the cut over the attacker's lip smeared across his cheek and painted Jonah's knuckles.

"You like to hurt women? Is that it? Has anyone ever hurt you?"

Jonah slammed his forehead into the guy's nose. A satisfying crunch of cartilage met his ears. A bubble of blood popped on the man's lower lip as he spoke.

"Whoever you think she is, she's lying. Bitch deserved it."

"The only one deserving of punishment is you."

"How heroic."

The guy cleared his throat and spat a wad of saliva and blood into Jonah's face. Out of instinct, Jonah released his hold and reared back, trying to rid his eyes of the vile fluid. As he blinked away the spittle, the man squirmed beneath Jonah, punching his vulnerable middle.

Yet, what Jonah felt wasn't the hard jab he'd expected. Instead, a sharp bite carved into the flesh to the right of his navel, followed by a warm, wet sensation that pooled over the waistband of his jeans.

"Jonah!"

Mac's cry echoed as Jonah slid off the attacker, unable to do much more than cradle the burning pain in his stomach. His head bounced off the grass. All that managed to pass his lips was a deep groan. Curled in the fetal position, Jonah pulled his hand away and was shocked to see his palm bathed in red. It was too much blood to have come from the other man, but if that were true, it had to mean it was his. Jonah's eyes wavered. When the man scurried off the ground, a steely smile caught his attention. Gripped in the stranger's fist was his knife, the one he wore on his belt in case he needed to make a quick cut in the fields.

"Think the little whore is worth it now?"

The asshole sneered and stumbled away as Mac jumped at him. The farmhand's punch sailed wide, and the attacker dodged Mac's other blow, Jonah's stolen blade winking threateningly. Helpless, Jonah watched from the grass. He tried to push himself onto his elbows, but searing pain flared in his midsection, prohibiting any movement.

A flash of neon green rippled across his vision. Numerous grunts and the thud of flesh on flesh provided an eerie soundtrack as Jonah struggled to keep his eyes open. Warm blood pulsed through the gaps in his fingers. He laid his head down. Everything hurt, but it felt good to rest. It would be so easy to fade away.

Soft hands cradled Jonah's head and cool fingers traced his hairline. His body responded to the familiar touch before his garbled thoughts could form. Avery's large brown eyes found his through the enclosing fog, but she wasn't happy. Tears ran from the amber pools, and her mascara painted black zigzags across her sun kissed cheeks. This wasn't right. Why was she crying? They were together.

Jonah lifted his crimson-stained hand and gently cupped Avery's face in his palm. Red smeared across her skin. "Hey, darlin'. Are you okay? I saw you . . . lying there. I tried to . . . stop him."

"I'm okay," Avery answered. Her tears fell harder.

"You're . . . okay?" Jonah confirmed, but his focus slid to the corner of his eyes. Away from Avery and her beautiful, sad face. His eyes rolled, desperate to find her again.

"Shh." Avery's gentle command was a balm and her hand ruffled his hair again. "Stay with me, Jonah. Please stay."

"I'm not goin' nowhere." He frowned. He wanted to sound reassuring, but his tongue was dead weight behind his teeth. "I love you."

"Jonah. Jonah. Please, open your eyes. Stay with me. Stay with—"

Chapter 39: Jonah

An incessant chorus of beeps roused Jonah from his medicated dreams. His eyelids flickered open, only to be met with eggshell white walls and a wavy turquoise curtain that barely brushed the mauve tiled floor.

A monitor cried to his left. Two long IV's descended from the box, their ends burrowed deep into the thin skin on the back of his hand. A paper hospital gown was draped across his chest, and his lower half was covered by a lightweight blanket with a scratchy square pattern.

Sunlight streamed in through the half-lidded blinds and alighted upon a figure, curled-up and fast asleep in the vinyl chair. Jonah's anxiety lessened. Avery was alive. Avery was safe. The urge to go to her and wrap her small body in his arms was overwhelming. He needed to see for himself that she was okay.

He fought with the medical tape on the back of his hand, but it was stickier than it looked. After a quick glance at the monitor, Jonah realized it was on wheels. Tossing back the threadbare cover, he swung his legs to the side of the bed, but a burst of tenderness erupted on his right side. The monotone beeps accelerated, and Avery stirred in the chair.

"Jonah?" Avery's voice was hoarse from sleep, and damn it if her raspy moan didn't make his cock throb, even through the pain. She blinked and rubbed her eyes. "Hey, you're awake."

Jonah grinned. "Yeah, though I hope I'm still more man than machine."

Avery slid off the chair cushion as he scooched over to make room for her on the narrow mattress. Her fingers threaded through his and a sense of calm settled over him.

"How do you feel?" Avery's voice was soft, intimate. Jonah didn't know if there was another patient on the other side of the curtain or if her gentle tone was reserved only for him.

He stroked the back of her hand as his fingers trailed up her forearm, indulging in the velvety skin. "My stomach is sore." Concern contorted his features, and he cupped her face. "What about you? What happened? Who was that guy?"

She answered with a heavy sigh. "His name is Todd. He worked for my father for a short while." Avery bit her lip. "I was responsible for getting him fired so he hatched this twisted plan to enact revenge and tracked me to the orchard."

Jonah frowned and brushed a lock of hair behind her ear. "I heard you scream. Saw you tumble off the deck."

Avery turned into his palm and kissed the rough skin. "I threw myself off after he ripped my shirt. I tried to make it to our cabin, but he hit me with a taser. The EMT's had to pull the barbs out of my back."

Jonah winced at the memory of Avery writhing on the ground. He dropped his hand and slipped it under her shirt. Two raised abrasions met his searching fingertips. Her skin was rough and beginning to scab. Guilt squeezed his gut.

"I'm so sorry he hurt you. I'm sorry I didn't get there in time."

"No." Avery shook her head. "You were amazing. You threw him off me."

Jonah gestured to his sore abdomen. He hadn't investigated the scar yet, but the glint of bloody steel clutched in Todd's fist was hard to forget. "Where did he hit me?"

Avery tightened her hold on his hand. "Your small intestines. The doctors said you were lucky the blade missed your liver."

"How long was I asleep?"

"Two days. They kept you sedated so you wouldn't go into shock, and until you passed the risk of the intestines perforating. You caught a slight fever too, so they monitored you for signs of worsening infection, but as of last night, you had shaken it. Your body just needed to rest."

Jonah scoffed. "Well, I should take up a grievance with Stan for working us fourteen hours a day for the last two months. Is he here?"

"He stayed for several hours the first night, but everyone is back at work."

"The orchard waits for no one."

"Yeah." Avery chuckled and snuggled closer into Jonah's uninjured side.

"What happened after I passed out? Did Todd get away?"

Avery snorted. "No. After he stabbed you, Mac and Jesse tackled him to the ground. Jesse saw the scuffle and radioed for Uncle Stan to call the police before he reached you. By the time the cops and ambulance arrived, they had Todd practically hog tied."

A low grumble of laughter reverberated in Jonah's chest. "You don't mess with country boys."

"A lesson Todd will not forget as he rots in jail."

"Isn't he rich enough to make bail?"

"Nope. He's broke. That's why he was so desperate to get back at me. He blamed me because he lost everything."

Jonah wrinkled his brow as he stared at the kind woman

before him. "I don't understand. Why would he blame you?"

Avery inhaled a shaky breath. He noticed the way she shied away from him, inviting a narrow strip of space between their bodies. "Jonah . . . before I came to the orchard, I wasn't a nice girl. I used people to get back at my father and selfishly hurt a lot of them. Todd was right when he called me a liar."

"No." Jonah pulled her against him, disliking the chasm she had created. "Don't you think for one second that this was your fault."

"I don't. Todd's actions were a result of his warped sense of justice, but it doesn't erase how I treated guys in the past. You're the first guy I've fallen for without an ulterior motive. I thought being with you would offer a fun escape, but I never intended to fall in love with you."

Avery's voice dropped to a hushed whisper. She stared at their joined hands, doing her best to ignore his gaze. Jonah's throat swelled with worry. He couldn't lose her, yet he could feel every brick she was layering between them.

"What are you saying?" Jonah asked. The tension in the room was palpable, a string pulled taunt, waiting for a pair of scissors to offer the fatal snip, and once cut, there would be no rejoining, no way to stitch it back together.

Avery's large eyes shone wetly. Her lashes clumped and tears trickled down her cheeks. The pain of being stabbed was nothing compared to the way his heart hammered and his chest constricted as he awaited her next words.

Her lips parted, and a tear hung suspended from the upper bow. "Jonah . . . I love you."

Chapter 40: Avery

Jonah sat in stunned silence for a moment as quiet sobs racked Avery's body. "But why is that a bad thing?" he asked.

Avery wiped her blurry eyes with the back of her hand. "Because I'm leaving. I love you, and I'm going back to the city."

The fear in Jonah's eyes lightened. "Darlin', the city is only a few hours away. We'll see each other all the time. We can make it work."

"No." Avery's words were muffled as she spoke into her hand. "We say that. We promise the distance won't change us, but it will. It always does. I've seen enough movies to know."

"Avery, those are fictional stories."

"Yeah, based on real life." She pressed the heel of her palms into her eyes. "I don't want that to happen to us. I don't want to fight and worry about you sleeping with some cute country girl, and eventually you're going to resent me for having to drive down to the city every weekend. It might work at first, but it's too much."

As her agitation increased, her sobs intensified, grief jackhammering her chest. The small bed beneath them shook. Jonah's warm hands steadied her heaving shoulders, and he placed a gentle kiss on her forehead.

"It's going to be okay. Sure, there's a lot to figure out, but we still have a few weeks to work out the logistics."

Fresh tears welled and her bottom lip quivered. "I'm leaving today."

"What?" Jonah's soothing rubs stilled. "What do you mean?"

"Uncle Stan called my dad, to alert him to the situation in case the press caught wind of it and connected us. My father was adamant I leave with him yesterday, but I convinced him to let me stay until you woke up so . . . so I could say goodbye."

Jonah's jaw dropped. "Can't you call him and tell him no? I'll drive you back to the city myself and—"

Avery sniffled and shook her head. "I told him the same thing. Suddenly, he's putting on a dramatic show, raving about how irresponsible Uncle Stan was for not having proper security at the orchard and allowing this incident to happen." She exhaled a frustrated breath and waved her hand in front of her face. "It's all to avoid any type of black mark or scandal on his end. He doesn't care about me." Avery grumbled the last bit under her breath and toyed with a loose thread that had begun to unravel in the middle of the blanket.

A pregnant silence ballooned. Avery didn't know what else to say. Jonah's expression was unreadable. She glanced at the analog clock. Her father told her the car would be there at four. She had eighteen minutes to say goodbye to the only man she'd ever trusted with her heart.

Jonah licked his dry lips. He looked nervous and uncomfortable. "What if . . . what if you don't go?"

"Jonah—"

He held up his hands. "I know but hear me out. If you don't want to do a long-distance relationship or don't believe it will work, then it won't. But I love you. I love you so much, Avery.

You can move in with me once Stan is set with the orchard. I'll go back to contracting, and we can find a career you'll enjoy, too."

"No, Jonah. No. It sounds wonderful, a simple, happy life with you, but you don't understand. I worked so hard for this position. I went to school and suffered through loads of misogynistic professors and bosses who all regarded me like a child playing pretend on bring your daughter to work day. None of them had any faith in me, but I'm smart. I can look at the market, anticipate changes, and adapt the products to better stand out and align with popular trends. I've worked so hard every single day of my life to prove I'm good enough for my father to take notice and hire me on as a proper executive, and I'm afraid that if I stay . . ."

Her words trailed off, losing steam when she looked at the wonderful man before her. "If I stay, I . . . I don't want to hate you for taking that opportunity away." Jonah sucked in a lungful of air as his features widened in shock. Avery fumbled for words. "I'm sorry. I know that's not fair to you, but I'm afraid that's what will happen. I never planned for this." She clutched her chest. "You weren't supposed to be here."

Jonah's mouth parted and he looked away from her for the first time. "Are you saying we were a mistake?"

Avery held his arm and shook her head. "No. Please don't think that. I've enjoyed every moment we've shared this summer. This has nothing to do with you. It's me. I need to do this."

"But I can go with you," Jonah said. Hope burned in his statement, yet it perched precariously.

"Come with me where?"

"To the city." Jonah propped himself up higher against the floppy mattress. "I'll help Stan finish up the season, then I can find a cheap place to rent and set up my contracting business down there. I'm sure the wealthy people of Manhattan require renovation projects."

Avery paused. "You'd move to the city? For me?"

"Well, yes. I mean, it's not my first choice of locations, but we'd be together."

"See, I don't want this."

Jonah wrinkled his brow. "What?"

Avery dropped her hands, and they bounced atop the sheet. "I don't want to steal you away from your life, your job, all your friends. You're going to feel trapped, and I won't have time to make it better. This job comes with long hours, and I need to dedicate one thousand percent of my energy to doing the best I possibly can, but I can't do that with you because I'll always feel guilty for choosing one over the other."

Strained cries boomed like hoarse cannons from her throat. She'd practiced this speech a dozen times in her head since the moment her father laid out the ultimatum. She knew it was going to be hard, but the reality of saying the words out loud was unbearable.

"I don't want to ever make you feel like that."

Jonah's voice was small, defeated. He looked so fragile against the backdrop of the hospital bed. The clock ticked. Her deadline approached with little remorse. Avery tucked her hands in her lap and slid off the mattress, letting her shoes hit the floor.

"Where are you going?" Jonah gently grabbed her arm.

"I have to go." She stood and moved just out of reach.

"Go? No. Please, can we talk about this? We can figure it out Av, I promise."

Avery bit down hard on the inside of her cheeks. "There's no time. My father has a car waiting for me downstairs. I'm going back to the city tonight."

Hurt rippled across Jonah's face. "I just woke up. We have to talk about this. You haven't even packed. Just take another day to think about it, and if you still want to go, I'll drive you."

"It's done. I packed everything this morning." Avery couldn't meet his gaze. Shame hung around her neck like an anchor.

"You packed?"

Those two small words were bullets to her heart.

"I'm sorry. My father gave me a choice and I made a decision." Avery took a step back and Jonah's face crumpled.

"Please don't do this. Don't go. I love you. Doesn't that mean anything?"

Avery slowly closed her eyes against the heartbreaking sight, and tears trailed down her cheeks. The voice in the back of her mind urged her to flee. She had made her choice and had to accept the consequences, even if that meant causing Jonah even more pain. Yet, she wasn't strong enough to walk away and never look back. She had meant it when she said she loved him, and her heart shattered into agonizing shards as his deep baritone broke with emotion.

"It means everything."

She rushed to him and took his face in her hands, her lips seeking his. His overgrown scruff scratched her palms. Forced to remain in the hospital, it was the longest he'd gone without shaving since she'd known him, and she relished the prickly texture against her chin as she kissed him with everything she had, her sorrow, her grief, and her regret over the things she wished could be different.

Jonah held her as close as the bed would allow and sighed, mistaking her affection for acceptance. He stroked the back of her head. "We'll figure it out. I promise."

Avery stifled a cry and buried her face in the warm crook of his neck. Her lips pressed against his ear. "I wish we had more time." She kissed him on the corner of his mouth one last time and used his momentary relief to slip out of his arms. "I love you."

Jonah's mistake was written all over his face. "Wait. Avery, no."

But she didn't stop. She rounded the metal edge of the bed and pushed aside the hideous curtain. Behind her, the mattress springs groaned in protest as Jonah attempted to follow.

"The IV's . . . I can't pull them out. Avery, please."

The doorknob was ice in her grasp, and she yanked it open with enough force to send it banging against the wall in her haste to exit. Jonah's cries echoed through the empty hallway before the door slammed shut with a solid click.

Her heart screamed at her to return, to erase the look of hurt and betrayal shining in his eyes as though she had been the one to stab him, and she wished she had. At least then his pain would be superficial, and he'd heal with the tiniest of blemishes. Instead, she would forever replay his forlorn misery and echoing pleas.

Her sneakers slapped against the reflective tile. The elevators loomed ahead, a steel prison to usher her toward her hard-won future.

Chapter 41: Jonah

The cabin door swung wide. Even before Jonah crossed the threshold, emptiness radiated. Gone were the handful of half-read books scattered across the little shelf along with the bottle of pink nail polish. Gone was Avery's collection of shoes piled against the wall that threatened to collapse every time he stepped on the loose plank.

His few shirts were now visible in the narrow closet, and they hung like bones that had been picked clean and scavenged by crows. All his things remained, but it felt as if he'd been robbed, his heart violated and abducted by a thief in the night. Yet, Avery was the worst kind of thief—the kind who stole in broad daylight—unconcerned with getting caught because she knew she'd never be found.

Jonah collapsed on the bed. His stitches throbbed, and he buried his face in the pillow. It had only been two days since she left, but the scent of Avery's shampoo had already begun to fade. He inhaled deeply as if he could bottle it within his memory and preserve the ghost of her.

Carrie had offered to walk him back after she ferried him home from the hospital, but he'd declined. He didn't want another lecture about lost love or how it wasn't meant to be. Since the moment Avery walked out of his room, silence was the only companion he craved.

He pictured her in her apartment in the city. Was she getting ready for her first day? He imagined her at a fancy salon, bleaching her sun-kissed hair back to the near platinum white it'd been when she first arrived. All that beautiful golden color would be leeched from the strands, the wispy ends sliced and trimmed.

Would she keep the clothes she'd bought with him? Throw on the denim shorts that made his pulse quicken to traverse Fifth Avenue? He closed his eyes, remembering her curves, and the way the wind caressed her shirt, rippling over the smooth skin of her stomach. The moment she got back home she probably threw them in the garbage chute, glad to be rid of everything that was soiled with dirt, sweat, and flour. Was she glad to be rid of him, too? To cast him off as easily as her muddy pair of sneakers and upgrade to a wealthy asshole in a Tom Ford suit?

Jonah liked to think he knew her better than that, but he also never expected to be blindsided by her departure. He knew it was going to be hard at the end of the summer, but he at least thought they'd have a chance to discuss it.

"Whatever," Jonah sighed and threw his arm over his face. "I can't change the fact that she doesn't want to be with me." He said the words aloud, but they were hollow. Two sharp knocks rapped from outside. He groaned. "Not now."

Stan's voice reverberated on the other side of the wooden door. "Open up, Jonah."

"I'm resting, Stan."

"This won't take long."

Jonah grumbled under his breath. He knew his friend wouldn't leave. Stan was as tenacious as his niece in that regard. He swung his feet to the floor and shuffled toward the front of the small cabin. Opening the door, he propped his forearm on the frame and leaned out.

"What do you need?"

Stan ushered him outside with two fingers and took a seat on the edge of the porch. He didn't watch Jonah to make sure he complied. Instead, he looked out toward the orchard. The sun hung like a molten globe in the sky, but clouds rolled across it, dampening its blaze.

Jonah stifled a groan and sat down beside him. He clapped his hands together and twisted his palms, rubbing ridge against ridge. "Look, Carrie already gave me the other fish in the sea speech, so you can save your breath."

"Not what I wanted to talk about." Stan continued to stare at the rows of thinning apple trees.

Jonah wrinkled his brow. "Oh, did something happen with the orchard while I was in the hospital?"

"Nah, orchard's doing fine. That was our best opening day in a while . . . least until you went and got yourself stabbed. That shut things down for a bit."

"Sorry about that." Normally Jonah would have cracked a joke, but today he didn't feel like laughing.

"It's fine. You protected Avery and put yourself in harm's way to do it." Stan turned to Jonah. The wrinkles around his eyes seemed more pronounced, and for the first time, his employer and friend looked old. He clasped Jonah on the back and pulled him in for a firm hug. "Thank you for what you did and . . . I'm sorry for how everything ended."

Jonah's eyes prickled with emotion. He hugged the other man back, then dropped his head. "It's my own fault. She was clear from the beginning that she wasn't looking for anything serious. I was the one who pursued her. I told her I loved her. Now she's gone, just like she said she would be, and I'm the fool holding a broken heart."

Stan fiddled with a fraying shoestring on his boot. "You're no fool, Jonah. We can't help who we fall for or how hard we fall. Avery didn't leave because of you. She left because of her. She's got in her head the perfect recipe for happiness and success, and just like my brother, the final ingredient is leaving this place, and the people who love them behind. They're scared that if they let someone in, they're weak. With that mindset, they can't see the advantage a partner creates, how they can lean on and count on that other person to support them when life becomes too much. And it will always become too much." A raspy chuckle interrupted his monologue. "They push everyone away and tell themselves they're better off."

Jonah frowned. "Are you trying to tell me I'm better off without her or not to push you away?"

Stan held up his palms in surrender. "I'm not trying to tell you what to feel. I wanted to thank you again for what you did, but I also want to make sure you know that validation and love doesn't come from just one person. Carrie and I love you. Jesse, Marissa, and hell, even Mac loves you." He patted Jonah's knee. "You're a grown man and you'll do what you wish, but we all care about you too much to watch you retreat behind your walls again. And even though you may be cursing her name now, I'm thankful for the magic she cast to bring you out from beneath that dark veil."

Jonah's cheeks warmed with color, a culmination of thoughts of Avery, Stan's declaration, and the comforting physical touch his friend offered. He inhaled a large, swirling breath and held it for a moment.

It wasn't that he viewed Stan as a replacement father figure—his own dad was alive and well—but rather that his dad was old school and believed fathers shouldn't hug their sons. Hesitantly, he reached out, grasped Stan's hand where it still rested on his knee, and expelled the breath. A sense of relief washed through him.

He didn't need to have the right answer. He wasn't expected to know what to do next. As Stan stated, all he had to do was not shut them out again and eventually, his aching heart would begin to stitch itself back together.

A heavy sigh broke the silence, and he released Stan's hand. His chest felt lighter, and the stinging nettles that had taken up residence around his heart dulled for the moment. Maybe he would be able to get through this if he didn't grieve alone.

"Wow, Stan. You know if the orchard ever falls on hard times, you should seriously consider a career in psychology. You actually made me feel better."

Stan's lips pulled back into a crooked grin. He dusted his palms on the front of his jeans, and the two men stood. "It's all those damn books Carrie keeps in the bathroom. I haven't replaced my *Hunting and Fishing magazine* yet and the other morning I needed reading material, so I read a chapter. I hope I said all of it right."

Jonah smiled and patted his friend on the back. "It sounded just fine. Thanks, man."

Stan bowed his head and flexed his hands. "You're welcome. Now, get back in there and lay down. I need you to heal up so you can come back to work. Some farmhand has been calling off for the last few days, and it's putting a bit of strain on the rest of them."

Jonah rolled his eyes and crossed his porch. "I was trying to take a nap, but some old man wouldn't shut his trap."

Stan shook his head and wiped the corner of his mouth with his knuckles. "People have got some kind of nerve."

"I hear ya."

Stan laughed as he hiked the short distance to the main house. Jonah returned to the cabin's stark interior and let the door close behind him. Regardless of whether Stan's story was legitimate and he was simply feeding him Carrie's words, he appreciated it just the same. He'd never been comfortable emoting feelings other than anger and passion, and the nice thing was that Stan didn't seem interested in giving him a good cry. Yet knowing how much they valued him and cared about his mental state gave him hope that he was going to emerge from this pain with only a few more scars.

Stan also wasn't asking Jonah to forget Avery. Thoughts of her and their relationship were healthy. No one saw him as lame or pathetic. It was important to remember the good parts too, for those were what healed the jagged edges and allowed his heart the confidence to love again.

Jonah laid down and spread out as much as the twin bed allowed while his thoughts drifted as they always did, to Avery. This time they weren't tinged with malice or despair. Instead, he imagined her walking into the big boardroom at the top of the building in her cutoffs, dragging one of the irrigation hoses behind her and throwing the snake-like body onto their polished desk.

If that girl could maneuver those beastly things around the orchard in one-hundred-degree heat with a sexy smile on her face, the men of her father's company were in for the shock of their lives when she came in and flipped the company on its head.

Chapter 42: Avery

Envelopes. Thirty-six identical alabaster envelopes lay scattered across Avery's desk. It would have been one thing if they were full, bearing carefully compiled sentences that would change her life. Alas, each one was empty, a blank canvas with no purpose or direction. She leaned forward and rested her head on the colorless surface. Maybe an idea would seep into her mind through osmosis if she left it there long enough.

The door to her office swung open. "Ah, hard at work I see."

Avery peeled herself off the folded paper and frowned when her foundation left a sheen of tanned product behind, marring the pristine sachet. "Well, it's not like I'm swimming in ideas for how to up envelopes' sex appeal." She leaned back in her swivel chair and cocked her head. "Why does Sterling Management represent this client? No one writes letters save for eighty-four-year-old women who send their grandkids birthday money, and the elderly don't exactly welcome change."

Her father crossed his arms. His expensive suit puckered at his elbows, giving the illusion that he was crafted from nothing but sharp angles and tapered points. Avery scoffed. No description had ever been more appropriate.

"You're thinking too small, Avery. Think about the potential applications for businesses, legal documents, or military personnel."

Avery pursed her lips and berated herself. The whole point of Sterling Management was their talent for marketing a product in a fresh, exciting way that made people pay attention. She should be thinking bigger, more abstractly, but her mind refused to focus.

"You're right. Thanks for the kick. It's hard to shake off the initial impression, I guess."

Her father raised one eyebrow and fixed her with a stern stare. "This position is meant to be challenging, Avery. Just because you earned the right to try doesn't mean it's yours to keep. If you don't impress me or the client at our meeting at the end of the week, you'll lose the account, and I can't have executives losing accounts. Do you understand?"

She shouldn't have been surprised, but her father's statement stole the oxygen from the room. If she couldn't find a way to expand the client's marketability to younger generations and a more diverse group of consumers, then she was done. She'd be kicked out on her ass before she could even set up her desk.

"Yes, sir." Avery returned his intimidating stare. She wouldn't be the first to break eye contact. He gave her this account on purpose, probably even hoped she'd buckle under the pressure so he could gloat for the rest of her life. The standoff raged for half a minute more before her father bowed his head. Avery blinked with relief as the back of her eyes burned.

"Excellent. Well then, I'll let you get back to work. You have a long day ahead of you." Her father's lips stretched into a practiced grin, then he pivoted and exited the small office.

Once the door separated them, Avery plunked her head back onto her desk and closed her eyes. She had wanted this, fought for it even. Yet the four walls, complete with a square window that offered a view of Central Park, were stifling rather than empowering.

She yearned to splay her toes atop the warm dirt and exchange her heels for a sturdy set of sneakers. She ached for the tender summer breeze and crisp scent of freshly mown grass. She missed the orchard, craved the bugs, and the heat, and the laughter that rippled along the rows as the little crew worked in tandem. Most of all, she longed for Jonah.

She missed everything. His calloused hands against her skin. His throaty chuckle when a rare laugh escaped. The hum of his body and the way he challenged her rather than catered to her every whim like the other men she'd been with. She'd thought returning to the city would feel like a homecoming, yet it was the orchard she pined for.

The urge to submerse herself in the orchard's magic propelled her out of her chair. It wasn't probable to physically drive up there, so she'd have to settle for the next best thing Manhattan could offer. Avery pulled open a drawer and withdrew a few plain sheets of paper. She grabbed her belongings and an envelope, then strode into the hall. Already, joy buoyed her steps on the short walk to the elevator while an idea germinated in her mind.

A short while later, noxious fumes and competing car horns overwhelmed Avery's senses. Her stilettos clacked atop the sidewalk, and she dodged a miserable white horse trussed up to an elaborate carriage that ferried gullible couples around the outskirts of the park. Gently, Avery laid her palm against the horse's neck.

Growing up in the city, horse-drawn carriages outside the park were a tourist staple, as permanent as the silver hot dog vendor perched on the cobblestone entrance. Avery never stopped to consider whether the horses dreamed of a different life, if they'd rather run on soft earth instead of hot asphalt and frolic with friends rather than compete against blaring yellow cabs for road space. Truth be told, until recently, she'd never imagined a different life for herself, either.

The choice, when presented, seemed so simple, but the horse was trapped, stuck in its wretched predicament and used at its owner's discretion. No such power dictated her life, yet there she was, wasting it in a concrete jungle where fresh air could only be found vented into expensive boutiques. Avery pressed her face to the horse's fur.

"I hope you get out of here soon," Avery whispered. The horse leaned in and nuzzled her hand.

"Hey, pretty lady." The driver called from his wooden perch. "May I interest you in a tour around our beautiful Central Park?"

Avery stroked the horse's face once more and looked away from its sad brown eyes. "No thanks. Do these horses work every day? Is there a stable nearby that offers room to run?"

The driver shifted atop the seat and rolled his eyes. "Geez, lady. You with PETA or something? I'm just trying to make a living here."

"By abusing an animal that doesn't have a voice or agency to say no."

The man hooked a thumb toward his chest and leered. His yellowed eyes nearly disappeared when his features scrunched into a scowl. "I got a license. I got every right to be here. You got an issue, take it up with the mayor, sweetheart. Now get away from my horse before I report you for obstructing my business."

The man flicked the butt of his cigarette to the ground where it landed inches away from her foot. Rage consumed Avery. It wasn't right what they subjected those poor animals to, but people didn't care when the abuse generated easy income.

She clutched her papers tighter in her hand and stormed away. Disgust roiled in her stomach, and fury made her jaw ache as she gritted her teeth. When she'd looked at the horse, she'd seen herself, a prisoner locked in a cell. But there was one crucial difference. She had the key.

Her steps quickened as she entered the park. Green benches lined the wide path and a break in the short fence led into the large, manicured meadow beyond. Instantly, she kicked off her heels and hopped onto the grass. An unrestrained sigh slipped from her lips at the cool sensation, and she started to run.

Avery didn't think about her dress slacks or what observers might think. She ran as fast as she could and lost herself in her long strides, in the playful wind tugging invisible fingers through her hair. She ran for the horse chained to the cart and for every day she'd forfeited the sun in favor of a screen full of trends and market stability calculations. She ran because she'd left the only place in the world that felt like home and abandoned the few people who truly loved her for who she was, not who she should be. Lastly, she ran for the little girl rooted deep inside, naïve to still believe that if she worked hard enough to please her father, he'd reward her with the love she so desperately craved.

She didn't know how far she'd traveled, but it was enough to exercise the demons that struggled inside, always insisting she would never reach the pinnacle her father demanded. The voices were quiet as she collapsed to the ground and stretched her limbs. Long grass tickled the underside of her arms, and fluffy white clouds punctuated the azure sky. The world was too big, and life was too short to surround herself with sadness.

The best one could do was find a place that mirrored Heaven and enjoy the simple blessings presented every day.

Avery rolled onto her stomach and laid the papers flat on the ground, the envelope supporting them. She pulled a pen from her pocket and began to write. At first, the words wouldn't flow, blocked by disappointing memories. Yet, soon after, the dam broke, and her pen couldn't scrawl fast enough.

An avalanche of regrets and dreams flooded through her, but in the end, she chose to keep it short and sweet. Unlike other letters, it wasn't a greeting or a goodbye. It was a moment of release, and as she penned what might possibly be her final words to her father, she included a springboard for the campaign.

Envelopes are modern-day treasure chests. Trusted to safeguard information until unsheathed by the one who holds the key. I hope, one day, you can be that person for me.

Avery left the park and returned to her apartment as the afternoon sun waned and the tall trees' shadows loomed like swaying giants. She crawled under the bed and retrieved her own personal chest that housed the few keepsakes salvaged from her childhood.

Shifting through the notebooks filled with drawings, she touched the one printed photo she had. Inside its crinkled edges, the scene depicted was a rare moment of love between father and daughter.

Seven-year-old Avery was dressed in a pink poodle skirt and Mary Janes with her long hair pinned in a high ponytail. Her arms were a blur as she flew, guided by her father's strong hands. He'd tossed her up and twirled her across the dance floor at the Sock Hop Dance. A genuine smile lit up her face, and her father wore a similar expression. They were two people, frozen forever in a beautiful moment of pure joy where all they needed was one another to create their own happiness.

Avery folded her note and tucked the picture alongside it. With a quick swipe of her tongue, she sealed the envelope and wrote her father's name on the front. She would give it to him tonight with her resignation. Now he would forever be able to keep that little girl trapped in the endless bubble of impossible perfection, for she had carved that pain and longing from her chest and gift-wrapped it for him.

She was done living her life in his shadow. It was time to run.

Chapter 43: Jonah

A high-pitched squeak sounded as the wagon wheels bumped along the disturbed gravel. Jonah sighed and bent down to readjust the janky hinge for the third time. He passed Marissa who was busy raking the loose rocks guests had kicked during the day back into a groomed path.

"You want to grab a beer after?"

Marissa grinned and placed her hand on her hip. "Sure. Let's hit up Bleacher's."

"You got it. I'll meet you by the cabins after a shower. If you see Mac or Jesse, let them know we're going. I already talked with Stan and Carrie."

"Cool." Marissa checked her watch. "An hour should be plenty of time to finish and get cleaned up."

"Sounds good." Jonah waved and corralled the wagon with the others outside the pavilion.

The last few stragglers were just pulling out. A large cloud of dust signaled their departure. It had been a busy day, but Jonah knew Stan had hoped for more traffic. Local attendance was up. However, apart from opening weekend, the orchard had yet to become a popular destination for folks in neighboring cities like Buffalo, Syracuse, or Rochester. Their operation was too small to stand out amongst the other farms in the area. It wasn't in danger of foreclosure or anything, but he wished there was some way to alleviate the pressures Stan faced.

Jonah grabbed one of the plastic bags from the weigh station and began scouring the common areas for trash. Half-gnawed apple cores were a given. Usually, they left the discarded fruit where guests dropped them among the rows for the animals, but closer to the picnic tables and store, abandoned apples attracted bees, and nothing chased guests away faster than Yellow Jackets.

Empty doughnut and popcorn bags littered the ground, along with trampled candy sticks that had fallen from toddlers' mouths as they played with the construction trucks and shovels. Once the garbage was collected, Jonah tied the handles, emptied the rest of the bins, and deposited the trash in the dumpster at the back of the store.

On his way back around, he stopped at the hand washing station near the Port-a-Johns and scrubbed away the accumulated grime and dirt. He was shaking the water droplets from his fingertips when Jesse's blond head popped out of the storage room door.

"Hey, man. I've been looking for you." Jesse jogged up the gradual hill. His neon reflector vest still covered his torso.

Jonah trudged down to meet him. "What's up?"

Jesse jerked his thumb over his shoulder. "On my way back up the drive, I saw two or three wagons down in the front orchard. I'd go grab them, but my dad just asked me to bring another load of pumpkins up."

"I got you, man." Jonah clasped Jesse on the shoulder. "Did you catch what rows the wagons were in?"

"I think like twenty-six or twenty-seven. Somewhere around there."

"Okay, no worries. I'll get them. We're heading to Bleacher's in an hour for a few beers."

Jesse waved. "Yup. I'll be there."

Jonah nodded and continued down the hill while Jesse veered toward the utility barn that housed the tractor and large cart. He let his mind go blank while he strolled down the long walk to the front orchard, but the sight of the maple tree conjured tender memories.

He was doing okay. Better than expected thanks in large part to his talk with Stan. The others treated him normally as well, even though he'd caught Marissa giving him the side-eye on more than one occasion as if she were waiting for him to shut down again.

The tree's shadow dappled half of his face. Visions of those moments with Avery beneath the canopy crackled in his mind. The contrast of her supple skin against his as the rough bark bit into his palms assailed him. His body remembered, and for a minute he indulged in the fantasy. Unlike he had with Laura, he allowed his heart to partake as well.

His feet carried him through the swaying grass, but all he saw was Avery. Her tousled hair, her squinting eyes, and her perfect lips upturned in a coy smile as she beckoned him closer. A flush of warmth enveloped him as he pictured her in his arms. His heart swelled with love. He didn't have to shun the memories. Didn't have to deny the happiness she'd given him.

Jonah sighed, and the images drifted away with the lazy breeze. It was okay to admit he missed her. Maybe one day, the allure of the orchard and the tart fruit suspended in its branches would lead her back to him.

A pair of wagons waited for him like stubborn cows who'd wandered off in the middle of row twenty-six. Jonah increased his pace. The trees down there still harbored a good number of apples. Most guests didn't feel the need to venture that far, especially for Crimson Crisps. These apples weren't coveted for pies, and their sweet, yet spicy taste wasn't preferred to the more popular Macintosh or Gala.

Jonah cursed under his breath at the thoughtlessness of others and scooped down to gather the handles. As he straightened, he noticed a pair of heels dangled from the tight branches, attached to long pant-clad legs, but the woman's upper body was distorted by leaves. His training kicked in.

"Ma'am, are you all right? Can I help you down?" Jonah frowned and dropped the handles. How long had she been stuck up there? Leaves rustled, and a tanned face surrounded by a halo of golden hair peeked back at him. Jonah's heart lurched. "Avery?" A jade green blouse was visible beneath her black suit, the perfect camouflage.

"Thank God you came. My ass was going numb." Avery chuckled and eased her torso around the numerous tree limbs until nothing but a few leaves obstructed her beautiful face. "Catch me." Her command was a purr, and Jonah complied without hesitation.

He grabbed her thick thighs and gently slid her down the skinny trunk until her heels wobbled unsteadily atop the fruit-strewn ground. Jonah glanced at the clumped branches. "How long were you up there?"

"Jesse snuck me in ten minutes ago." She smiled, yet Jonah sensed she was holding back. She kept her arms at her sides, and the tightness in her eyes relayed nerves that simmered beneath her calm façade.

"Why? What are you doing here?"

Avery flinched. Jonah hadn't meant his question to wound like an accusation, but he couldn't understand her motives.

Why was she messing with his head? She fixed her doe-like gaze on him.

"I didn't plan on coming back. My father kept his promise and made me an executive. I was struggling to understand my first account and took a walk to Central Park when I saw a horse tied to one of those tourist carriages."

The energy between them popped and the desire to capture her lips and erase all the heartbreak was a physical need he had to actively restrain himself from satisfying. But as nice as it would be to forgive her abrupt departure immediately, Jonah first needed to hear what she had to say. He nodded and waited for her to continue.

"It broke my heart to see him strapped and restrained, forced to carry happy strangers who refused to acknowledge how miserable he was because it would impede their own lives. He should be on a farm, running free around a grassy pasture, and I realized we were the same. The only difference was that I had chained myself to misery and could run if I wanted to."

Jonah smirked. "You got all this from a horse?"

Avery swatted his arm. "Yes." She wrinkled her nose, but her smile brightened. "The point is, I don't want that life. I want the orchard, and the grass, and the clear sky, and . . . you. If you'll have me."

Her words should have made him leap for joy, but he hesitated. Jonah worked the denim folds of his jeans between his thumb and forefinger. "What if this life isn't enough for you? What if in a few months you decide you made another mistake? I love you, Avery, but I don't want to give my heart to someone who has no qualms about breaking it."

Avery clasped his hands and placed a kiss on his fingers before a flash of black fluttered out of the corner of his eye. Her heels lay scattered across the grass a few yards away from where she'd kicked them off. She reached up onto the tips of her toes and nudged his nose with hers.

"I can't promise we'll be happy here forever. We don't know what the future holds any more than the next couple. But I can promise that I'll never leave you again. If I start to crave something different, we'll talk and discuss moving forward together. Plus, I have a bunch of ideas to help elevate Sterling Orchards' image." Avery wiggled her eyebrows, and excitement flared in her eyes. She was serious. She had chosen the orchard over the city. Chosen him.

Relief and joy surged within Jonah's chest. He dropped one of her hands and snaked his arm around her waist. "I like the sound of that. So this city girl is finally ready to switch sides to the good ole country life?"

Avery tilted her head and a mischievous glint sparked in her eyes. "Not quite."

Before Jonah could ask what she meant, Avery gripped the edge of her blouse and yanked it over her head. Her hair brushed back, and her ringlets were wild as they framed her face. Without pause, she unlatched her belt and let her dress pants puddle at her feet. She stood in a matching white lace bra and panty set, awaiting his next move. The apple trees provided a sultry backdrop reminiscent of Eden, the perfect setting for his lovely Eve.

Jonah traced her curves and followed the swell of her breasts, memorized the graceful column of her throat, and became lost in the wave of her lips. His cock hardened behind his zipper and the narrow breadth of space that separated them was suddenly too much.

Avery caught the desire in his hooded gaze and slowly reached behind her. A quiet click sounded, and her bra gave way, spilling out her beautiful breasts. Jonah fisted the material at the back of his neck and tugged his own shirt over his head. His ball cap tilted forward, but he reached up and turned it around. He didn't want anything between them ever again.

Avery purred, and the reaction went right to his cock. Jonah sank to his knees and hooked his fingers into the lace band of her panties. As he forced them to the ground, a small gasp fell from Avery's lips. He pressed his mouth to her sweet center, his warm tongue circling her clit with unbridled need. Coming up for air, he dropped his head back while his hands cupped her ass and drew her even closer to him.

"Say you're mine," he ordered and pressed his lips to her sex again.

Avery groaned and gripped the back of his head, leaning into his kiss. Jonah slipped a finger into her wetness while his tongue lapped at her sensitive bundle. Avery squirmed beneath him.

"Say it."

"I'm yours, Jonah. Forever," Avery surrendered in a breathy moan.

Jonah growled, and his tongue dove deeper. He plunged another finger into her, then rose to his feet. His hot mouth covered her nipple, and she responded with a delicious mewl. She was his. This beautiful, engaging, stubborn mare chose to run alongside him. He was wrong before. He didn't want to tame her. He adored her wild rebellion and was proud of her for walking away from a future she'd cultivated out of necessity to please the one person who wished to see her broken.

Jonah swore he'd never break her. Only when she begged for it. And right now, with her hips rolling against his palm, trying to force his hand to reach that exquisite point inside, all he craved was his name in her mouth as he carried her into the sweet abyss of orgasm.

With a practiced hand, Jonah undid his jeans and shimmied them off his thighs, followed by his boots, until he matched Avery's nakedness. She moaned and wrapped her fingers around his length. He elicited a strained groan of pleasure in return.

Avery stepped back and playfully pulled him after her. She leaned against the tall trunk of the apple tree and propped her foot on the rough bark. Her knee pivoted to the right, baring her center he'd made slick with need. She aligned the crown of his shaft with her slit and rubbed it along her opening.

Jonah didn't care that she'd left. He didn't care that they had no plan once the season ended. The only thing that mattered was that she had come back to him. He couldn't wait to fill her and remind her where her home truly existed.

"Fuck me, Jonah," Avery whispered and pressed her clit harder against his cock.

Jonah cradled the back of her head while his other hand gripped her hip. Avery gasped when he thrust and sank into her. Her eyes rolled back, and she tried to drop her head, but he forced her to look at him before he devoured her lips. Their passion quickly caught flame and they tore at one another's bodies, unable to get close enough.

Avery reached up and took hold of the lower-hanging branches while Jonah steadied her hips and increased his pace. He wasn't interested in going slow or dragging out her pleasure. This woman was his to claim, to mark, and he had to prove that leaving him behind wasn't an option. Whatever the world threw at them, they would tackle it together.

She moaned into his mouth again, and their tongues twirled as Jonah withdrew his cock, only to slam back into her with a need that bordered on fury. Avery's whimpers of pleasure cascaded down the long rows, heedless of being overhead as she screamed for him to thrust harder, faster, deeper.

Jonah's lips trailed from her mouth to her jaw, to her neck, to the vulnerable flesh before her shoulder. Overwhelmed with his own building release, Jonah dragged his teeth along the soft skin and bit down. She tasted like a newly harvested apple, fresh and sweet with a spicy kick that left him licking his lips.

Always hungry for more.

269

270

Acknowledgements

The inspiration for this novel began with a simple idea of two lovers getting caught in a thunderstorm. Turns out, the characters had quite a bit more to say as their stories—Avery's in particular—helped me to confront my own demons that I'd been running from since childhood.

I am forever grateful to my editor, Samantha Moran, without whom this book would not have been possible. Thank you for transforming my jumbled fragments into eloquent sentences. To my cover designer, Neil J Hart, you truly astound me with your beautiful designs and friendship.

To Reisinger's Apple Country in Watkins Glen, NY for the magic your orchard wields and the inspiration for this fictitious setting.

To my incredible friends Brad and Jimmy, your sweet words of encouragement always brighten my day and remind me how wonderful life truly is. To my amazing friend Kelsey, your character art is beyond compare and I am forever grateful for all the time you spent bringing my books to life. I hope you enjoyed chapter thirty. To Andi McClane, thank you for explaining that romance books must end happily ever after, no matter how tempting a different outcome might be.

To my husband, Daniel, thank you for your patience during the countless weeks of late nights and early mornings. To my children, Jack and Joanna, thank you for understanding every time I said, "One more chapter."

And lastly to my seven-year-old self, captured in the Father Daughter Dance photograph, you are enough.

273

About the Author

Caytlyn Brooke is an award-winning author known for writing thrilling stories where no one is safe. She attended UAlbany where she majored in psychology and cut two or three French classes to hang out with a cute boy. They are now married with two children and a fat orange cat. Autumn is by far her favorite season, and she yearns for chilly days and a pair of slippers. This is her first romance novel.

275